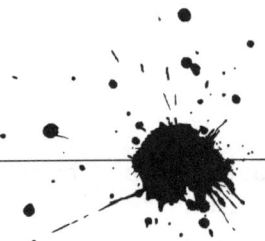

Freud's Revenge

by
PJ Adams

Freud's Revenge is a work of fiction. Any references to real events, businesses, organizations, and locales are intended only to give the fiction a sense of reality and authenticity. Any resemblance to actual persons, living or dead, is purely coincidental.

For information:

http://pjadamsbooks.com/

Freud's Revenge

ISBN-13: 9780615477237
ISBN-10: 0615477232
LCCN: 2013911311
PJAdamsBooks

The very emphasis of the commandment Thou shalt not kill, makes it certain that we are descended from an endlessly long chain of generations of murderers, whose love of murder was in their blood as it is perhaps also in ours.

–Sigmund Freud

Chapter One

Fits and Starts

A being in the clutch of madness has a sound like no other; like a fetus fighting death in the womb, the life force begs: love me, save me, redeem me from this abyss. Psychotherapist Amanda Carlisle listened, transfixed, as the voice bled through the walls.

"Stay away from me, you goddamn Nazis. Keep your hands off me, assholes." Furniture crashed somewhere then a new burst of epithets broke through. "Goddamn, fucking assholes..."

"Damn." Amanda sighed. She closed her eyes and leaned back in her black business suit against Seaside's old elevator as it lumbered to the clinic's second floor. "Sounds like Carl again."

It was Monday of course. Monday was the day things happened at Seaside Mental Health Clinic. Psychotic patients saw demons on the ceiling Sunday night. Couples separated after a boozy weekend. Teenagers got high or busted, then hauled into the clinic first thing

Freud's Revenge

Monday morning. People had panic attacks, found out they had cancer, lost their jobs, learned about an affair.

The screams grew louder. Amanda thought she heard running, banging. Carl was probably midway through a psychotic break upstairs. She adjusted her bulging briefcase stuffed with files, ready to bolt from the elevator. Pain shot from her right elbow cramping badly from the weight. She ignored it.

The voice welled up, garbled, anguished. "I hate you, get away from me. Don't hurt me. God, oh God, please help me, somebody please help me."

Amanda listened, assessing the degree of pain. The elevator doors finally wheezed open and she strode quickly out into the waiting room. She turned a sharp left as her auburn hair swung out behind her, and then tossed her keys into her bag, freeing a hand. About thirty feet in front of her, a small-headed, pock-faced man in filthy khaki pants and a salmon T-shirt was writhing on the floor, spewing vitriol.

Definitely Carl.

"I hate you, don't hurt me. Help, help..."

The waiting room was an unholy mess. Lobby chairs were upended near the reception desk; magazines and papers were scattered across the wood floors like garbage. One of the green floor lamps lay mangled on the striped area rug. Light bulbs crunched underfoot as people scattered. A shrieking woman with a toddler under each arm sidled around Carl as she rushed for the stairs. On the long blue couch to the left, an elderly man cowered with his knees pulled up under his chin. A pair of teenage boys in baseball caps snickered at a safe distance to the right, filming the mayhem with their cell phones.

Carl Fillmore. Or was it Fellman? Amanda racked her brain. She remembered that Carl was one of Sandra Daniels' therapy patients. With sixty plus cases divided between her two student interns, Sandra and Gary, Amanda couldn't possibly keep all the patient names straight anymore. Added to her own busy caseload, the three of them handled the Marriage and Family Therapy department treating nearly ninety families in all. Right now, however, Carl F. was critical.

1

She studied him. Carl lay squirming in some kind of mental hell; he was either off his meds or on street drugs, so an intervention was tricky. She suddenly recalled his history as she stepped toward him: thirty-six-year-old paranoid schizophrenic, in and out of inpatient treatment, heavy medication, domineering mother named Edna, absent father, no siblings. He'd had another episode like this last year. His mother most likely had left town to do some gambling in Las Vegas; Carl must have decided he could handle life without his meds. He'd probably had his first symptoms during breakfast, and then remembered his regular Monday counseling session. Haldol or no Haldol he knew to keep his appointments.

Amanda swerved left as she tripped on the jumbled area rug. Maybe her new three-inch Manolos weren't the best choice for today. She balanced herself, and then detoured and dumped her bags against the north wall. She grabbed her cell, and then swept forward toward Carl. Suddenly, Al Naylor, the clinic's 230-pound security guard, dashed in from the file room. Before Amanda could reach Carl, Al swooped down to the flailing man and tried to get him in a headlock.

"Come on, buddy," Al coaxed. "Calm down. No one's gonna hurt you. You cooperate, no one'll get hurt. Hold still."

Amanda watched the grappling pair. Carl looked like he'd been digging in a dumpster. There was something blue smeared on his knuckles. Paint? Makeup? Candy wrappers stuck out of his khaki pockets and his fly was down. Orange underwear peeked out. Carl suddenly glommed on to the edge of the oak coffee table with his fingers, and then clamped his legs around the table base.

"Carl, it's OK," Amanda shouted at the two grappling men. The table abruptly crashed over toward the couch as the elderly man bolted over the couch. "Carl, stop!"

Carl wrenched toward her when he heard Amanda's voice again, then he scrambled up to all fours and shot through Al's legs. "Help me, help me! You've got to help me!" He flung his arms out like a hungry infant.

"Carl, calm down, we can only help you if you calm down!" Amanda ordered as Carl scrambled toward her. Al whipped around

3

Freud's Revenge

in a blur of tan uniform snatching Carl by the feet but not stopping him.

"Go man, go," shouted one of the teenagers.

From a side chair, a ponytailed man in paint-splattered overalls brusquely thrust a leg out, corralling Carl as he slithered toward Amanda. Al jumped. An agile Hispanic man with terrorist training, Al grasped Carl's waist with both hands, then flopped him flat on his stomach and spread-eagled him.

Drooling and sputtering, Carl screamed, "You goddamn fucking Nazis. You can't do this to me. You goddamn asshole prick...get off me..."

Al pressed the man's face into the carpet, and then cranked Carl's arms up behind him on his back. A moment passed. Amanda leaned forward, barely breathing. Then Carl reared up and suddenly puked into the carpet. When he was done, he wept like a five-year-old.

"Don't hurt me...don't hurt me. Help me," he begged Amanda. Snot ran down his chin.

Amanda's heart twisted. She wanted to reach out, but in this state a psychotic could be unpredictable—might attack in an instant. Tears pressed against her eyes but she held her position. Out of the corner of her eye, she spotted someone in dark trousers racing toward them from the hallway. It was Mark Huston, the clinic director, Taser in hand. Mark, his face ashen against his thin black hair, crouched down to the struggling men. He held the Taser at Carl's back, ready to fire. With his other hand, he hit speed dial on his phone.

"Now, Carl," Mark soothed, waiting for the line to connect. "We don't want to hurt you. You need to calm down and let us help you." Mark looked up at Amanda, mouthing "God, what a mess." Suddenly he shouted into the phone, "Got a 5150! Seaside Clinic. Del Mar, downtown, on Pacific Coast Highway. Come now! This is Dr. Mark Huston. Come NOW."

When he heard the call, Carl wrenched his arm free, twisted toward Mark and hurled a mouthful of spit at the psychologist. Eyes flaming, Carl jabbed his finger at Mark: "He's Hitler, he's Hitler!

4

Don't you see? He'll get me, don't let him get me! You goddamn fucking Nazis..."

Mark slid adroitly to the right as the writhing man nearly snagged Mark's blue polo shirt. Amanda watched Carl's gleaming spit slide slowly down Mark's pants onto his Italian loafers. There was a thwack as a People magazine slid onto the floor near Carl's head. He promptly snatched it up and thrust it into Mark's face; Mark parried the jab with his cell. Al grunted and reached over, whipping the magazine out of Carl's hand. It flew across the room toward Jackie Forrest, the clinic's receptionist, who was peering over the counter. As she ducked, a stack of patient charts hit the tile.

Carl collapsed, sobbing. "Don't hurt me, don't hurt me. I'll be good, I'll be good..." Exasperated, Al grabbed the back of Carl's neck with one hand and the back of his pants with the other and pressed the man to the floor. Mark crept to Carl's side once more, ready to fire.

Jackie leaped up. "Police are here!"

Amanda and Carl locked eyes as pounding footsteps came from the stairs behind them. Al paused, not loosening his grip, but Mark stood up still pointing the Taser. Amanda backed up a few inches until her back was nearly against the elevator door as a pair of police officers burst from the stairwell. One, a heavily armed woman, moved into Al and Carl, then focused her Taser on Carl as she surveyed the room for others. Mark backed away when she waved him off. The cop knelt beside Carl as Al pulled the man's stained hands together across his back for the cuffs.

Wrenching forward with a Herculean effort, Carl lunged once more for Amanda, throwing off both the female officer and Al. The police Taser went flying.

"Help me, they're killing me!" he begged, snagging Amanda's left leg, digging his dirty nails into the tender skin along the front of her ankle. Instinctively she kicked him off, barely missing Carl's head with her high heel. At exactly the same moment, the police Taser rolled to within inches of her right foot.

Amanda and Carl saw it at the same time.

Deftly, Amanda thrust out the toe of her right Manolo and slid it under the Taser. With a snap, she lobbed it to the female officer. The cop scooped it up, pointed, and fired.

Carl spasmed, and then went limp. He convulsed a couple of times, then his bowels released. Stench filled the room. Amanda knelt down, trying to comfort him.

"You bitch!" Carl sneered at her weakly. "You should 'a helped me!"

The two officers jerked Carl facedown and cuffed him. Lifting him up, they dragged the hobbled man across the floor toward the elevator.

"Good job, Amanda," Mark whispered as he moved past her to hold the doors open for the officers. The cops and Carl disappeared into the old elevator and Carl's moans faded as the elevator dropped slowly to the ground.

"God, Mark, this is not my favorite way to start the week."

Mark moved to Amanda and put his arm around her shoulders. "You did well, Amanda. Carl must have been on meth or PCP the way he kept going and going. Are you OK?"

"I'll recover," Amanda said quietly, noticing Mark was clammy with sweat. "We had to keep him from hurting himself. Poor guy."

"The good news is we knew how to handle it." The crinkle around Mark's eyes returned as he smiled. Amanda instantly felt better. Mark had a wonderful way of engendering confidence. It was one of the reasons she liked working with him.

Mark turned toward Al who was picking up furniture and quieting patients who were emerging from various hiding places. Mark moved over to assist, but he glanced back at Amanda's leg and called out, "Better check that out, Amanda. First aid kit in the kitchen."

She hesitated, wanting to help, but then she felt a throbbing pain beginning to creep up her leg. First aid first. Amanda picked up her bags, and then headed down the long hallway to her office at the back of the clinic. She passed half a dozen clinical offices on either side of the hall, her heels clicking on the parquet. She could hear crying from one of the rooms. Reaching the second-to-the-last green fire door on the right, Amanda twisted the knob and slipped inside.

Relief swept over her as she entered her sanctuary. Scent from a dish of last week's gardenias on her corner table sweetened the air. She could see the tall, familiar pine trees swaying outside the west window in the sun. Very faintly, she could hear the Pacific crashing up on the beach about a mile away. Sanity. Amanda slowly limped toward her mahogany desk and chair where her yellow sweater still hung from Friday's sessions. Her head was pounding. She dumped her briefcase and bag near the file cabinet, and then bent down and reached into her desk drawer for wipes and Band-Aids. Absently, she waited for the door to close. There was nothing.

Amanda looked up, puzzled. Then she gasped as a hand curled around the door's edge. The door whipped open. A man peeled in.

Chapter Two

Blood and Sympathy

Gary Bowman zipped around the door and collapsed onto Amanda's tan couch as the door banged shut behind him. She exhaled slowly and closed her eyes, frankly relieved.

"Gary!"

"Geez, Amanda!" Gary shouted, face flushed, his red hair sticking out on one side. Her intern flung his stack of files on the table and slumped back. Amanda noticed the young man's white shirt hung out on one side. "I was finishing up a session when I heard the noise. Holy crap, Amanda, who...who was that?"

Amanda willed her face into a calm, professional stare as she moved around her desk to sit, but her knees buckled slightly and she finally sank gratefully into her leather chair. "Sorry if it frightened you, Gary. It was Carl Fellman. You know, Sandra's patient. Must be off his meds again."

Amanda's voice sounded strange, like from the bottom of a well. She closed her eyes a couple of times to clear.

"Sounded like there was a gang war going on out there!"

"Close." Amanda smiled wanly. She looked down. Her leg was really bleeding now, rapidly turning her blue pump into a bloody tie-dye. She snatched a wipe and dabbed at her leg, grateful for something constructive to do.

"Did he hurt you, Amanda?" Gary watched her, concerned, but she waved him off.

"It's OK...just a scratch," she assured him, applying a Band-Aid. "Carl was...out of control for awhile. It's scary in the moment, but most patients like this won't do anything really serious. Sometimes we go years before something like this happens."

Her rational mind was talking along, but somewhere in her psyche, images of Carl flailing, screaming, grabbing, flashed in and out. PTSD. Post-traumatic reverb. Shaking it off, she was about to say something to Gary when she heard Carl's voice again. But not in her head—outside in real time. Sweeping around to the window, she saw three officers down in the parking lot struggling to get Carl into a squad car. Gary stood up behind her and the two watched as the police finally got Carl into the backseat, slammed the door, and got inside. When the vehicle reversed, Carl thrust out his tongue and licked the car window, bottom to top. As the car pulled out to the highway and turned south, Carl rubbed his chin back and forth through the spit.

Amanda turned to Gary and shook her head. "I feel sorry for him really. Getting him in a safe place is best for him now. And back on his meds."

"I guess I wasn't rrr...ready for it. Honestly, Amanda, I'm glad he's Sandra's patient, not mine."

"Understandable. That's why you get so much supervision before you're licensed from people like me. So you see most of this before you go out there on your own."

The door suddenly burst open again. Al Naylor poked his head in. "All clear, Ms. Carlisle." Al's shirt gaped open; the middle buttons were gone. And his right ear was bloody.

"Thanks for the update, Al. Great work, by the way. You're bleeding, you know." She handed him a tissue.

Al grinned, sopping up the blood. He liked Amanda. Liked being a hero too. "Just missed a kick in the groin by that nut job, but other than that, everything's OK." He laughed. "You two OK?"

"Fine, fine. I hope your back can take it, Al."

"I'm tough," he said, glancing over at Gary. "You look a little green, though, Bowman." He turned to go. "Looks like one of your patients is about to pass out in the waiting room."

"Yikes, I completely forgot!" Gary leapt up, remembering his 9:30 bipolar patient. He bolted out the door, sweeping past Al.

"Good luck," Amanda called out after him. Al gave her a thumbs-up, and then followed Gary, letting the door slam behind him. Amanda flinched. Damn fire doors. Louder than hell.

"Get hold of yourself, Amanda Carlisle." She shook her head a couple of times and tried to focus on what was left of Monday. Seaside Clinic was typically a place of solace, known for helping people, not jailing them. Carl was an aberration. Rubbing her neck, Amanda turned to her in-box, grateful to get back to the mundane. She hoisted three inches of case files out, and then separated the work: read, sign, file. She stood up to take some of the weekend files out of her briefcase, but her eyes caught something odd at the bottom of the tray: a folded piece of gray paper. Carefully, she picked up the note. Opening it, she read:

BACK OFF AMANDA CARLISLE. YOU'RE PUSHING HER TOO MUCH. I'M WARNING YOU.

It was signed: D.

Amanda stared at the words, stunned.

Now what?

Chapter Three

Kid Dreams

The kid was itching to get out.

Man, I'm bored. Talk, talk, talk. Nothing but talk. So sick of these two pinheads. How do they do it? Screw up every time. She tries, I guess...just keeps screwin' it up.

The kid sat, watching, seeing but not seen. Seething.

I blame him. Asshole. Jerk-off. He did this to Her. Glad the old prick is dead. If it hadn't been pneumonia, sooner or later it woulda been me. Ol' man finally got his due.

The kid smiled.

Saw it a few times there at the end. Knew I was gonna take care of things if he made one more goddamn move. Kinda fun, watchin' him get it. Out on the porch that morning, both us seein' the rat goin' for the old man's breakfast. Thought I was too soft to do it. But he saw. Saw me jump that stupid thing. Thwack.

Freud's Revenge

Man that rat's head popped right off. Ol' man shoulda been proud. He taught me, man. But he just looked at me—then that friggin' rat jumpin' around, blood goin' everywhere. Me laughin'. Laughin' at that stupid rat. Laughin' at the ol' man.

The kid chuckled.

Yep, ol' bastard got it then. He SAW. Kept his eye on me after that. I showed him...who he was dealing with, man.

I did it for Her. Crap. Always do it for Her. But, man, I get so dang tired of havin' to fix things for Her. Like that Amanda chick. Shrink needs to back off. That chick should have Her back, you know? If she won't do it, goddamn it, I'll have to make her. But I have to go slow. I know, I KNOW. But it's got to be done. For Her. For the both of 'em. Stupid bitches.

The kid sat, mulling things over. Thinking about guns needing cleaning. About the shooting range, seeing the boys. Trying out the new rifle, loving that twenty-five-yard range. Indoor. Private. Nobody caring who you were, what you were. Just how many bullets it took you, 'til you were done. The kid was good at it. Very good.

The kid waited, thinking about guns and old pricks and people who hurt Her and assholes who screwed her, and about getting even, while the voices droned on and on and on and on.

But I'm in charge. They'll see.

Soon.

Chapter Four

Murmurs

S he read it again.

BACK OFF AMANDA CARLISLE. YOU'RE PUSHING HER TOO MUCH. I'M WARNING YOU. D.

Drumming her fingers as she stared at the picture of ripe vineyards on her wall, Amanda ran through the possibilities. "OK, somebody is peeved," she said to herself. "Paranoid, maybe. Definitely unhappy. But why be so cryptic? What's the point? Why not be direct, tell me to my face? And why in my in-box? Why not text or e-mail? Must be someone who has clear access to this office. But who? D? Who the hell is 'D'?"

Amanda's eyes narrowed; she was annoyed now, especially after the morning's events. But this is how things happen sometimes, she reminded herself. When you treat people with mental health issues, you get mental health *dynamics*. Still, threatening notes are special. The more she thought about it, the more violated she felt.

"Who would come into my private office and give me feedback this way?" she said aloud. "Make a threat, 'I'm warning you.' Then not tell me directly what I'm doing and to whom?"

Amanda reasoned it out, doodling on a pad with a colored pencil—pencils she usually kept on her desk in a big plastic jar for kids doing therapeutic drawing. This had happened before, she suddenly remembered. When she'd first come to Seaside as the Marriage & Family Therapy supervisor a few years ago, a patient began stalking one of the senior therapists. Tim Hutchens got anonymous notes; he found cookies or toys on his car, his desk, sometimes even on the front porch of his home. It went on for weeks. They finally discovered it was a teenage patient named Julie. When Tim tried to work with her on her misplaced feelings, the girl attempted suicide. She ended up in Aurora Hospital's psych ward for a month. Tim moved to the Bay Area, chastened about blurring boundaries with young, unstable girls.

Other than that, Seaside Clinic was usually contained and quiet. Extreme patients like Carl and Julie were rare. Mark and Barbara Huston, the clinic owners, preferred it that way. Amanda was well aware of their story. With California real estate so pricey, Mark and Barbara had taken a big risk. Instead of building from scratch a decade ago, the couple bought a crumbling, Tudor-style hotel in downtown Del Mar and morphed it into clinical offices. The old rooms had been tiny for holiday guests, but they made perfect counseling offices. Seaside was now a full-service mental health organization, treating everything from chronic mental illness to marital strife. Mark served as clinic director and lead psychologist. Barbara, his ash-blond, Austrian wife, was the administrative psychologist.

Even the old honeymoon suite was put to good use. The Hustons modified the expansive suite into a palatial executive wing for themselves, complete with double offices and a conference alcove. The staff giggled behind their backs about it though. Ed Michael, the clinic's acerbic psychiatrist, once asked during a staff meeting there, "Barbara, do you think there once was an enormous vibrator bed right here where we are sitting? The stories this room could tell! Maybe still does..."

Barbara, born and reared in Europe, snapped back: "Projections—all of you. You Americans are so sexually repressed. You want it to happen to you so you fantasize about it."

She was probably right. However, there definitely wasn't a lot of honeymooning going on in there now. Barbara and Mark argued—often. They grappled with soaring costs and dwindling funding. California managed care parceled out funds one dollar at a time it seemed; low- and no-pay indigents clogged the appointment book. Fundraisers became the norm, much to Barbara's distaste. Her Austrian accent rose to a clipped staccato when she'd had enough of Mark's nonchalance about money. Or if something dicey happened that affected the reputation of the clinic.

"Barbara, Barbara, calm down." Mark sometimes stood behind her chair, rubbing Barbara's neck with slow, languid movements. After a time, Barbara's demanding voice softened into a pleasant Austrian lilt. Their door closed quietly. Honeymoon suite indeed.

Amanda looked down at her pad and laughed. She'd drawn a huge purple bed surrounded by waves and dollar signs. In the center of the bed was a bull's eye.

A sharp knock on Amanda's door jolted her from her reverie. She stuffed the pad in her drawer and put the note back in the bottom of her in-box, facedown. "Come in," Amanda called out.

Sandra Daniels stepped in. Amanda's female intern seemed composed in her sober gray suit and plain straight hair. The girl, in her early thirties, sat gingerly on the couch and smoothed her skirt as she spoke. "Hi, Amanda. What a weird Monday already. I'm so, so sorry Carl went nuts, Amanda. He's usually pretty good in our sessions, as you know, since we've talked through his case often enough. But this is crazy! God, Amanda, it sounds like he even went after you!"

"I'm OK. Just a scratch really. Were you here?"

"Yup. Tied up in the playroom with a mother and her kids. I heard all the noise. Couldn't get out there until after the cops took Carl away. So sorry."

"Nothing you could do about it..."

"Well..."

"Yes?"

"I...I have to tell you something."

Sandra looked down at her hands, and then cleared her throat. "Carl left a message last night—actually three—on my cell. I had my phone turned off yesterday. Forgot to turn it back on."

Amanda listened patiently.

"Didn't pick up the messages until this morning. Sounded like he was off his meds big time, Amanda. He wanted me to call him, and when I finally did, he didn't answer. I guess I really screwed up, Amanda. It's just that sometimes...I guess I...just need a break. I'm so sorry."

"Well," Amanda measured her words. "That's a tough one. I know sometimes you'd like to get away from it. Believe me, I can relate. But we're really on call most of the time—at least roughly from eight in the morning to eight or nine or so at night. Especially with patients as unstable as Carl. That's the hard part of treating the severely mentally ill."

Sandra's eyes clouded. "Oh, Amanda, I really am sorry. It won't happen again, I promise."

Humiliation rolled over the girl. Sandra tried hard as a student therapist. "OK. I know it's a wake-up call for you. The good news is he came to us first thing." Amanda softened the feedback, but Sandra had to learn it. Had to learn while she was in training because when she was out on her own, apologies wouldn't mean anything to a managed care company getting sued or a patient—or the patient's family—if that patient jumped off a bridge or overdosed because they decompensated and couldn't reach help. Realistically, patients could always call an emergency room. Morally, therapists make an agreement to do everything they can to be available—with reasonable limits.

Sandra started when her beeper went off. "Gotta go. Next patient. Thanks, Amanda. I promise I won't let this happen again."

"OK, I know you get it. See you tomorrow for supervision. We can work it through."

"Right. Thanks, Amanda." The girl smiled as she scooted out the door.

Supervising interns could be tricky. Amanda wasn't their boss, strictly speaking. More like their shepherd, guiding her two charges through the hills and valleys of the human psyche, helping them assist people by getting involved, but not caught up. Even handling threatening notes like the one sitting in her in-box was all part of the therapeutic process. She flipped the note over again and studied it.

"D? D who?"

Just then her com line went. It was Jackie. "Hey, Amanda, your patient is here. Shall I send him back?"

"Yeah, thanks. By the way, how're you doing, Jackie?"

"Man, that Carl guy is a total nut case. Good thing you had on your Manolos—you could 'a gouged his eyes out if you'd had to, Amanda."

"Not a great use of my new shoes, Jackie." Amanda chuckled.

"Yeah, but in a pinch...Anyway, I feel better now. Got to see Officer Hernandez again at least." Jackie smacked her lips loudly. "A fine-lookin' man. Said he might have to stop back by to see how we're doin'."

"Well you have fun, Jackie. Go ahead and send my patient back."

Amanda stood up to open the door for Bradley, her favorite obsessive-compulsive accountant.

Chapter Five

Obsessions

"Oh, God," Amanda groaned as she stood in the doorway and peered down the hallway. "He probably saw the police cars."

Bradley had a variety of compulsions. Hand washing. Locking and unlocking doors. Arranging and rearranging his shoes. He was thirty-eight, prematurely balding, and afraid of many, many things. She watched him propel himself down the hallway like he was wrapped in cellophane. Clutching his planner like it was armor, Bradley subtly averted his eyes as a young woman passed by. When he finally reached Amanda's door, he slithered around it, neatly avoiding both the doorknob and his therapist.

Amanda watched as Bradley took his favorite seat as far away from the door as possible. He leaned over, adjusted his socks eight times, and then began a breathless verbal download even before she sank into her chair.

"Oh my God, Amanda!" Bradley's eyes bulged. "There was this icky man screaming and fighting with the police as I drove into the parking lot. It took me fourteen minutes to find a suitable parking place! I thought I even saw him drooling on the window!" Sweat glistened through Bradley's sparse brown hair. His right hand felt in his lap for his planner and found the clasp, which he began snapping and unsnapping like a metronome on speed.

Open. Closed. Open. Closed. Open. Closed.

"Unfortunately there was an incident this morning, Bradley," Amanda explained, her voice low and warm. "I'm sorry you had to see the aftermath. You're OK now, safe." She smiled genially and adjusted her back pillow. Her eyes fell on the gray note; she moved it nonchalantly to the top of the patient files on the other side of her desk. She was determined to ignore it.

"I had all this great stuff to tell you too," Bradley leaned forward intently, opening his planner to today's date. "I only checked the locks nine times this morning before I left. That's an improvement, don't you think?"

Amanda nodded.

"Yesterday I couldn't leave for work until I'd done fifty-one," he added, studying his notes. Bradley documented everything. Notes on his condition. Things he saw. Things that upset him. He was a model patient that way. The bad news is his biggest obsession was himself.

"But now that awful man in the car really set me back. How do people live like that? If I ever get that bad, I don't know what I'd do." His chin commenced jutting back and forth like a chicken pecking for food. Sweat seeped out across his yellow shirt like blood spreading from a punctured artery. Suddenly he sat up, shuddered violently, and then his right cheek began spasming at regular two- or three-second intervals. His facial tic was back. As he hyperventilated, the twitch picked up speed.

Amanda made eye contact, commanding: "Breathe, Bradley, breathe." She inhaled and exhaled with him in slow, methodical breaths, as her eyes wandered over to the nasty little gray note. *I won-*

der who wrote this, she thought, all the time smiling and breathing, staring at Bradley.

BACK OFF AMANDA CARLISLE. YOU'RE PUSHING HER TOO MUCH. I'M WARNING YOU. D.

Who is that? I can't think of anyone who's particularly pissed at me right now. And who I'm "pushing too hard?" D? Darrel? David? Douglas? We had a Dick Abbott in here recently...

"Amanda," Bradley shouted. "I remember now!" He sat up, the tic forgotten. "I had a dream! A nightmare, I guess? I made some notes." He drew out a sheaf of typed pages from his notebook with relish.

"Bradley, are you calm enough for this now?"

"It was my mother again," he rushed on. "She was this tall, scraggly person in my dream. Wearing a gigantic lipstick-pink dress... chasing me around the house...grabbing at my clothes! There were no doors so I couldn't keep her out. She just kept coming at me and I couldn't move very fast. Huge fangs came out of her dentures...her hands were all hairy...and her fingernails were *filthy*! Filthy! I started to scream. Then I woke up. I had asthma most of the night after that. It was terrible, terrible!"

"Yes, I see." Amanda listened but her mind wandered. *Donna? Diane? Delia? Doctor, maybe?*

Suddenly Bradley's tic returned and he began snapping the planner's clasp in rhythm to it.

"OK, Bradley, you can relax here," Amanda affirmed, raising her hands in front of her like Moses stilling the sea. "It was just a dream. Breathe. One, two, three. Yes, that's it. Look at me and breathe. Good. Good."

Bradley's head finally relaxed.

"OK, let's work this through. Close your eyes and breathe. Good. Now, what are you thinking of right now, Bradley? Free association." She spoke in a soothing voice, using her favorite Freudian technique.

"Sounds. Snapping."

"Keep going," Amanda urged.

Freud's Revenge

"Chomping. Teeth. Eating. Jaw. Hands, uh, grabbing. Arms. Legs. Oh, stomach, I guess. Groin. Penis. Moist. Hairy. Crunch. Crunching." Bradley squirmed on the couch.

"Relax and keep going."

"Well, let's see. Um...crunch. Crunching. Eating. Being eaten. Pain. Hurt. Hurting. Losing myself. Losing parts of myself. Disappearing. Swallowed. Digested. Eliminated. No more," Bradley finished, morose.

"OK, come out of it now, open your eyes, and take a deep breath." Bradley complied. Then he burped.

Amanda ignored it. "Now, what do you make of all that?" She glanced again at the note, inwardly swore, and then slapped a file on top of it. She'd be damned if it was going to ruin her entire session.

"Well," Bradley said gleefully. He loved free association; he was unusually good at interpreting himself even if he wasn't good at controlling his actions. "I guess somewhere in my head I think my mother is...I don't I know...eating me alive?"

"Hmm. And...if you're eaten alive?" Amanda said delicately.

"I don't...I don't...exist?" Bradley answered.

"And if you don't exist..." Amanda kept on.

"I will be gone," Bradley said flatly. He stopped breathing.

"Breathe, keep breathing. Now, Bradley, you and I both know you're not gone. You're here. You're sitting right here in this office, with me, and we're OK."

"Yes, I'm here. I can hear my breathing," he answered, connecting with her steady gaze.

"So you know rationally that you're *here*. But a teeny little part of you wonders...wonders if you may be disappearing? Especially with your mother. She's so strong, so powerful, isn't she? Almost makes you disappear—as a separate person?"

"Yes, yes! But doggone it, I AM here. I do exist. And it's a dream, isn't it? Only a teeny piece of me."

"Yes, and we're making peace with that piece of you. Connection is the first step toward wholeness. So now let's breathe."

"In, out, in, out," Bradley repeated. Ten more times, twenty more times. He exhaled more fully with each new cycle. Slowly he sat back, calm. She watched him as she drummed her fingers on the desk. Her mind wandered. *Darn it, who in hell sent me that frigging note?*

Bradley was watching her now. She sat up. "All right, let's see where we are. You might want to journal about how you're a separate person from your mother, Bradley. Does that sound like something you'd like to do?"

"I can try," he responded brightly.

"OK, that's probably enough for today. Write more of your thoughts between now and next time and we'll pick up with that next week. And keep breathing," Amanda reminded him as she got up, ending the session.

He stood up, and promptly cracked his shin on the coffee table. He yelped, then gathered up his things and headed toward the door, limping. He stood before it and savagely snapped his planner several times. "You see?" he smiled back at her. "Only eight times today before I go. I *am* getting better. Thank you, Amanda!" Dramatically, Bradley flung open the door and strode through it, a renewed man.

Amanda made a few notes about her patient's condition. His obsessive-compulsive behaviors had clustered into some debilitating rituals, but the more he controlled them through treatment, the better he would function. Eventually he might lead a happy, productive life.

Bradley, however, was a fairly moderate OCD case. Amanda knew well that there were plenty of other obsessive personalities out there, many who were severally ill. Substance addicts. Self-mutilators. Internet obsessors. Arsonists. Kleptomaniacs. Sex abusers. Serial murderers. Personalities bent on self-destruction. Or other-destruction. She'd read once that the biggest fear about human behavior was not that people in rule-based society misbehave. It was that ruleless people do whatever they want, whenever they want, without remorse. For them, there are no rules. Take or be taken.

Freud's Revenge

Amanda checked her watch. Something hot could help clear her mind. She stood up to head to the kitchen. After a few steps, she winced. Her ankle pulsed with pain. It reminded her. Reminded her that people in pain sometimes inflict pain as a way to still their compulsions. But Amanda was determined not to be a victim today, despite the nasty note and crumpled Carl grasping at her feet. She was slightly off balance—but not off guard. Coffee called.

She headed down the hallway to the right, passing by Dr. Ed Michael's psychiatrist office next door, and on toward the break room. As she turned left into the kitchen area, she caught Ed's baritone droning on in a long discourse for the interns seated with him at the table by the window. The students laughed. Seeing her over his spectacles, Ed waved her over but someone suddenly grabbed her elbow.

Chapter Six

Down the Rabbit Hole

She stared at Mark Huston's hand as it gripped her arm. "Hey, Mark, it's you." She looked up and noticed he was holding a fresh cup of coffee. His mug read: Head Shrink.

"Just me. I wanted to check in with you on Carl," Mark said, releasing her arm. He paused for a swallow, and then continued. "Carl needs to stay on his meds, for God's sake. Another one of those and he'll have to go to residential treatment."

"I agree."

"How's your foot?"

"Mending, thanks. But you're the one who got the loogie."

"Executive privilege."

Amanda laughed, relaxing. She followed Mark over to the employee mailboxes along the wall. Her mailbox was empty.

"By the way, Mark," Amanda began in a low voice, "I found something odd in my office..."

Freud's Revenge

At the moment, Barbara Huston swept toward them from the hallway.

"Donnerwetter! I was on the phone but I heard all the banging about." Barbara often lapsed into her native language under stress. "Mark said you were attacked, poor dear!"

"I'm all right, really, Barbara. Mark and Al did all the work."

"God though, the shouting. And that Hitler nonsense," Barbara continued.

"You know Carl's psychosis, Barbara. He's lapsed into that Hitler fixation before. Nothing to worry about."

"Yes, of course, but it's the scene in the waiting room...and his language...what must the patients think..."

"It's disturbing, I know," Mark soothed. He placed a reassuring hand on his wife's shoulder. Barbara stared at him, and then brusquely shrugged him off.

Amanda felt slightly uncomfortable. There was an unspoken conversation going on between Mark and Barbara. Barbara opened her mouth to continue but Mark's hand on her arm again stilled her.

"Don't mind me, dear." Barbara softened, swinging her long blond hair off one shoulder. Turning back to Mark, Amanda noticed Barbara's jaw clench. "It's just that we can't have him disturbing the other patients, Mark," she hissed. "We need to keep the clinic running smoothly or it will affect the business. You know how iffy the state grants are."

Mark shifted his weight. Barbara stood rigid, a blue vein rising in her neck. Mark glanced at Amanda who he knew was registering the rising tension.

"Barbara, let's discuss this in our office." He scooped up his mail, took her arm, and propelled her out. "Sorry, Amanda."

"No problem. It's happened before and undoubtedly will again. We'll try to keep Carl under control."

"Oh, by the way," Mark turned back to her, "what was it you were saying about something in your office?"

"Never mind. We'll talk later."

Barbara looked blankly at Amanda, then suddenly smiled brilliantly and said, "Thank you, Amanda dear, for dealing with all this." Barbara patted her. "Sorry I'm—you know—I guess I'm just under stress." Turning back to Mark, Barbara continued, "Mark, this really can be a problem if..."

"In our office, *please*, Barbara." Mark pulled Barbara into the hallway and the two disappeared around the corner.

Another private dialogue for the honeymoon suite, Amanda mused. Barbara was on edge about the business most days now. Amanda knew Mark felt they could keep the clinic running on their local contracts and walk-ins even *if* the state funds went bust. Barbara disagreed. She thought they were dependent on the funds if private and managed care insurance tightened or if walk-in traffic diminished from bad press. Barbara had been stung more than once by her family's old Nazi connections during the war. The local *LA Times* edition had done a story on the rise of neo-Nazism in San Diego early last year; Barbara's family and others had been mentioned peripherally. She was distraught when swastikas appeared on the clinic walls. Then, last year, there had been rumors of a financial scandal when Barbara fired the clinic's billing agency due to accounting irregularities. The next weekend, graffiti appeared again, this time on the front door.

"Carl's certainly not helping things," Amanda muttered as she reached for the coffee pot and filled her cup. Turning, she noticed Jackie lying on the brown suede couch against the wall. Midforties, single, a bit high-strung, Jackie usually had to take half a Valium and a "lie-down" whenever a patient went "whacko." Lila, the temp, must be answering the incessant phones. Over at the window, her interns, Gary Bowman and Sandra Daniels, along with Margaret Tanaka, one of the psychology interns, sat with Ed.

Jaunty in cuffed shirt and bow tie, Dr. Ed was sipping from his teacup while the three students listened raptly to his latest tale. As the clinic's lone psychiatrist, he saw the most gravely ill patients, and handled prescribing for the entire clinic. Eccentric by his own account, he was a native New Yorker, divorced several years, with no children. No fan of the California lifestyle, Ed was fond of saying, "I am lost in a land of brown bodies and tapioca brains."

Ed loved psychiatric jokes—the raunchier the better. Right now he was lecturing the three students on Carl's psychotic break.

"Yes, the delusions come back," Ed said with relish.

"But why the Hitler stuff?" Sandra asked, sitting forward, twisting a strand of stick-straight hair between her fingers. She smiled as Amanda stepped toward the group.

"Not sure. Carl's delusions may have nothing to do with anything he's experienced directly. But he's fixated on symbols. Symbols of fear and hate. His internal voices prodding him, seeking a target."

"Why focus the delusion on Dr. Huston?" Margaret Tanaka asked impatiently, her Asian eyes open wide. Margaret was an intern for the clinic's other supervisor, psychologist Nancy Davis.

Ed paused, grinning. He enjoyed shocking students with psychology's seamy side. "Authority figures get demonized in Carl's paranoid head," Ed explained, his eyebrows twitching up and down ominously. "Picture Carl, pulsating with all manner of maddening voices, whispering, and then shouting to him. The unreal real. The real unreal. When he sees Dr. Huston, his voices cluster the delusion around a power figure—a violent one due to the added paranoia—and Dr. Huston magically becomes Hitler in Carl's mind. Classic transference. Carl feels persecuted. Dr. Huston—Hitler—is doing the persecuting. So he goes for him—rather than be gotten!"

Ed sat back, satisfied when he got a stricken stare from the three students. Then he burst out laughing.

"OK, OK, kind of dramatic, but still basically that's the dynamic, right?" said Sandra, pushing for the kernel of truth in Ed's game.

"Yes, my dear, basically that's it. But you should see your faces. You'll have to learn to control your display of emotion!"

"Yeah, yeah, OK. But why did Carl go off his Haldol?" Gary Bowman pressed.

"Carl may simply have been feeling well, and, without his minder—it's his mother, isn't it—he neglected his medication. Of course he decompensated. Then the poor bugger slid into a full-blown acute episode." Ed took a swallow of mint tea.

"But by the time he got here then, he thought they—we—were going to kill him. Why?"

"He probably became disruptive as soon as he got here, shouting, tearing things up. Al comes in like a bulldozer, constrains him, and Carl's delusions escalate, fueled by all that adrenaline. I remember an instance a long time ago when a psychotic patient bit my leg—thought he was a pit bull and I was his dinner!" Ed snorted at his own joke. Sandra giggled but Margaret smiled wanly, twisting her watch around her wrist. Gary frowned.

"Debriefing Carl's eruption, are we Ed?" Amanda interjected.

"Yes, our students seldom get to see paranoid schizophrenia in action," Ed answered, smiling at her. "Like our Sandra here who gets to see Carl each week as his therapist while he's in medicated, docile bliss. An *unmedicated* eruption, however," he leaned in, placing his cup on the table with a bang and gleefully rubbing his hands, "gives us a delicious peek into the patient's messy, inner world. The delusions come out. The voices are made real, and we get to experience psychosis in action! Delightful."

"The violence scares me," Margaret said quietly.

"Well I kind of wish he'd keep his delusions to himself and use his meds," Gary shuddered.

"We can explore some treatment options in supervision tomorrow," Amanda advised.

"Quite motherly, aren't we, Amanda?"

"Cut the crap, Ed," Amanda shot back. It was the interns' chance to laugh now. "You'll lead my interns down the rabbit hole if I let you." It was true that Amanda was protective. It was also true that Ed enjoyed mucking around in people's psyches until he hit something. "Be careful or we'll have to explore why you wear all those bow ties."

"OK, truce," Ed demurred. "I defer to the matriarch."

The buzzer board went off, lighting up Amanda's name. Seconds later, Gary's lit up also.

"Got to go." Amanda headed back to her office before the mass exodus from the kitchen. She could hear Sandra and Margaret pepper Ed with still more questions as she and Gary left the room, followed by Jackie. As she passed down the hallway, Amanda heard Nancy Davis on the phone in her office opposite Amanda's. Nancy was the clinic's supervising psychologist and Amanda's direct peer. Nancy supervised the two psychology interns, Margaret Tanaka and Thomas Wong. She and Nancy often conferred about the challenges of guiding students.

The door was open; she could hear Nancy talking quietly into her phone. Amanda paused when she heard Ed Michael's name mentioned. As Amanda peeked in, Nancy said, "We need to do something..."

"Just a minute." Nancy covered the phone when she registered Amanda standing in her door. "Hi, Amanda. How're things? Heard about the tussle this morning. Everything OK?"

"Yes. I'm sure we'll debrief fully at five o'clock. By the way, have you gotten anything strange in your mailbox?"

"Not that I've seen. What's up?"

"Show you later."

Amada paused. Nancy kept her hand over the phone until Amanda finally turned and grasped the doorknob to her own office. As she did so, Nancy got up, unhooked her office door and let it slam shut. Just before it closed, Amanda heard Nancy say, "Yes, OK. But we have to do something. He's out of control...and it could be real trouble..."

"Odd," Amanda said under her breath as her own fire door closed behind her. What was Nancy on to now?

Chapter Seven

Love and Liability

Amanda hoisted her briefcase and dumped the contents on her desk next to her other files. It had been a rough start to Monday, but she knew exactly what to do to get things back on track: work. She dug into the piles, ate her sandwich, saw two more patients, and gulped one more cup of coffee. At one minute to five, Amanda entered Mark and Barbara's executive suite for their weekly staff meeting.

Mark was already seated at the round conference table on the left, signing papers. He'd changed his shirt and now had on a light blue dress shirt and dark slacks. On the right-hand side of the suite, Barbara was on the phone at her desk. As always, Barbara looked classy in an elegant white blouse opening at the throat to chunky gold and a black pencil skirt. Right now, she was in a heated discussion, her accent punctuating certain words. Judging from the liberal use of "patient responsibility" and "clinic liability" it was most likely an attorney on the receiving end. Barbara stabbed her brass letter opener into the blotter each time she made a point.

Amanda sat at the far side of the conference table where she had a view of the entire room. Watching Mark and Barbara work, Amanda remembered the story of how they met. Mark first encountered Barbara as a colleague while on sabbatical in Europe. He was in his late twenties and both of them were married. They were friends, but no more. At the time, Mark taught developmental psychology at the University of San Diego. Just a year later, his first wife and young son were tragically killed on a holiday trip to visit her parents. A drunk driver in St. Louis had been knocking back Jack Daniels for two days straight when he climbed into his truck the day after Christmas. Minutes later, he plowed head-on into Mark's wife and young son as they drove to the airport to return to San Diego. The man lived. Mark's family didn't.

Mark had returned early on Christmas day to help a suicidal patient. Oddly enough, it was another psychologist, a close personal colleague. When he got the news, Mark was inconsolable. Sadly, the colleague took his life anyway a few weeks later. Burying himself in his work, Mark's special love for human development took him on a summer program to Vienna in the 1980s. There he worked with Erik Erikson, the famous developmental psychologist who studied under Sigmund Freud. Erickson grew famous modernizing Freud's concepts and loved training new disciples.

While there, Mark ran into the beautiful, brilliant clinician named Barbara Keller. Flirtation turned to courtship and Barbara went through a contentious divorce from her German trucking magnate husband. Mark and Barbara ultimately married in a quiet ceremony in Napa at a friend's vineyard. They returned to San Diego where Barbara earned her US clinical degrees and her American citizenship in the ensuing years. They never had children.

Mark's devotion to Barbara was legendary. Amanda knew less about Barbara's upbringing but she gathered that Barbara had been born a few years after World War II ended. Her father, a village doctor, had apparently been coerced into service by the Nazis and forced to leave his young wife in Austria to tend to prisoners in one of the infamous death camps. Later, Dr. Keller became a key collaborator with the allies. Barbara said her family lost loved ones killed by both the Germans and the Allies. However, once the war ended, the family was apparently looked on with suspicion. The locals found it hard to like the smart little blond girl whose father collaborated with the Nazis on the one hand, then aided the allies on the other—and made a fortune through it all.

Dr. and Mrs. Keller sent their only daughter to the best institutions of learning. Barbara had gone on to graduate school in psychology, and then hastily married a wealthy former patient. Klaus was a controlling man; their divorce was bitter. But Barbara had fallen completely in love with her American colleague Mark Huston, and she was set on a new life in the States. Finally married, Mark and Barbara worked in other clinical settings in California before they scraped together enough money to open Seaside. It was their life's work together. Neither wanted to jeopardize it in any way.

Watching Barbara now as she took a seat near Mark, Amanda saw a loving look pass between them. Things had definitely warmed up since this morning. Mark's hand briefly rested on Barbara's arm and she visibly relaxed at his touch.

Turning to Amanda, Barbara explained, "Amanda dear, that was one of the University Hospital attorneys on that Nunez case. We're still wrangling on the key issues, especially the mismedication part. We just don't want it to impact our Healthy Families relationship."

"Tough situation. Anything I can do to help?"

"No, not really," Barbara reached over and patted Amanda's hand. "Just keep those little interns in line, please."

There was movement at the door. Ed Michael sauntered in. "Hi, all," he said cheerily and slid his glasses jauntily up on his head. He sat next to Amanda then slapped his latest psychiatric cartoon down in the middle of the table. Despite his Harvard background, Ed loved bawdy jokes.

"You'll enjoy this," he announced. "Not too blue."

Freud's Revenge

Amanda cringed as she looked down remembering the penis envy cartoon Ed produced last week. This cartoon was a benign picture of a psychiatrist sitting on a chair. On the couch lay a humanized bottle of nonalcoholic beer. Mr. Beer was dejected. He told the doctor: "Sometimes, I get so depressed. I say to myself, 'Why am I here?'"

Amanda laughed. So did Mark. Barbara frowned. She opened her mouth to say something but stopped when Nancy Davis whipped around the door and shut it behind her.

"Come on, Barbara, a little humor is good for you," Ed said, goading her.

"Yes, if I could find some," Barbara retorted. She tapped her pen impatiently on the table, studying Ed. Ed grinned rather like a schoolboy watching his teacher sit on thumbtacks he's left on her chair.

"Greetings," Nancy said as she sat down across from Ed. "Sounds like we had a little episode this morning. Carl, was it? Are you over-medicating again, Ed?"

Ed, his bubble burst, slid his glasses back over his face. "No, Nancy, our illustrious Carl apparently took it upon himself to stop taking his meds and then come to our very own little clinic to have a meltdown," Ed retorted. "Psychotic episode number three by my count."

"Hmmm," Nancy responded. Ed tweaked his bow tie and leaned back.

"Apparently, he decided this time that I was Hitler trying to murder him," Mark added. "I think the staff handled it pretty well, though." He was attempting to waylay Nancy; she seemed bent on confronting either Ed or Amanda about the patient's treatment regimen.

Nancy, a very experienced psychologist, had a running argument with Ed about medication management. Trained and originally licensed in Louisiana where psychologists could prescribe medication, Nancy knew as much as Ed did about psychotropics. She'd spent years prescribing. Once in California, however, things

36

changed. In California, only psychiatrists or physicians were licensed to prescribe medication. Psychologists like Nancy were barred from dispensing meds. So she had to stick to testing and basic therapy and leave the medication management to Ed. As such, she made it her job to keep Ed on his toes.

Ed didn't necessarily welcome the intrusion, but he enjoyed the challenge. He and Nancy sparred regularly. She was outspoken and assertive, especially about her African-Hispanic heritage. She'd climbed the clinical ranks, raised three sons, and juggled a busy household—all despite a chronically unemployed husband and ailing mother. No cheeky psychiatrist was going to intimidate her.

Mark continued, ignoring the undercurrent. "Everyone remained calm. Al jumped in right away. The good news is there were only a handful of patients in the waiting area. The police arrived in less than ten minutes." Mark had a skillful way of keeping his minions focused on positive outcomes. Barbara looked bilious, however.

"Well that may well be, but we can't have that sort of thing happening in the clinic with county mental health coming to assess us for a new grant," Barbara warned. They all knew Seaside was on the short list for several hundred thousand dollars of next year's funding. "The good news is they didn't show up today. Who the hell is seeing Carl, anyway?" Barbara testily scanned the table. "Isn't it one of your students, Amanda?"

Amanda took a breath to reply, but Nancy jumped in. "Yes, it's Sandra. Frankly, Barbara, I wonder if she's in over her head. Sandra may be a two-year intern, but Carl is still a complicated case. I wonder if one of my psych interns is better prepared. Thomas has two more years than Sandra and lots of experience with acute schizophrenia."

"Yes, Carl is volatile, but Sandra has been doing a good job with him and his mother. You know we're treating them for family therapy, not Carl's psychosis," Amanda responded. "Ed's medication seems to be working as long as Carl complies with his behavioral contract and takes it."

Nancy eased back. She'd been round this argument with Amanda before.

"Thanks, Amanda," Ed murmured, "I appreciate the vote of confidence."

Nancy turned to Ed, readying a new argument. "I wonder then if you are prescribing the right meds, Ed. Some of the newer ones you're using don't have enough clinical testing with Carl's type of paranoia."

"Perhaps the two of you could debate Carl's medication after the meeting," Mark cut in. "Let's reassess Carl's progress in a week. For now, we'll leave things as they are."

There was silence around the room, but Ed's face brightened. He glanced at Amanda for reinforcement. She gave him nothing.

"Moving along, we need to talk about the new grants," Mark spoke quickly. "They're very important to the future of the clinic."

"We've got to demonstrate competence, especially when the reviewers are here. Please be sure you and the rest of the staff are doing everything you can to comply with good clinic protocol," Barbara added loudly. "How do you think the temp, Lila, is doing?"

"She's jumping in and working hard as far as I know. I've seen her stay late a couple of nights to finish up filing," Nancy commented. "She could do with a little less makeup though. At least she got rid of her nose ring."

"I heard Al flirting with her last week." Ed chuckled.

"And what did she do?" Barbara asked.

"I believe I heard her say she didn't want to be bothered by an old macho man with too much time on his hands," Ed responded. The room erupted in laughter.

"Good for her. An assertive woman," Nancy observed. "Al can be a little much sometimes."

"She and Jackie seem to get along all right. Are you going to hire her?" Amanda added.

"We'll assess her progress in two weeks and make our decision," Mark concluded.

"OK, keep in mind we have auditors coming through this week; try to keep your patients down to a low roar," Barbara directed. She stabbed her pen into her notepad for emphasis as she turned to Ed. "I still need that report on the Larson suicide, Ed. The authorities keep calling."

Ed was notorious for putting off writing lengthy reports. "Yeah, yeah, yeah, you know I'm pretty busy. I'll get it to you by the end of the week."

"Too bad about that kid," Mark said. "Acutely depressed, I guess. Still, the hanging was a shock."

"The mother is just as depressed," Ed said ruefully.

"Nevertheless, I need that report by tomorrow, Ed." Barbara leaned into him.

"Will do, old girl," Ed said nonchalantly, winking at Barbara. "Do we need to relax a bit, Barbara dear?"

"Don't patronize me, Edward. Just do your job, please, and all will be well."

"Amen," Ed intoned. Then he winked again.

"OK, anything else?"

Amanda reached in her handbag. "Well, there's this." She laid the cryptic gray note in the middle of the table. The group studied it.

"God, Amanda," Barbara spoke first. "Here's *another* misguided person leaving stuff."

"Well, Amanda, just who are you pushing?" Ed asked. "You're such a motherly sort, I'm surprised anyone would attack you."

"Come on, Ed, stop fooling around," Nancy cut in.

"Did anyone else get something like this?" Mark asked. No one spoke. "Well, after this morning, maybe it's Carl. That would fit."

"Yes, Mark, but it says, '*her*'" Barbara corrected, studying the note. "Unless it's Carl telling you to back off his mother or something..."

"You don't personally treat the mother, do you?" Mark asked.

"No. But I've got plenty of other female patients who someone might feel I'm being too hard on."

"Well," Nancy piped up, "you're not alone. We used to have plenty of things like this in Louisiana—and some down in Chula Vista. Just be on guard, I guess."

"Yes, and let Al know, will you?" Mark directed. "Alert the rest of the staff, Barbara. Nancy, you'll inform your interns of course?"

"Sure."

"OK, and Amanda—you're taking precautions?"

"Of course."

"I can lend you a .38 if you'd like. Got one at home," Ed added helpfully.

"Ed, don't even kid about it," Barbara snapped.

"Let me know immediately if there's anything else unusual," Mark cut in, looking first at Ed, then at the rest of the group. "That's all for today. Thanks, everyone."

As they left the suite, Amanda followed Nancy out. Thomas Wong, one of Nancy's two psych assistants, was waiting outside the door. He stopped Nancy for a question, and then waited for Ed to enter the hallway. When Ed emerged, the two men began chatting about a case and went into Ed's office. The door closed behind them.

"Amanda," Nancy called out, ushering Amanda into her office. "We still need to talk about that problem between Thomas and Sandra."

"Yes, we do. Thomas seems intent on making life miserable for her regarding that Korean family," Amanda said. "I know he thinks she doesn't know enough about Koreans but he still didn't have the right to interfere with the family directly."

"Well, Amanda, he has a point about how she got blatantly angry with the husband."

"Yes, you may be right. But for Thomas to talk to the family directly just because he's also Korean, and then denigrate Sandra to them, is not acceptable either."

"I guess we need to have a powwow with the four of us to clear the air. How about tomorrow morning at nine? We can check in with the interns and confirm via e-mail," Nancy suggested diplomatically.

"OK, tomorrow then. We'll get this worked out," Amanda agreed, not willing to make the issue bigger than it was. She turned to head to her own office.

"Amanda," Nancy touched her arm, "sorry you received that weird note. Very disturbing. You got a double whammy today."

"Yup. Thanks for your concern. See you later."

Amanda went in to her office, feeling drained. Neither the note nor Nancy was really bothering her at the moment. The tension between Ed and Barbara, however, was palpable. Ed was a gifted psychiatrist even if he was a conundrum as a man. He'd followed the classical path of psychoanalysis with an expensive Harvard degree. She still found it odd that Ed had landed at a small clinic in Del Mar. Needling Barbara seemed to be one of his favorite pastimes these days. She wasn't sure what the gun was about.

She glanced at the clock: 6:20. Time to meet Shelby, her best friend from college. Shelby was going through a tough time right now. She'd been divorced for only a few weeks from Bill, a tax accountant, who'd left Shelby for an heiress named Carolyn. White-blond and green eyed, Shelby's looks were a sharp contrast to Amanda's auburn hair and topaz eyes. Midthirties, the women had each been through a serious relationship that ended sadly. But Shelby's was fresh. She'd phoned to meet up with Amanda at the Fish Market near the racetrack at 6:45 tonight. It was a fifteen-minute drive so Amanda knew she'd have to hustle.

She quickly tidied up the cushions and chairs, and tossed some therapeutic toys back in the toy box. Snatching up her purse and keys at 6:30, she grabbed her briefcase and mug, and then headed out to her car, all thoughts of Carl and the curious note forgotten.

Chapter Eight

Watchers

Amanda rode the elevator to the first floor and stepped out. She walked quickly down the long hall to the craftsman doors at the entryway and popped out of the building nearly on a run despite her bandaged foot. The evening breeze whipped her wavy hair back as she turned left toward the parking spaces. The chilled air felt good—like a fresh breath from the lips of Mother Nature herself.

As she turned, Amanda heard a man's voice at the far end of the parking lot. As she walked toward her car, she saw it was Mark Huston, deep in a cell call, standing near the bushes out of sight of the windows in his office above. Something in his manner made her study him as she beeped her car open.

Mark looked up. He waved and covered the phone. "Hey. Glad you're finally going home. Long day."

"Yeah, you know it." Amanda called out.

"Trying to get a good signal," he shouted then he turned back to his conversation.

Amanda opened the back door to her Audi, dumped her briefcase inside, and then opened the driver door to slide in. As she did so, she could hear Mark's voice clearly.

"Yes, I understand that, but you have to give me some more time..." After a pause, he continued, "Yes, I get that, but I need some more time, I tell you..."

Amanda closed the car door. Eavesdropping was not usually her style, but this was certainly the first time she'd seen Mark doing business in the parking lot. Buckling up, she checked the mirror, and then reached in her bag for lip gloss. "It'll have to do," she groaned and fluffed her hair up in back, then popped the mirror back into place.

Starting the Audi, she backed up then drove through the lot toward the street, glancing at Mark in the rearview mirror. He waved as she pulled away. Turning out onto Pacific Coast Highway—PCH to locals—she headed north to the Fish Market. A glass of wine sounded really good right now.

If her mind hadn't been on merlot, Amanda might have noticed a battered black Nissan make a U-turn on PCH, then tuck in behind her Audi. The Nissan sat low with dark windows. The driver, in an old blue hoodie, stared intently at the Audi ahead.

Opening the driver's side window, Amanda breathed in the salty air. She gazed over the rooftops to the blue ocean stretching for miles to the west with no end in sight. As she inched through town, Del Mar bubbled with tourists. June was when they poured in despite the cool marine layer that grayed the mornings until the sun finally burnt it off by afternoon. June Gloom the papers called it. Although actually June Gloom started in May and often hung around until August before the sparkling summer days emerged that all the travel brochures depicted. Amanda drove along as the red-yellow sun began to set. Knots of tourists and locals wandered along the street, some pushing baby strollers, others lugging surfboards.

Del Mar was a love-hate kind of place. At the turn of the nineteenth century, it had been just a sleepy village on the southern railroad's Santa Ana-to-San Diego line before the celebrities descended. Bing Crosby and his cronies loved the area so much they built a race-track, which opened in 1937 with a little help from the WPA. The Thoroughbred Club soon made harness racing a worldwide attraction. Jimmy Durante, Desi and Lucy, Esther Williams, Pat Obrien, Ann Miller, and others turned the area into a stars' playground. Decades later, the tiny Del Mar coastline bristled with hotels like L'Auberge Resort and million-dollar-view homes overlooking surfer shacks.

Speeding on PCH past Fifteenth on a green light, Amanda passed L'Auberge on the left and sped down the hill toward the race-track. She heard tires squeal behind her but drove on, oblivious to the hooded driver behind her cursing at the cross traffic.

"Goddamn," the kid spat out, braking hard as a teenage boy in cut offs and a skinny girl in short shorts drifted across the crosswalk, stopping traffic. The light was red. But the reckless teens crossed anyway, daring the cars to do something. Fuming, the kid jammed the accelerator once the teens had passed, and nearly clipped a star-tled biker who darted into the crosswalk. Flipping him off, the kid sped north, eyeballing the Audi as it dropped into the valley where the racetrack rose from the sand.

She's movin' fast tonight. Wonder where she's goin'? Home if she turns soon. To her rich little beach condo, Rich Bitch. Oops, passed it up. Man, she's movin'. Well, you can't get away from me, lady. No matter how smart you are. Got you in my sights.

The kid glanced at the backseat where the new rifle waited, wrapped in brown paper. New. Virgin. Bullets close by in a bag. The kid was itching to try her out, but right now there was Amanda.

Let's see where you're goin'.

Amanda pushed through several stop signs until she finally passed Dog Beach on the left. She glanced over and saw a few dogs dragging their owners across the damp sand as the sun met the Green Flash at water's edge. At Via de la Valle, she swung right, then raced the last few blocks to the Fish Market, parked, and got out. She crossed the lot quickly, her feet slapping the pavement. Glancing south, Amanda saw the racetrack's graceful arches and grandstands jutting above the turf. She smiled, feeling good for the first time today. Entering the glass front door, she moved quickly toward the bar through the crowd, inhaling the smell of fresh crab and shrimp, looking for Shelby.

Accelerating hard, the Nissan barely caught the Audi at Via de la Valle, and then followed when it turned east. The kid parked on the street once Amanda wheeled into the parking lot at the restaurant. Turning off the engine, the face from the Nissan watched as Amanda passed into the restaurant. The kid sat, patient, sometimes glancing at the prize in the backseat, waiting for the right moment to unwrap her.

"Soon," the kid said to a fly buzzing the window. "Soon."

Chapter Nine

Shockwaves

"Taking your half in the middle again," Amanda said to Emily the next morning. The cat lay curled next to her, snoozing. She opened one eye, slapped her tail in acknowledgement, and then lapsed back into sleep. Amanda's window stood slightly open across from her queen bed; she smelled the crisp sea air and watched as a seagull glided by. "Another perfect Tuesday in paradise."

Rising, Amanda winced. It felt like she'd stepped into cement. "Damn those new shoes." She loved how trendy they made her look yesterday, but after a couple of hours those Manolos were hell. The scratch from Carl didn't help much either, but it seemed to be healing nicely. As she headed to the kitchen for tea, Amanda thought about Shelby. She'd been in a great mood last night. They'd shared a couple of glasses of St. Supery merlot and reminisced about old boyfriends and vacations they'd taken together, especially the one to Aspen. Shelby had unfortunately broken a wrist while learning to snowboard on that trip, but she'd been rescued off the mountain by a pair of cute snow patrollers, so the week had a silver lining after all. One of the guys had recently found her on Facebook, so Shelby was busy with a budding online romance. Amanda was pleased that Shelby was feeling upbeat and hopeful again.

Tea made, Amanda sipped while she reviewed today's schedule: Nancy at 9:00 a.m., divorcing couple at 9:30, a bulimic at 10:30, a depressed teen at 11:30, lunch, a bi-polar mom at 1:00 p.m., then intern supervision at 2:00, and out by 5:00 p.m. if all went well. She moved quickly through her morning routine: cereal, CNN, toiletries, makeup. A few minutes in her walk-in closet and she emerged in a blue skirt, cream silk blouse with a colorful scarf at the neck, and regular pumps—but in purple—to complete her outfit. Checking her phone, Amanda saw no messages. She stepped into her office nook off the kitchen to answer a couple of e-mails, when she caught a musty smell. Peering down, she saw that Emily, Siamese huntress, had caught another mouse. This one lay pulverized on the beige carpet.

"Emily, you're missing your moment," Amanda called. No response. Huffing, she got the dustpan and scooped up the dead thing. Gazing at its pathetic remains, Amanda had an ominous feeling in her gut. Ignoring it, she made a hurried trip to the dumpster, then returned to dab her carpet and spray Lysol. Glancing at the clock, Amanda saw she was now late; sighing, she grabbed her briefcase and bag and rushed out to her Audi.

Coffee—the thought flashed as she slid into the driver's seat and turned on the ignition. "Damn. Forgot my travel mug. Oh well, paper it is." She sped to her favorite coffee drive-through a few blocks away. Later, with a steaming latte beside her, she drove on. Gulping coffee, she suddenly had to slam on the brakes when the woman in front of her stopped short at the train tracks. Glancing down, Amanda watched as a smear of brown sludge slid down her silk blouse.

"Crap. I'll have to blot it when I get there."

Pulling into her Seaside parking space a few minutes later she grabbed her bag, briefcase, and latte and raced into the clinic.

The lobby was peaceful. Jackie sat at the front desk, answering the phones; Lila stood in the file room behind Jackie, prepping charts for the day. Amanda heard Al's voice booming from the break room. As she passed down the hallway to her office, she noticed Mark and Barbara's office door was half open. She could hear muffled voices from inside. Slipping inside her office, Amanda dumped her belongings and picked up the phone to call Nancy. She was interrupted by a quiet tap on the door. Lila entered with Amanda's revised schedule and her charts for the day.

"Good morning. Hey...looks like you splobbed." Lila eyed Amanda's latte stain.

"Yeah, don't drink and drive. Could be a sign I should cut down on my caffeine."

"My mother did that when she was going through the big M. She switched to herbal tea. Man, she was even crankier than usual. We begged her to go back to coffee." Lila snorted.

Lila's long brown bangs popped up and down when she blinked. Pretty girl though, Amanda thought, despite the twelve-inch snake tattoo curling up the length of Lila's left arm, its iridescent blues and greens undulating as she moved. Amanda noticed the snake's tongue peeking out from Lila's neck where the tattoo disappeared into her cami strap and reemerged near her throat, like the snake was tasting her flesh.

Lila watched Amanda studying her. "Sorry, noticing your colorful tattoo," Amanda covered.

"Yeah," Lila shrugged. "I get that a lot."

"It's striking. Really. How are you anyway, Lila? Are you liking it here?" Amanda added cheerfully, trying not to stare as the snake arm stretched out with today's charts.

"Oh, I'm good," Lila said, flipping her hair aside, "for the most part. You guys are cool. Some of those patients are jacked, though. Sorry, 'distressed.'"

"Sometimes they are, it's true."

"That Carl is really whacked. Man, that dude drools. Al was on him yesterday like the LAPD." Lila rolled her eyes.

"Yes, thank God for Al. Hopefully, today will be better. Keep up the good work, Lila."

Lila shrugged and headed out, neatly balancing four more stacks of files while she wrangled open the fire door. Amanda glanced down at her calendar then began dabbing the ugly latte spot. The next moment, she heard a gut-wrenching scream.

Amanda sprang into crisis mode. She rushed toward her heavy office door, yanked it open, and sped into the hallway. Something moved to the right. It was Lila, standing paralyzed, in Ed Michael's doorway. She was gasping, unable to speak. As Amanda moved to Lila's side, she saw that the files had fallen all around the girl's feet, blocking the door from closing. Following Lila's line of sight, Amanda saw it.

Deep inside the office, Psychiatrist Ed Michael sat upright at his desk, eyes bulging, face contorted into an ugly grimace. Ed's neck was wrenched up and back by a window shade cord that stretched across from the double windows to his right. The cord looped several times around Ed's neck and was pulled taut; Ed's mouth gaped open. His bloated tongue hung halfway out.

Amanda stared at the scene for several seconds, and then she swiftly stepped around Lila and waded through the avalanche of spilled files. As she moved toward Ed's desk, Amanda gasped when she realized that Ed's right hand was impaled on the desk, palm down. A blade was driven through the man's entire hand clean through to the wood beneath. As she stepped closer, Amanda clutched her stomach when she realized there was also a knife sticking out of Ed's groin. Her eyes followed the red-black stream of blood that spilled from his groin onto his leather chair, then puddled in the thick carpet below.

"Oh my God, the stench," Amanda choked.

Her eyes darted to the other side of the desk; there were some kind of marks on the top of the desk. Covering her mouth she swallowed the urge to bolt or barf, and forced herself to come around to the left side of the desk and look closer.

F-R-E- something.

Freu or *Frew* was crudely spelled out in—blood maybe?—with an additional letter trailing off. R? P? B? D? It looked like the letters had mixed with some kind of liquid from Ed's teacup, which lay smashed to the right. Bending slightly, she saw Ed's left arm as it hung lifeless, some kind of dried muck caked on his fingers.

Amanda felt sick. She staggered back then crunched on something. Glasses. Reeling around, she glimpsed Ed's certificates on the walls now splattered with blood. A second more and she had to get out. Amanda half stumbled toward the door, right into Lila as Mark Huston suddenly appeared in the doorway.

"Holy Hell, what happened in here, Amanda?" Mark's nostrils flared as he caught the scent. Amanda saw the reflection of her own horror in his eyes. The three of them stood there, transfixed.

"Argh, ugh, I...I...can't...ugh..." Lila whimpered, and sank slowly to the floor.

"Lila, move back," Mark choked out and grabbed the girl as she sagged. "Amanda get out of there."

"Lila, look at me," he shouted, dragging Lila backward out the door. "You're fine. Look at me," Mark ordered. He got her into the hallway, and jerked his head at Amanda, signaling her to back out of Ed's office. The door finally swung shut, and then stuck at the disheveled files. Amanda gaped at Mark and Lila, then back to Ed, too stunned to move.

There was noise as Jackie and Al burst from the break room. "Jackie, move Lila to the couch in the back," Mark instructed. "Al, call 911."

"What is it? What's happened?" Jackie screamed. She stopped halfway down the hallway, registering the stench and Lila's near catatonic state.

"Mark, what?" Al shouted.

From the opposite direction, Nancy Davis raced from the front of the clinic toward Mark. "Nancy, the rest of you, it's an emergency! Clear the waiting area, Nancy; check for any patients in session and clear them out. Use the alarm if you have to." Nancy blinked, and then started to say something, but Mark's face made her turn and jump into action.

"Al, call 911 NOW. Tell them there's a body. Jackie, take Lila to the couch. NOW. Don't look, just go."

Al moved toward the lobby talking into his cell. Jackie began to cry but grabbed Lila's arm as instructed and swept her up the hallway, nearly colliding with Barbara who rushed out of the master office.

"What's happened?" Barbara scanned Lila's chalk-white face.

"Barbara, Jackie...take Lila into the break room. *Now!* Barbara, I don't want you to see this," Mark shouted.

"See what?" Barbara demanded.

"Never mind, just GO!" He dashed back into Ed's office, grabbed Amanda's arm, and pulled her through the files into the hallway. Savagely kicking the files aside, he let the door slam behind him. For a split second, Barbara looked back and read Amanda's revulsion. Then she saw Mark's glare and quickly turned back to Lila and Jackie. The three women finally disappeared into the kitchen.

"My god, Amanda. What happened in there?" Mark whispered, leaning with her against the wall.

"I don't know, Mark." Amanda felt like a bomb had imploded in her gut. She struggled to breathe, but gagged, every breath bringing in more of the stench. She grabbed Mark's shoulder.

"Lila...Lila...had just delivered my case files to me. Then she must have...gone into Ed's office to deliver his. The next thing I knew, she was screaming...I came out, saw her standing there, then came behind her and saw...Ed. I went inside...and it's...horrible... Mark. Ed's...my god, he must be dead..."

As Mark steadied her, Amanda noticed vaguely how putrid green the walls were. Like diseased snot. Nausea suddenly swept over her. She clamped her teeth together and sucked air into her lungs through her nose. *I will not lose control*, she told herself silently. *You are OK, you are OK.* She said it over and over, a life-or-death mantra.

Mark paused, studying her. "I need to go in for a look. Are you OK out here for a minute?" She nodded. Mark pushed the door open, and stepped into Ed's office. Steeling himself, he moved toward Ed's desk. More composed, Amanda turned, swung her scarf up over her mouth and nose, and ventured a step or two back into the room behind Mark. The door shut behind them.

"This is unbelievable," Mark wailed as he paused at the edge of the desk, surveying the scene. They stood together in silence. Suddenly Mark pivoted and charged toward Amanda. "Come on, let's get out of here, Amanda." He grabbed her arm and pulled them both out of the room. "Let's wait for the police. Come on...in my office."

"I need to sit down, I guess," Amanda said weakly. Her knees were shaking.

Mark guided Amanda to the couch inside the suite. She sat heavily. He went over to his desk, pulled out a large piece of paper, wrote something on it in black marker, left for a moment to tape it on Ed's door, and then reentered, closing the door behind them.

"I put a *Do Not Enter* sign on Ed's door. The police can handle this."

They jumped when Barbara abruptly entered from the side door connecting to the large conference room. She tripped, seeing their reaction, but managed to stay upright. "My God, Mark, what is it? Amanda, you look like death! What's happened?" she shrieked as she moved toward Mark.

"It's Ed," Mark said quietly. "I want you to prepare yourself, Barbara. It's something...horrible. It looks like Ed's been killed. Al's calling the police."

"Oh my God, it's not possible," Barbara screamed in English, then followed up with a stream of angry German. Mark went to her, his face drawn, but Barbara waved him off. "Let's all just sit down and wait, Barbara. The police are coming."

Barbara looked like she wanted to hit him, but she finally sank next to him on the couch and slumped forward, hugging her knees. "Mark, can I see...?"

"You don't want to see it, Barbara. Believe me."

Barbara watched Mark, and then looked at Amanda. Amanda shook her head sadly and closed her eyes.

"Goddamn," Barbara blurted and lay back. Mark put his head in his hands. Minutes later, the intercom blared.

"Police are here, boss," Al's voice boomed.

"At last," Mark sighed.

"Mark...?"

"I will handle this, Barbara," he said firmly and went out.

Barbara and Amanda looked at each other. Neither spoke.

Chapter Ten

Murder Most Foul

San Diego PD arrived quickly. Officers Boyd Fredrick and Debbie Lyle happened to be less than two miles away at the fairgrounds, working their way through a robbery. When the Gem and Mineral Show opened up for its second day, one of the jeweler's displays was smashed and several thousand dollars in gemstones was missing. The officers were finishing up interviews with peripheral witnesses, and Debbie was bent over paperwork as Boyd went on the prowl for coffee when they got the frantic call from Seaside Clinic. The two left on a run for their patrol car.

Boyd Fredrick was a brawny, thirty-seven-year-old beat cop. He'd been to the clinic a few times over the past year during routine calls. Nothing major—a schizo or two. Leaving junior officer Logan to secure the robbery scene, Boyd and Debbie Lyle, his thirty-five-year-old partner who had homicide experience, sped south on PCH to Seaside. Debbie was driving.

"Seaside's usually pretty quiet," Boyd told her as they crawled through beach traffic. "A dead body is kind of unusual, though." He focused on the crosswalks as they hit all the regular stop signs. Tourists juggled coolers and squirming children as they strolled along; surfers crossed barefoot, boards in tow. Boyd noticed a couple of graying beach types. The dude in the yellow hat looked familiar. Boyd was pretty sure he'd arrested the guy for selling pot at least once, probably down by the Poseidon Restaurant. The two beach bums eyed the cop car, and then they sauntered across the crosswalk when the light changed, trying to look relaxed. Yellow Hat averted his eyes. Debbie drove on once they passed, then she sped up the hill to commercial Del Mar. Whipping into Seaside's parking lot two minutes later, Debbie stopped short. People streamed out the front door. Easing in, she parked as close to the door as possible, and the two jumped out. Debbie smiled over at Boyd.

"Need an antacid?" She knew that Boyd's experience with dead bodies was limited.

"Nah," he teased. "I know you'll catch me if I faint." She chuckled, and then the two moved quickly through the front door, all business. Boyd led them up the clinic staircase at the left, avoiding the elevator altogether. Seconds later, they popped out onto the second floor. Reception was straight ahead. Boyd spied Al right away. He was standing next to the reception desk, waiting. He knew Al from previous visits, hauling out the 5150s. Right now, Al looked amazingly white—particularly since Al was Hispanic.

"What ya got, Al?" Boyd asked as Debbie scanned the scene.

"Shrink's d...d...dead we think, officers." Al gasped for air.

"Take it easy, Al," Boyd soothed. "Go slow."

"Someone killed the guy, I guess. Come on. Down here." Al moved unsteadily, then got his stride and led the officers at a run down the hallway.

"It's bad. Not seen it myself, but Dr. Huston says it's real ugly." The officers slipped on thin crime scene gloves as they trailed Al. Debbie heard someone weeping in one of the left-hand rooms. Al finally stopped at an office near the end of the hallway.

Looks like he's about to hurl, Debbie thought. She flipped her note-book open and Al stepped back as the officers stepped up to the entrance. Debbie jotted down the name on the door as they entered: *Dr. Edward Michael, Psychiatrist.* She noted the handmade *Do Not Enter* sign. Boyd went first, pushing the door open all the way. The officers walked on into the room and signaled Al to wait outside. The door sucked shut behind them.

Boyd caught the smell first. "Oh man. Shit...and piss, I'd guess."

"Blood...old blood, maybe some other stuff," Debbie added. They noted the files and papers littered at the entrance and moved in slowly to the desk to study the male body trussed up in the leather chair behind the mahogany desk.

"Yup, this is a good one." Debbie cautiously moved to the side of the desk. "Looks like somebody didn't like the shrink too much... if in fact he *is* the shrink." Methodically, the two officers explored the room, limiting contact. They noted the shade cord around the neck of the victim, the impaled hand, the weapon sticking out of the man's pants. "Yup," Debbie said to Boyd, "definitely a good one."

Boyd called for crime scene backup. He relayed the message: homicide. Debbie continued documenting, shielding her nose periodically from the stench. She knew from experience the stench bugged you for only about three minutes. After that, your olfactory nerves went numb, and you couldn't smell it anymore. Oddly reassuring. Especially with fresh death.

Over the next hour Boyd corralled the staff and remaining patients in the large general conference room next to Mark and Barbara's office adjacent to the kitchen. Then he and Debbie interviewed Lila. The girl blubbered throughout the entire interview and had to have smelling salts. They moved on to Amanda Carlisle and Mark Huston, getting all the preliminary details lined up for the detectives who'd do the in-depths.

Back at the front desk, Jackie hurriedly cancelled as many patients on the day's schedule as possible. Others who arrived were turned away by the yellow crime scene tape now stretched across the front of the building. The phone rang off the hook. Jackie gratefully forwarded it to voice mail, and then unplugged the main line. She finally joined the others in the conference room at the back, sat down, and burst into tears.

Chapter Eleven

Nick

Out on the street, the murder buzz drew a crowd. PCH slowed to a crawl. A throng of shop people and tourists clogged the lot by the time the detectives and forensics people began arriving.

Detective Nick Caswell was avoiding writing a report, checking baseball scores on his BlackBerry, when the call came in: homicide in Del Mar. Could be the name of the next big cop movie, Nick thought. *Death in Del Mar.*

Hopping into his black Crown Vic, Nick drove north on I-5, then headed over on Del Mar Heights toward the water. "God, the summer traffic here is as bad as ever," Nick said to himself. He had a momentary twinge when he turned north at PCH and saw the ocean rippling out over the pine trees. "Man, what a beautiful set of waves," he exclaimed. He'd surfed there plenty of times, board in hand, wading into the surf, feeling the cool rush of water on his legs.

Suddenly he hit the brakes. A couple of preteens stepped off the curb right in front of him, jaywalking. The lurch pulled him back to reality. "Damn, focus, man." The Crown Vic plodded up PCH, waiting at each of half a dozen stop signs between Del Mar Heights and the clinic since the foot traffic was so heavy.

Nick knew this was the calm before the screws began to turn. Caswell, thirty-eight, was a fifteen-year veteran; he'd been a detective now for five years and had a pretty good reputation for applying pressure until perps coughed up the truth. He'd moved over to homicide three years ago. Divorced four years, he'd come up through the ranks. Nick's father, Hal, had practically run the Escondido Police department. Hal had been convinced his surfer son would end up a "no good surf bum with knotty knees and friggin' skin cancer." But Nick had done well. He'd made detective in his early thirties and cracked a few high-profile cases like the Gaslamp transient murders and the Imperial Beach strangler case where a string of college kids were murdered by a lunatic fond of sailing ropes and slipknots.

Despite forty dawning, Nick kept his surfer look. Long and lean, his dirty blond-brown hair fell over his eyes and always, always he had a day-old beard—no matter when he'd shaved last. His ex, Lauren, had left him a few years ago. Ditched him for a high-profile real estate broker famous for selling horsey estates in Fairbanks Ranch. Good riddance, Nick thought at the time. Nothing he did was good enough, according to Lauren. But in the eyes of their seven-year-old, Tracy, Dad could do no wrong. He hadn't seen Tracy much though in the past six months. She'd been busy with her new horse, Candy. And Nick had been inundated with spring murders. Something in the air, he figured. Something about San Diego June gloom that starts in April and doesn't end until fall makes people want to murder somebody.

By the time Nick reached Seaside he had to wade through a crowd. Nick was in charge of the core homicide investigations for this area of San Diego. Despite its incorporation as a city, Del Mar still depended on San Diego proper for homicide investigations. Nick got support from other investigatory personnel from San Diego

PD—evidence collection, photography, medical examiners, forensics, and the evidence storage unit. Boyd had checked the database while Nick was driving to see if Seaside popped up, then e-mailed Nick the results. A couple of 5150s showed, nothing serious. There was a defacing incident—something to do with neo-Nazi sentiment or something.

Easing out of his Crown Vic after he parked at the back, Nick ducked under the crime scene tape at the front door, entered the building slowly, and climbed the stairs. He emerged on the second floor and meandered into the waiting area. It was empty except for one officer standing guard. He called Boyd.

Debbie and Boyd were sequestered in the clinic's large conference room with the staff and a few patients. Debbie had called in backup so the entire group could be isolated and watched. The group had been instructed not to confer, but the officers were having a hard time keeping everyone quiet. One kid about twenty kept crying, "I want my monkey, I just want my monkey."

"I hope that's a patient," Boyd said to Debbie under his breath. He got up to retrieve Nick from the front. "OK, here we go."

Nick walked slowly toward Boyd when he appeared at the end of the hallway, scanning everything. Front desk. Waiting area. Exits. Elevator. Escape stairs off to the west near the restrooms. Plenty of places to hide then ditch a murder scene, he noted.

"Hey, Nick," Boyd said, striding toward him. "It's a good one."

"OK, show me the way." Boyd led him down the hall to the murder scene.

Continuing his methodical cruise, Nick noted various doors: Observation Room, Play Room 1, Play Room 2, numbered office doors, labeled offices marked Nancy Davis and Amanda Carlisle. There was a room marked Interns next to Davis's office. Beyond that was one labeled Lounge. Boyd stopped just beyond Amanda Carlisle's door.

Carlisle.

Nick remembered the name, but couldn't place it. Boyd pointed to the door on his right. Noting the name Dr. Edward Michael, he cocked his ear and turned slightly at voices coming from the opening elevator in the lobby he'd just left. He watched his crime scene staff emerge. Gail Burton, forensic investigator, and Marcus Roberts, assistant medical examiner, spied Nick down the long corridor and walked rapidly toward him when he beckoned.

"Welcome," Nick greeted them. "Just got here too. Officer, give us an update."

The three turned to Boyd and Debbie, who had now joined them, leaving two other cops with the sequestered clinic group. The pair gave a quick update on their findings.

"Enough to get us started," Nick said when the officers finished. "Let's go." Snapping on gloves, shoe booties, and floater masks, Nick, Gail, and Marcus turned and pushed inside through the crime tape. As they entered, Gail snapped photos. Boyd followed the threesome in and stood just inside the door. Debbie anchored the outside, barring anyone else from entering. There was silence for a moment while the trio scanned the room, taking it in.

"No obvious blood on the door or on the nameplate," Nick said mostly to himself as he glanced behind him. The team moved gingerly toward the desk at the far end. Everyone caught the smell, but kept going.

Marcus and Gail conferred as they stepped around the sides of the desk. Then they moved in for a closer look. Gail snapped a flurry of pictures of everything, especially the body getting stiffer by the minute. She made notes in her old leather notebook while Marcus began examining the body, recording his observations with a hand recorder.

"Body," Marcus spoke clearly, "male. Caucasian. Possibly late forties. Business dress, white shirt, looks like an untied bow tie, dark slacks. Sitting upright in a black—looks to be leather—chair. Cord from south facing window blind stretches over to the desk area and... OK...wraps at least two...no...three times around the victim's neck above the prominentia laryngea. Looks like it's yanking said victim back into an upright, slightly arching position. Eyes bulge, tongue extended."

"Interesting. Knife...approximately six-inch blade...is plunged into victim's groin area. Looks like his fly is open—hard to tell at this point. Victim sits in a pool of what looks to be blood and...urine maybe...and something else...Semen possibly? Smell suggests bowel release at time of death."

"Right hand is impaled on desk by a...letter opener...or small kitchen knife...six to eight inches long, thrust between victim's middle and fourth fingers. Blade goes through the soft tissue clean through to the desk surface. Judging from the position of the body in the chair, the victim might have been immobilized so the perp could do the stabbing and strangling afterward. I doubt if he would've held still for a knife to the groin without a struggle if he'd been fully conscious. Could have been dead already, or poisoned, or had a heart attack, or something else."

"Clothes fairly neat. Shirt disheveled but tucked in. Looks like the guy's glasses were smashed down here off to the left behind the chair. Could be the perp's glasses though. Blood flows off the desk top from the impaled right hand, but there's not a whole lot of it."

"This brings us to some marks on the desk. Victim appears to have scrawled something with his left hand. Looks like he was try-ing to write...let's see...F-R-E-x-x or something. Definitely trying to tell us something. Left arm hangs down to the side. Blood's caked on the...left index and middle fingers. A blood smear goes from the last letter off the desk and down. There's blood residue on the carpet under the dangled left hand next to the guy's chair. Also a three- to four-inch puddle of blood perhaps mixed with semen on the carpet beneath his legs where the groin injury flowed out and downward. A couple of drips from the left fingers are on the carpet underneath."

Marcus snapped off the recorder and looked up at Nick waiting for feedback. "What do you think? I'd guess our vic wrote it before he died, judging from the blood on his fingers—but you never know. What's it say?" The team conferred for a minute and agreed the first three letters were *F-R-E-*. The last ones were unclear.

"Freds? Frees? Freed?" Nick guessed. "If we've got the right guy, he's the shrink here, right? Some message about his killer? A patient?

A good-bye? We'll have to check his ID and prints when we get him to the morgue. For right now let's assume it's this Ed Michael guy listed on the door."

Marcus hit the recorder button and continued talking. "The victim's right hand doesn't seem to show any defense wounds per se. Just a clean thrust into the back of the hand with the implement to pin the guy to the surface beneath. Nails seem to be clean. Not much blood. So he may have been nearing death—or paralyzed somehow—when the thrust was made."

Marcus's voice trailed off and he stopped the recorder again. "I don't know, Nick. Maybe the killer left, thinking the victim was dead or dying. Our guy may have had just strength to pull his left index finger through the seeping blood from the right hand, and spell out his message before he went completely unconscious."

"Or croaked," Gail offered.

"Paralyzed? Paralyzed how?" Nick asked, studying the body. "From an injection? Pills? What about that white cabinet in the corner?"

Gail and Marcus checked inside. "Door unlocked, plenty of drug samples inside though. Nothing looks disturbed but stuff could be missing," Gail said, uncertain.

Looking closer at the desk, Nick said, "How about this cup? Looks like whatever was in this also spilled across the desk."

"Saturated the mouse pad too," Gail added.

Leaning down to catch a whiff of the pad, Marcus looked puzzled, and then pushed record again. "There's a broken white porcelain tea cup on the far right side of the desk. Liquid has seeped toward the impaled hand and into the mouse pad. Smells like something herbal, but it's hard to tell without analysis." Marcus leaned close to the victim's face, and sniffed gently.

"Anything?" Nick pressed.

"Maybe. Could be tea or coffee and something more. Lab results will be able to tell us."

"Poison maybe?" Nick said to Marcus.

"Dunno at this point," Marcus replied. He stopped the recorder.

"The good news is it looks like we've got plenty of residue. Still a little in the cup pieces, even," Nick said. "The killer was clumsy. Rushed maybe. Inexperienced?"

There was silence for a moment.

"Looks like the guy's phone has messages," Nick said, seeing the blinking light. "Need to check it out." Nick suddenly heard the hum from the computer. Gail noticed it at exactly the same time, her head snapping toward it. Marcus hit record. "Looks like the computer is live. Please note for the records: I'm hitting the return key to see what comes up." All three watched as the computer screen came to life.

Within seconds a grainy image of a young girl, perhaps seven or eight years old, appeared. Redheaded and dimpled, she looked out from the screen, head toward the camera, her face blank like she was drugged. Her arms were outstretched, grasping the back of a kitchen chair. She bent forward from the waist. Her panties were around her ankles, and a pock-faced old man in profile was standing behind her, fornicating her in the rear end. He had on a ratty T-shirt, but no pants at all. His flabby, tattooed arms held her butt in place. The man smiled wickedly toward the camera.

The three investigators gasped.

Gail stood up in disgust and blurted, "Pervert."

Even Nick flinched. "Damn. The shrink must have been into child porn."

The group stood silent for a few seconds glancing at the screen, then at each other. Marcus, father of four grown children, looked particularly grim. He finally spoke into the recorder, detailing the picture onscreen.

"Be sure you get a picture of that, Gail." Nick glanced up at the plaque on the wall behind Marcus's head. *Edward D. Michael, Psychiatrist.* Next to it was a second plaque: *Specialization in Child Psychiatry.*

"Sick bastard," Gail spat out seeing Nick's line of sight.

"Maybe, Gail. If he had it on for himself. Maybe not if somebody planted it there."

"Yeah, OK. Could be motive."

"Perhaps. Too soon to tell," Nick frowned, rubbing his beard. "We'll need to get Scotty Jones to check out the hard drive."

"Phone too. The messages might help fix the time of death."

Within half an hour, Marcus made a preliminary finding. "The body's been dead probably since last night, judging from the lividity and rigor mortis—maybe twelve hours or so."

"That would put it at about eight or nine last night, right?" Nick said.

"Maybe. We'll know more once we do a full work-up."

"Any idea which thing actually killed the guy?" Nick asked ruefully, pushing his hair back from his eyes.

Marcus grunted. "You mean the strangulation or the knifing or possible poisoning or something else? Dunno. I'd say definitely the perp wanted this guy dead. We'll know more later."

"OK, we'll need to check out the kitchen and bathrooms, and any attendant areas as well," Nick instructed. "Any place substances, chemicals, knives were kept. Looks like two entrances. I guess we came through the guy's main office door off the hallway. Where does that door lead?" Nick pointed to the south door.

"Goes to the head guy's office," Boyd said. "Dr. Huston. Uh, Mr. and Mrs. Huston. Both psychologists. Own the clinic."

"OK, so we've got two exits. The killer could have used one or both—in one and out the other maybe," Nick speculated.

"Hey, Boyd," Gail asked, "what's down on the first floor?"

"Storage rooms plus a small auditorium for training events and big meetings. And a few more therapy rooms."

Nick's phone went. The Field Services Unit had arrived to take prints, track the evidence, and study the forensic detail. After a preliminary overview, Nick summarized: "Dust everything you can find...don't miss the floor, the walls, all surfaces, the door handles, the other guy's office next door here, the body obviously, kitchen, bathrooms. You know the drill. Don't miss the mouse and monitor. Killer may have touched them too."

Over the next several hours the team dusted every possible surface and began fiber analysis. The body was carted off to the morgue.

Gail sketched and measured the scene, and the removable evidence was taken down to headquarters.

As the crew finished, Nick entered the Hustons' executive office where he realized there were three entrances: one to the dead guy's office, one to the corridor, and one opening into a large conference area off to the far left where Debbie Lyle and some other officers were guarding about a dozen people. Several of them looked up expectantly when Nick poked his head in. Debbie hastily handed him a list of names as Gail popped in from the victim's office.

"OK, let's begin taking these people's statements. Where have you set up to do it?" Nick asked Debbie.

She gestured to the Hustons' round conference table. "The owners' executive suite here seemed like the best place now that forensics is done in the murder room. Mark Huston and his wife, Barbara, share it."

"Guess this place used to be a hotel, Nick. They were telling me this room used to be the honeymoon suite." Boyd smirked.

"Great," Nick said, not particularly amused. "How many people we got in total, officers?"

"Fourteen. Three patients. Eleven staffers."

"OK, well it's going to be a long day, folks," Nick said. "Remember, the killer could be sitting in there right now, so be bright."

"Gail and I will be interviewing. We'll start with the head guy, Mark Huston. Boyd, I want you to control the flow of people. We'll release them one at a time if we don't find anything. Nothing leaves the building without a search."

Gail and Nick set themselves up at the round conference table. Nick studied the list. "Huston? I think I remember them from a break-in and suicide case. About three years ago. Stolen drugs. Patient overdosed."

"Don't remember it but I'll take your word for it."

"You ready?" Nick asked her, throwing some of his business cards on the table. They both knew this was the toughest part of all. Sift and sift and sift until you uncover a killer. Sometimes not. Way too many times it was the latter.

"Sure. Notebook, recorder, Rolaids. Good to go."

He rolled his eyes in acknowledgement, and then paused. He was about to ask her if the porn got to her. Gail had a young daughter, maybe seven or eight years old, about the same age as his daughter, Tracy. But he thought better of asking. Bringing up Gail's kid would make him worry about his own. Right now, he had to focus. Murder was number one.

"Send in Dr. Huston. Uh, Mark Huston," Nick signaled Boyd, putting on his crime investigation face. Inwardly, there were times Nick really wished he were surfing. This was one of them.

Chapter Twelve

Mark and Barbara

The door opened and Mark Huston, visibly shaken, stepped into his own office. Nick gestured for him to take a seat across from him. Mark complied. Gail punched the recorder. Mark and Nick studied each other for a moment.

Serious. Officious. Eyes a little close together, Nick thought. Do shrinks kill other shrinks? Had a case about eight years ago. Love triangle. Shrink shot a colleague for boffing his wife. Self-defense, he'd said. Three shots, though. One to the stomach. Two to the head. Pretty deliberate—for self-defense.

"I'm Dr. Huston." Mark extended his hand. Nick reached over and shook. Smooth, Nick thought, as he grasped the man's hand. Like buffed leather.

"I'm in charge of the clinic," Mark continued. "And...I'm...I'm here to help in any way I can."

Nick introduced himself, then Gail. "Tell us what happened."
Nick watched the man's eyes. Unblinking, Mark related the events
of the morning. Then he sat back, jaw clenched slightly.

"And you're sure the body is that of Dr. Edward Michael?"

"Yes. Our staff psychiatrist."

"How long had you known the victim?"

"A little less than twenty years," Mark answered. "Ed came to us
here about four years ago from another clinic. He's a fine psychiatrist
and a good doctor."

"Did he have any enemies, someone who would do this?"

Mark paused slightly. "Well, he was our only psychiatrist, so
he had a unique place. He was a bit eccentric, tended to enjoy the
humorous side of mental health work."

"Explain 'eccentric.'"

Mark blinked twice. "Well, he teased people sometimes. You
know, shared jokes, comics. Sometimes a bit slow on paperwork.
Seemed to do well with his patients, though, and most of the staff."

"Most?

"Well he could sometimes push a joke a little too far."

"With...who?" Nick noticed a photo on the credenza behind
Mark's shoulder. It looked like Mark with a tall, blond woman, smiling from a beach with the waves rolling in behind them.

Mark hesitated.

"This is a homicide investigation, Dr. Huston. We need you to
be completely candid."

"OK. He sometimes butted heads with Nancy Davis, our psychologist intern supervisor. Figuratively of course. A fine woman,
very professional. But she doesn't like a lot of nonsense. And I guess
he could sometimes rub, uh, Barbara, the wrong way. Me too at
times."

"Barbara?"

"Yes, Dr. Barbara Huston. Administrative psychologist, my
wife. Ed bucked the system a little. Barbara's job is to keep it running. There was a little creative tension, nothing serious."

"Anyone else he 'rubbed?'"

"Well, that's hard to say. He treated dozens of psychiatric patients, any number of whom had delusions, paranoia, drug addictions, suicidality, homicidal ideation. Ed had to hospitalize several of them."

"OK. Lots of crazies around. Anyone specifically you know who might want to kill the guy now, this week? Enemies? Old girlfriends?"

"I know of no one specifically," Mark replied, eyes crinkling. "I wish I could help you more but this really came out of the blue... horrible."

"And what about proclivities this guy had?"

"Such as...?"

"Sex, drugs. Gambling. Women. Men. Boys...?"

Mark frowned and looked back and forth between the officers. "Ed...Ed seemed more interested in other people's obsessions as far as I know. He was a scholarly kind of guy. Was he a deviant? Not as far as I can say."

"Married? Girlfriend? Boyfriend?"

"Divorced, no children. I don't know about the rest. Ed usually came alone to clinic get-togethers. He had family back east, but I never met any of them. He didn't mention anyone he was seeing now. I guess I really can't be very helpful to you in this area."

"How about drug use? Heroin? Gambling?"

"Not as far I knew."

"Took his own samples? Prescribed for himself?"

"Not that I ever saw."

"Where were you last night after seven, Dr. Huston?" Nick asked without changing his casual slouch.

"I left the office about seven to join some friends for dinner. A dinner meeting actually. At Bully's. Down the street. Barbara met us also...a little later."

"Later?"

"Well she had some paperwork and a few calls to return first. Got there about eight or thereabouts, I think."

"Who did you meet?"

"Mary and Tom. Maynard. Friends from San Francisco."

"And after?" Nick could hear Gail breathe beside him.

There was a beat as Mark prepared to answer. "Then we all left. Around nine thirty or ten, and went home. I don't recall the exact time."

Nick noticed the man seemed agitated, subtly tapping his left fingers on the table, buffed leather in action. Mark spotted Nick's glance at his fingers; he stopped tapping. Nick suddenly pointed at the photo behind Mark's head. "Is that her?"

"My wife? Yes. Taken in Hawaii a couple of years ago. She really loves it there."

"Is it possible your wife was romantically involved with the dead man?" Gail interjected.

"Barbara? Hardly." Mark half smiled and sat back. "Not Barbara...not with Ed."

"OK, Doctor," Nick leaned in. "I have to ask this. Did you kill him?"

Mark's eyes narrowed slightly. "Of course not, detective. I run a mental health clinic. I'm in the business of helping people not killing them."

"OK then, how about your wife?"

Mark moved slightly in his chair and a red flush inched up his neck toward his chin. "My wife would never do such a thing. She and Ed sometimes had conflict, but she would never dream of doing anything like this."

"There's an incident on the books about a defacing on the premises last year. Any idea why that might have happened?"

"An unfortunate incident. We don't really know where that came from."

"I understand from the other officers that your wife has a pretty thick accent."

"Austrian. But she's been in the States for a long time." Mark sat back and folded his arms across his chest.

Nick stared at him. Mark stared back. Neither breathed. Finally, Nick exhaled. "Anyone else you think might be especially homicidal in this place?"

"I've racked my brain, believe me, detective. I can't think of anyone who would do such a horrible thing. Especially here."

"Yes, why here, Doctor? Why not at his home for example? Or on the street?"

"There must be something. I agree with you. Something about his accessibility here. Or his proximity. Something."

"You saw the crime scene, right?" Mark nodded. "What did you think?"

"Well I was overcome...but it looked like it happened...last night or something. He had on yesterday's clothes, I believe. Looked like he had been working...when...it happened."

"What about the marks on the desk?"

"I thought I saw...an *F*...and an *R*...or something..." Mark's voice trailed off. "I saw it only very briefly."

"What do they mean? *F-R-* and what else?"

"Can't recall, really."

Nick watched him for a moment, and then he sat forward. "OK, I'd like to have personnel files on all your staffers, as well as everyone's schedule from yesterday if you can provide it. I can get a search warrant if you like, but it will go faster if you all cooperate."

"We have nothing to hide here. We'll provide whatever you need. Jackie Forrest can help you with that. She runs the front desk."

"OK, that's all for now, Dr. Huston, thank you for all your help." Nick rose from his chair. "My cards are on the table there if you need to reach me. Please stay in town, as we'll need to contact you further. One last thing: please don't confer with anyone, including your wife, until we have interviewed everyone in the conference room."

"I understand. May I take my briefcase?" Mark asked, indicating a large valise beside his desk.

"No, we'd like to see everything before we release it back to you...including your phone, if you don't mind. Please feel free to contact me if you think of anything else."

"I understand. I hope you find this person...as soon as you can, officers." Mark took a few cards and was escorted out of the office to the parking lot below.

Nick turned to Gail once he was gone. "What do you think?"

"Hard to say. The guy's probably used to masking what he feels. And being in charge. Strong though, physically. Could have done it."

"Maybe. He kind of bothers me."

"Because he's a shrink?"

"More because his wife's here. He reacted more about her than himself."

"Could be a sign."

"Let's do her next."

Gail smiled. "Seems fitting we're in the old honeymoon suite." It was just too good to let pass.

"And?" Nick said, opening the door for the inevitable.

"I'm just wondering if they mix business with pleasure." Nick laughed. "Could be relevant, Nick," Gail added, "since there was sex porn on the vic's computer."

"Yeah, yeah, OK. When Mrs. Huston comes in, you can ask her," he said lobbing it back.

"If it fits, ask," they both said at once. After three years together and dozens of cases, Nick knew Gail pretty well. And vice versa.

"OK, bring in Mrs. Huston, please," Nick called to Boyd, back in murder mode.

Seconds later, Barbara Huston walked into the room. She scanned the two officers and the pile of business cards on the conference table. She then sat down across from Gail, pushing some stray blond hair behind her ears as she crossed her legs primly under the table.

"Hi, I'm Dr. Huston." She extended her hand to Gail first. Her bracelets clinked as she shook. She reached over to Nick next as if he were the second banana.

Nick glanced over at Gail, who was stifling a grin, knowing that Nick hated power plays. Nick introduced them both, and, after a pause, Barbara turned her chair reluctantly to engage him as chief interrogator.

"We'd like to go over what you heard and saw just before the victim was found." Nick studied her. She was blond, lithe, bony. Sharp nosed, like her husband.

"Vell," Barbara answered as she smiled and tilted her chin fetchingly to the side. "I was in my office, preparing some reports, conferring with our attorney on the phone. I heard this horrible screaming out in the hallway. I looked over at Mark, who was at his desk over there. Mark rushed out the door. It took me a few moments to end my phone call, and then I rushed into the hallway as soon as I could. Lila and Jackie were there, absolutely hysterical. I tried to calm poor Lila who was about to faint. Apparently, she'd discovered, uh, Ed. Mark directed me to take them into the kitchen. I saw Mark and Amanda go back into Ed's office. After a few minutes in the kitchen, I came back into our office and Mark and Amanda were already here. Mark looked like death. Amanda too."

"Do you have any idea who did this Dr. Huston?"

"God, I don't know. Ed treated dozens of patients. And we'd had the problem with Carl yesterday." Barbara reached up to adjust a strand of hair that fell across her check. Nick noticed her hand shake slightly.

"Carl?"

"Yes, Carl. Carl Fellman. Paranoid schizophrenic. He'd had an episode in the waiting room. Off his meds, you know. He'd shown up here for his Monday morning session, and then suddenly broke—screaming, spitting, causing a commotion. Al and Mark had to restrain him. We had the police come and take him. Nancy—Nancy Davis, one of our supervisors—had been very upset about it...and Amanda. He'd tried to grab Amanda. Nancy was annoyed with Ed that maybe his prescribing might be off."

"Nancy?

"Our third psychologist. She supervises our psych interns, Margaret and Thomas."

"And Amanda?"

"Amanda Carlisle, Marriage and Family Therapist. Psychotherapist. She supervises our other students, marriage and family therapist interns, Sandra and Gary."

Turning to Gail, Nick said, "We need to find out where this Carl guy is right now." Redirecting to Barbara he asked, "Did Nancy and Dr. Michael ever argue?"

"They didn't always agree. But they were professional with each other."

"And you?"

"With Ed? Frankly, sometimes Ed was annoying."

"Annoying?"

"Late with paperwork, a bit lax in his record keeping. His joking around was a bit much." Barbara's lip curled up slightly.

"So you really disliked him?"

The bracelets clinked as Barbara slid her wrist across the table. "No, of course not. He was just sometimes...inconsistent and...a little immature." She sat back and folded her arms, bracelets jangling again.

"Anything else you can tell us about him—or your relationship?"

"Not really." She sat there, unmoving.

But Nick noticed something. He wasn't a shrink, but he'd seen a lot of people hiding things. Hiding things by flattening their faces. Somehow this woman's face was like a mask—but a mask that moves. He waited for it to move again. It didn't. He scanned the list in front of him. "How about Amanda...Carlisle, is it? What was their relationship like?"

"Ed loved her. As far as I know she got along well with him. No complaints that I ever heard."

"'Loved her.' Did they date?" Nick said.

"Ed and Amanda?" Barbara laughed. "Hardly. She wasn't Ed's type, I'm sure."

"What was his type?"

"Not Amanda," Barbara said with a slight edge, then her face went flat and she sat back, mask in place.

"How would you know that?"

"Because I am a psychologist, detective, and I know how to read people." She paused letting Nick grasp the implication. "Ed was not interested in Amanda, in my opinion. They were colleagues. No more."

"So what *was* he interested in?"

Barbara cocked her head to one side, and closed her eyes briefly. "I really can't say definitively what Ed was 'interested in' other than cartoons—and the latest psychotropic."

"Did he use drugs?" Nick asked.

"Not as far as I knew."

"Anything else unusual about him?"

Barbara subtly licked her lips, taking time. "Not really," she said. Her pupils were large and black.

"How about the students? Did they work with Dr. Michael as well?"

"Sure. They'd confer on medication management, you know, and other psychiatric issues. All the interns needed to work with him since he was the only one of our staff who prescribed."

"OK. Where were you last night from seven o'clock on?"

A beat. "Let's see," her eyes darted over to her desk and her calendar, trying to remember. "I was at the clinic until after seven or so. I had a chat with Ed about some clinic matters, and then I left to join my husband for dinner."

"Where did you and Ed talk?"

"In his office."

"Was he alive?"

"Of course." She frowned. "He was doing paperwork...and holding court with the interns who were in and out. We finally finished up privately after fifteen minutes or so. Then I left."

"Did you argue?"

"No. We had an update meeting, that's all. Then I left."

"And you went on to...?"

"Bully's. Down the street. To meet some friends of ours from San Francisco. The Maynards."

"Drove or walk?"

"Drove."

"And after dinner?"

"Then we...I went home."

Nick looked puzzled. "Do you mind me asking if you and your husband were in one or two cars?"

"Two, of course. We often keep separate schedules, so we drive our own cars most of the time. Since we live up in the hills here, it's not far."

"Did you arrive home together?"

"Ummm, no." She paused, and then brightened. "Mark stayed longer. I was tired, so I went home first."

"And your husband came home when?"

"Oh God, so many questions! An hour or two later, I guess. I was falling asleep so I'm not certain. It'd been a trying day, with Carl and all."

"OK," Nick paused for emphasis. "So if you went home without your husband, is it possible Dr. Huston returned here and killed Dr. Michael?"

Barbara's jaw clenched ever so slightly, and then she laughed. "That's ridiculous, detective. Don't be an imbecile. We're civilized people. We don't go around bludgeoning people to death." She turned to Gail and asked. "Do I really have to answer all these ludicrous questions?"

"We are just trying to find out who did this."

Nick waited. She sat back eyeing him. Stalemate. "OK. One last thing," Nick asked. "Where were you raised? Germany?"

"Austria," Barbara answered quietly.

"Were you and your family involved with the Nazis or something?" The air sucked completely out of the room. "I understand there was a graffiti incident involving swastikas some time ago. Sorry to bring this up but we need to consider all relevant facts."

After a long beat, Barbara answered, leaning in as if talking to a retarded child. "I do not know where any of that came from, detective. I am a lawful American citizen...for more than ten years. My childhood years and my family are past history, long forgotten. I am offended, frankly, that you seem to be hinting at something—sinister." She cocked her head for emphasis. "I am trying to be sensitive to the fact that you deal regularly with the criminal element. And that you tend perhaps to deal with everyone this way. I'm sure it must be very isolating for you." She paused for emphasis. "Now, if we're done, I'd really like to leave—unless of course you need me further."

"Ed Michael. Psychiatrist." Nick cocked his head to one side, listening to the name. "Was he Jewish?"

Coolly, Barbara answered. "I believe Ed had Jewish heritage. This is a heinous crime and I'm so very sorry that Ed bore the brunt of someone's hatred like this, Jewish or not. I don't know what else I can tell you, detective."

"OK," he spoke slowly. "Thank you for your assistance. You can go for now, Dr. Huston. But all paperwork, phones, and other pertinent items except for your handbag stay, please."

"Don't you need a search warrant for that?"

"If we need one. Typically cooperative folks don't mind helping us."

"Very well. I will leave everything and allow your officers to search my bag."

"Thanks for your cooperation."

"It's been charming, detective," Barbara replied coldly, about to rise. Then, after a pause, she softened, rewarding him with a dazzling smile. "I'm sorry if I was a little high handed, detective. I acknowledge that I sometimes revert to that style under stress. Please accept my apology. Know that I am available to help you in any way."

"Thanks." He pointed to his cards. "Please call me if you remember anything else that might be helpful."

She eyed the cards askance. "My husband undoubtedly took your number. No use in wasting paper—right, detective?"

He smiled, and then called Boyd to have her escorted below. Once she'd gone, he turned to Gail. "What'd you think?"

"Well, I don't think I'd see her for marital counseling anytime soon," Gail quipped.

They laughed, breaking the tension that hung in the room like a bug bomb. "Yup," Nick agreed, "She's tough all right. Icy for a shrink. Hiding something though. Do you think she could have done it?"

"Maybe. Under the right circumstances."

"Yeah. Do you think she dislikes men? Or Jews?"

"Maybe just cops," Gail said, smiling.

"Maybe just male cops. By the way, you didn't ask about their shrink sex."

"Maybe later. I want to be prepared before I question Frau Blucher again."

Nick smiled. "What's that from?"

"*Young Frankenstein*—my favorite film."

"Right. OK, time later to analyze the Doctors Huston." He studied his notes. "OK, two more senior people: Amanda Carlisle and Nancy Davis."

He flagged Boyd to bring in the first one, then sat back and waited. Something was bugging him about the next two names, but he couldn't place it. He figured he'd know soon enough.

Chapter Thirteen

Amanda and Nancy

Amanda was relieved as she entered the familiar suite. The image of Ed, so horribly violated, ran relentlessly through her mind and she wanted to talk about it. She sat across from Nick and cocked her head to the side, searching her memory. Suddenly she grinned.

Nick studied her, confused. She seemed familiar. *Where have I known her before? Previous case? An arrest? God, not from some bar somewhere, I hope.*

Amanda introduced herself, watching first Nick and then Gail react to her words. "I'm Amanda Carlisle. You may not remember, detective, but we know each other." Gail raised her eyebrow; Nick squirmed in his seat. "I consulted with you and your partner—a different one—a few years ago on a case. Child kidnapping."

Nick remembered. "In Torrey Pines? Mother was a hit and run, I think. Child disappeared. About six years ago, right?"

"Yes. Ultimately the child was found safe and sound and returned to his father. The mother was killed, though. That part was very sad."

"OK, it's coming back. You were somewhere else then, weren't you? La Jolla?"

"Yes, La Jolla Medical." Memories came flooding back—of Nick in uniform, shorter hair, but always the day-old beard.

"Well, OK. Nice, to see you again," Nick mumbled. *OK, OK, we've worked together, but now is now. She could be a suspect.* "You discovered the body, right?" Nick said firmly.

"Well actually, Lila, our temp, found him first."

"What happened exactly?"

"Lila delivers our case files every morning. She goes from office to office, you know. When she got to Ed's, she opened the door and... and...found him." Amanda shuddered and gripped the table.

"Do you need some water?" Gail asked.

"No, I'm all right." She took some deep breaths. "It was just a shock, seeing him there."

"You went in?" Amanda nodded. "Did you touch anything?"

"Well...I may have brushed past the door with Lila...perhaps the doorknob...nothing else. Nothing on or near the desk or...or...Ed... that I can recall. Oh. I stepped back on his glasses. Sorry."

"What's that on your shirt?"

"What?" Amanda recoiled. Then she followed Nick's eyes and remembered the latte stain. "Oh, I spilled coffee on myself on the drive in this morning."

"You didn't touch the body, then?"

"No," she said emphatically. A wave of nausea came over her. "I should be better at this, but it's always a shock."

"Why should you be better?" Suddenly it hit Nick. "Carlisle. I know a Phil Carlisle. Cop. Oceanside."

"Yes. My Dad. Retired now. He had some pretty grisly cases in his time."

"Phil Carlisle ran a tight ship up there. Tough but fair." Nick nearly smiled but he sensed Gail's eyes boring into his head. "OK, so you've been around this sort of thing before. Do you know of anyone who'd want to kill this guy? Somebody who wanted drugs maybe? Somebody he committed and came back to get even?"

"I don't know really. I'm sure you've heard we had an incident yesterday with Carl. Carl, however, is a hopelessly disorganized schizophrenic off his meds. Ed wasn't even around in the morning. He came in later after Carl was taken away by the police."

"Who *was* around yesterday evening?"

"Patients in and out, all the regular staffers, our students." Amanda toyed with one of her hoop earrings—a lifelong habit when she was trying to figure something out.

"What do you call the students? Interns?"

"Yes, I've got two: Gary Bowman and Sandra Daniels."

"Any obvious weirdnesses?"

"Well I don't know what your measure of weird is," Amanda answered trying not to smile, "but Gary's a little anxious. Sandra's a bit serious. Both are excellent therapists."

"How'd they work with Ed?"

"They seemed to like him pretty well. Sandra spent a lot of time with Ed."

"Were you jealous?"

"Jealous?" Amanda repeated the word. "Honestly, I appreciated his expertise. The interns need exposure to that. From a motherly sort of place, I may have had a little irrational attachment to their not always turning to me for the last word, I guess."

"Enough to harm him?" Nick asked.

"You mean kill him? And then nearly pass out upon finding him?"

He studied her, then moved on. "Tell me about Nancy Davis. She's your peer, I guess?"

"Yes, basically. But she's a psychologist like Mark and Barbara. She supervises the psychology interns Margaret and Thomas. Margaret's from UCSD. Thomas is from USD. Margaret is third-generation Japanese, Thomas is Korean. His parents came over ten years ago or so."

"Did they work with Ed like your students did?"

"Yes. Perhaps more closely since they saw the more gravely ill patients like psychotics, for example."

"Did Nancy's people like Ed?"

"As far as I know. Thomas seemed to spend quite a bit of time with him."

"And Nancy Davis? What about her?"

"An excellent, skilled colleague. She and Ed had their moments." Amanda caught herself. "Well, what I mean is that she wasn't afraid to challenge him—sometimes thought he was too cavalier, for lack of a better word."

"Enough to kill him?"

Amanda frowned. "I don't think so, really, detective. Nancy doesn't strike me as someone who'd resort to that."

"And the Hustons?"

Amanda paused. "I guess I'm uncomfortable going there. They're my bosses."

"But in your opinion? Remember this is a criminal investigation."

"They can be intense sometimes. In general they're good people, great to work for." Amanda gazed at Nick as his eyes bore into hers. She particularly noticed the crease between his eyes when he was thinking hard. Very appealing. She caught herself and cleared her throat.

"OK." Nick broke the moment and shifted in his chair. "What about anyone else? Girlfriends? Exes? Boyfriends?"

"As far as I know he was divorced, didn't date much."

"Did you two go out?"

Amanda laughed heartily. "No way. Absolutely no interest."

Nick scrutinized her. She was pretty when she smiled.

After a very long pause, Gail piped up and said, "OK. So who in your opinion would do this?"

"Someone highly enraged, perhaps?"

"Enraged?"

"From the way Ed was...mutilated. Someone who really wanted to...make their mark."

"Carve him up?"

"Somebody gripped with murderous anger. The kind where there's no going back."

"A druggie? PCP? Heroin?"

"Isn't a PCP-fueled attack more random? This feels like extreme rage to me, but expressed in a calculated way."

"Interesting." Nick listened hard. "What was Ed 'into'?"

"You mean addictions? Liaisons?" He nodded. "He loved cartoons, of course. Keeping up on new meds. Being kind of a know-it-all, I guess. Not much social life, as far as I knew."

"Where were you last night, by the way?"

"Let's see, I left the clinic about six thirty to meet a friend for dinner."

"Go on."

"My best friend, Shelby, at the Fish Market. We were there until after nine or so. Then I went home."

"Straight home? Did you drive by the clinic?"

"I drove back up PCH, but I turn before I reach the clinic. I live down in the valley."

"One last thing," Nick asked. "Did you happen to notice the markings on the desk?"

"Yes, barely. I think there was an F or something, then maybe an R and an E? Can't remember the rest. I think five letters in all, if I recall."

"F-R-E- smudge smudge. What does that mean to you?"

"F-R-E...E...D? Oh. F-R-E-U-D? Freud?"

"What do you make of that?"

"It's certainly a name we use often enough around here. Don't know what Ed could have meant by a message like that...in those last...moments." Amanda remembered her own cryptic note and reached down for her bag as she spoke. "Speaking of messages, I got this yesterday...in my in-box."

The detectives read the typed note: BACK OFF AMANDA CARLISLE. YOU'RE PUSHING HER TOO MUCH. I'M WARNING YOU. D

Gail spoke first. "Any idea who gave you this?"

"Somebody like a patient or a family member who's upset with me, I guess."

"Let's check for fingerprints." Nick signaled Boyd to bring in an evidence bag.

"Unfortunately, lots of us have handled it. I showed it at our staff meeting yesterday and later to Shelby."

Gail bagged the note and laid it on the table. "Have you gotten any other notes like this? Did Ed get one?"

"No. I don't think Ed got one or he would have mentioned it in our meeting."

Nick studied her for moment then made a decision. "OK, that's all for now. You probably need to watch out for yourself, Ms. Carlisle. You'll report anything else unusual, right?"

"Of course. Um, can I ask you a question?"

"Sure."

"What will happen next? Will you close the clinic? We have a lot of patients that need to be seen..."

"We'll have to shut you down for now...until the investigation is complete. Maybe you can transfer people somewhere?"

"OK, I can work on that."

"Thanks. The officers will see you out. Can we look at your phone, by the way? We'll return it of course. You can take your other belongings but nothing else, please, no files or anything. Sorry. Please call if you think of anything else."

"I understand." Amanda stood up with her bag, took a business card, and exited the room.

Once the door shut behind Amanda, Nick turned to Gail. "What'd ya think?"

"Well there was definitely something going on there, but I'm not sure if all of it had to do with this homicide investigation!" Gail burst out laughing.

"OK, OK, I've known her before and it threw me for a second."

"I'll say." After three years, Gail thought Nick was completely transparent, especially around certain kinds of females. Nick, on the other hand, thought he was perennially cool, inscrutable.

"OK, OK. Focus, Burton. She's a suspect. So do you think she did it?"

"Hard to say," Gail answered. "Unless she plays against type. Maybe she hated the shrink. Jealousy maybe? Doesn't really fit though, unless she's a real cool liar."

"Doesn't seem like the type. OK, OK, I guess I am not completely objective," Nick admitted.

Gail grunted. "You didn't ask her if she saw the porn."

"Not sure she even saw it. OK. Lots of questions. We'll have some alternative interviewers if we need to with that one."

"Could be a good idea." Gail enjoyed seeing Nick off kilter.

"Let's keep moving. Who's next?"

"Dr. Davis."

Moments later, a tall, dark-skinned women with jet-black hair and a wide mouth entered and sat down across from Nick. "Nancy Davis," she said to both detectives. "Psychologist and clinical supervisor."

Nick and Gail introduced themselves.

"How can I help you? I know you have lots of questions so fire away."

"Tell us what you know about what happened."

"Well, I came in at my usual time this morning, around seven thirty. Did my early morning coffee prep and started making calls, reading reports in my office, like normal, then I went out front and got snagged on a phone call."

Nick observed Nancy as she spoke. She was all business: careful speech, very direct, educated, ethnic, slight southern accent, maybe a mix of African and Hispanic. She had on a dark business suit, worn flats, and very large handbag with a beanie baby—no two—hanging off the handle.

"I was talking to an irate mother when I heard this god-awful screaming." She rolled her eyes. "Got off as soon as I could, then ran down the hallway. Mark was there, with Amanda, and the girls. He had me clear the waiting area and release all the patients that were in the building."

"How long did that take?"

"I don't know, a few minutes."

"Then what?"

"Then I returned to the back of the clinic and went into the lounge area with Jackie and Lila. Got out smelling salts and tried to revive Jackie who was having a conniption. Barbara left and came back in here. I guess Mark and Amanda were here already. Didn't get the details until later when we were herded next door here." Nancy pointed behind her.

"Were you surprised?"

"Surprised it happened here. But I've seen it before."

"Where?"

"I did some of my early years in the jail system in Louisiana. Saw a couple of prison murders, inmate violence, you know," Nancy smiled, secure.

"What was your relationship to the deceased?"

"OK, what I think you're asking me is if I liked him or not. Well the honest answer is: not much. I tolerated him; we were colleagues. He was the clinic psychiatrist and we all had to work with him. Including me." She clucked her tongue.

"Sounds like you disliked the guy quite a bit actually."

"He could be a prick, if you really want to know."

"How so?"

"Arrogant. Loved dumb jokes. Tried a practical joke on me once. Put him in his place though." She paused, considering the implication then she shrugged and went on. "Nicely of course. We disagreed on his medication management sometimes. Always wanted the newer drugs. I pushed for the old ones. My students got a lot out of him."

"So did you kill him?"

Nancy smiled broadly, nearly laughing. "Good one. Of course I didn't kill him, detective. Didn't need to. Simply learned how to deal with the guy. Like last night. We had words at the end of the day about some clinic issues...the Carl problem and such. He thought we had a rivalry going."

"Did you?"

Nancy paused, folding her hands carefully in front of her on the desk, and leaning in. "I didn't avoid confronting him. Some men see that as competitive, detective." She glanced over at Gail, then back to Nick. "I wanted him to model respectfulness, that's all. Especially for my students."

"Were you jealous of him?"

Nancy hissed slightly. "Why would I be jealous of him? I thought he had some problems...tried way too hard to be funny...as far as honest emotion, he was a dullard, in my opinion."

Nick studied her but she remained silent. "Who would want to kill the guy, in your opinion?"

"Could be anyone really. Some of the killers I treated in Louisiana were the nicest people 'til you provoked 'em. 'Course some were outright sociopaths—so cold they'd stomp on a baby for an ice cream cone."

"Are you that cold?" Nick asked quietly.

"I've raised three sons mostly without a husband around, maintained a professional career, and provided for my family. I'm tough more than cold, I think, but you be the judge." She smiled and sat back.

"OK, so when did you leave last night?"

"After I talked with Ed for a bit, I did a phone session, then left. I don't know...sometime after seven, I guess."

"Was Ed alive?"

"As far as I know but then I didn't check his pulse."

"And you didn't hear or see anything?"

"Not really. Voices maybe. People about."

Nick watched her. Nancy stared back. "And what about your students? Tell me about them."

"Margaret's very focused. A wonderful student, pretty good counselor. Thomas has a good handle on the Asian culture. Solid with clinical testing."

"How were they with Ed?"

"Margaret laughed at his jokes. Thomas hung around Ed quite a bit, sometimes saw them huddling. Male stuff? I don't know." Nancy pulled some Juicy Fruit gum from her massive handbag and popped it into her mouth. Then she offered a stick to her interrogators. Both declined. Nick watched her; Nancy smiled back, chewing.

"Who else was close to Ed?"

"As far as lovers, friends, or fuzzy objects he hugged in the night, don't know. He was pretty private, as far as I could tell. Lots of psychiatrists are. They're a strange breed."

"Are you glad he's dead?"

"Hmmm, glad is going some. On the one hand I feel really terrible. On the other hand, I think, well, what goes around comes around."

"Interesting phrase for a psychologist."

"Yup. And I've seen some interesting justice in my time."

Nick paused for a moment, on to something. "Do you own a weapon, Ms. Davis?"

"Sure. Handgun. We live in south bay. Not so safe there."

"Do you have it with you?"

"Nope. Just my Taser today."

"Mind if we take a look at it?"

"Nope. I'd like it back though." Nancy fished in her bag and pulled out a lady's Taser. It was pink. She handed it to Gail.

"Have you used it?"

Nancy smiled. "Not in California."

"Previously?"

"Sure. Couple of times. And my handgun."

"Any arrest record?"

"Nope. Both shooting incidents were self-defense. You can check it out."

"Thanks, we will," Nick nodded. "By the way, what do you think of the Hustons?"

She stopped chewing for a moment. "Well, they've always been good to me. Sometimes a little too tolerant in my mind, but I enjoy working with them."

"Are they murderers?"

She considered it. "Can't really say. You're the detective."

"And Ms. Carlisle?"

"Don't think so. Not enough steel in her belly."

"Interesting," Nick waited. Nothing more came. "OK. Boyd will escort you out. Only your handbag goes. No files, etc., please. And we'd like to look at your phone too."

"Sure. Thanks Officers. It's been a pleasure." Nancy got up and took one of Nick's cards. "I'll let you know if I think of anything else, detectives."

"Very interesting," Nick said after the door slammed and they were alone.

"Could be her," Gail said, staring at the pink Taser.

"Maybe," Nick agreed. "Plenty of 'steel.'"

"Yup."

"Any way to order up some coffee?" Nick said, stretching. "I sure need some caffeine about now."

"When it comes to coffee, I got you covered." Gail rose to order in.

While she was out, Nick studied the suspect list. There was a veneer of cool sanity from all these suspects so far. Dr. Ed Michael, however, had clearly been the target of somebody completely unhinged. At this point he couldn't tell if the perp was a deranged, garden-variety killer, or a disguised psychopath hidden among the supposedly sane. The four students were up next. They were probably pretty green. Less veneer, more emotion. Maybe even a killer among them.

Chapter Fourteen

Powwow

The sun had dissipated the morning mist and an afternoon breeze was whipping the pines toward PCH by the time Amanda emerged from the building. She passed a lone cop standing near the yellow tape, keeping his eye on the crowd and anyone leaving the building. He nodded to her and waved her out. She walked around the corner to her Audi, and saw the Hustons leaning on Mark's silver SUV. They were talking intently.

"Hey," Mark called out.

Amanda walked slowly toward the couple who grew silent. She was drained, wary, wanting their familiarity but apprehensive that the most mundane encounter might veer into something macabre. Cautious, she found herself working hard to balance the reptilian side of her brain screaming *be on alert* with the rational side telling her to *chill out*.

"God what a mess," Barbara said as Amanda joined them. Her blond hair swept back in the breeze, exposing a one-inch scar on the right side of her neck. "My God, who would have done such a thing to poor Ed?"

"Yes, it's absolutely unthinkable."

Mark put his arm around Barbara and pulled her close. "Horrific. Absolutely unbelievable. I can't imagine what happened. Or when it happened. Amanda, how're you doing now?"

"Uh...trying to cope, I guess."

"Who are they talking to now?" Mark asked.

"Nancy, I guess. I heard them call her as I was leaving."

"God, Mark, what are we going to do?" Barbara wailed. "This is absolutely the worst thing that could have possibly happened to us... and the clinic. I can't believe that someone would do this."

Amanda put her hand on Barbara's arm. "Barbara...Mark...I'm so sorry this happened. I had that awful note yesterday and now this... it's..."

"Unfathomable," Barbara finished for her.

"Do you think Ed's...death...has any connection to that note?" Mark leaned in to Amanda.

"God, Mark, I have no idea."

"I wonder if we're all in danger," Barbara said to the others.

"I hadn't thought of that. It's possible." The three stood silent.

Mark spoke. "We need to get hold of ourselves. We'll close the clinic for now...of course. Amanda, you and Nancy will need to work with me to refer all the patients...to other places. And you'll get together with the interns..."

"Yes."

"Barbara, you'll probably do better with pending cases, clinic business, by contacting them first, of course..."

"Oh, God, yes...before they read about it in the papers."

"Yes. I think I need to be the point person for any interviews, queries," Mark added, glad to have something other than the corpse upstairs to think about.

"Oh, here's Nancy."

Nancy Davis came around the corner, smiling. "Hi," the woman called out to the other three. "What a day! Are you all doing OK?"

"We're coping," Barbara answered as Nancy neared them. "You're almost cheerful!"

"Well I don't know about cheerful, but all those years I spent in the prison system probably helps. Seen it before...not quite like this of course...but it certainly happens..."

"Are you sure you're OK, Nancy?"

"I'll manage. You know it's just bravado, but it's my way, I guess. Probably pop a beer and have a good cry when I get home. Maybe even a cigarette. I think this calls for one, don't you?"

"You may be right. I was just saying, Nancy, that we need to contact the patients...get the interns together...you know, help them process it...and come up with a prepared statement that we can all read to anyone we're talking to. I'll work on it and we can do a conference call in the morning. OK?" Mark looked at the three women.

"Sounds good," Amanda said. Nancy nodded.

"In the meantime, Barbara, you'll deal with the staff, right?"

"Of course."

"And I think we all need to be cautious. Amanda got threatened, and Ed..." he stopped, avoiding the word. "Yes, now that I think about it, we might all be targets. Let me know immediately if anything else happens—even if it seems small." They nodded. "Barbara and I will call you at ten tomorrow morning. The police said they'd return all of our cell phones by nine in the morning if at all possible. Take care of yourselves, and call immediately if anything else comes up."

Amanda slid into her Audi and started the engine. She watched Nancy walk to her Buick. Mark got into the SUV and Barbara unlocked her green Mercedes convertible and slid in. Amanda pulled out first, looking through the rearview mirror as the line of grim-faced drivers fell in behind her. It felt like a funeral procession as she led the way to the highway, only the dead hadn't been buried yet. And the demons had only just begun to dance.

Chapter Fifteen

Margaret and Sandra

Up in the former honeymoon suite, one of the beat cops had made a run to Starbucks at Fifteenth and now a comfortable coffee aroma filled the air. Nick and Gail caffed up and took a progress check.

"Of the four we've interviewed so far, who's our killer?" Nick stared into his straight-up double espresso, which wasn't very hot.

"Couple of good candidates." Gail swallowed a gulp of her half-caf half-decaf latte with chocolate on top. "I'd say any one of 'em could have done it, really. Maybe not your friend...unless she's a well-honed sociopath with a stabbing fetish."

"She seems iffy for it to me, but you never know. Looks more like someone who had serious issues with the guy—and various parts of his body."

"Kind of a stabber-strangler Lorena Bobbitt sort?"

"Maybe. Somebody who wanted the doc to suffer."

"Feel the pain, so to speak."

"OK, who else have we got?"

"Four students—interns, I guess they're called—got to learn the lingo. Support staff—three of them. Plus three patients."

"OK, let's do the students, first the two women, then the men. Then we can split up the rest." Nick drained his cup. He called to Boyd who brought in the first of the female students, Margaret Tanaka. Margaret came into the room and perched delicately on the chair across from Nick. "Ms. Tanaka?"

"Yes. Margaret Tanaka. I'm one of the psych assistants." Margaret posed barely breathing in the chair, twisting her watch around her wrist. Dark eyed, she was a young Japanese-American woman in her late twenties with short black hair and long bangs swept over one eye. She was dressed neck to toe in black. Even her fingernail polish was black; her only flash of color was a pair of pink flamingo earrings hanging from her tiny earlobes. She set her iPhone gingerly on the table.

"So, Ms. Tanaka, what do you know about what happened?"

"I...I...didn't see anything really. Only...only Lila and Jackie... are so upset...I understand that Dr. Michael is...dead." She blinked several times as if trying to orient herself.

"When was the last time you saw him?"

"Well...yesterday...uh...last night, last evening, I mean."

"When exactly?" Nick asked, leaning forward.

Margaret shifted. "I...I...guess I saw him about six...no, six thirty. I had my last patient at five...a lawyer...and then I finished up my notes, talked a little to Ed. I left right after."

"Where did you see Ed?"

"After my last patient, I went into the kitchen for tea and Ed was just leaving with his."

"Was Ed alone?"

"I think he was walking out with Thomas." She frowned and looked down, remembering how the men were laughing about some joke about penile implants. She looked up to Nick's stare. "Thomas Wong. The other psych intern. I don't think you've seen him yet. Nancy Davis supervises us both."

"What does that mean? Is she your boss?"

"She supervises our clinical work. Mentors us, signs off on our clinical hours."

"Hours?"

"Yes. We have to earn so many supervised hours in order to get licensed."

"What do you do in return for her? Help her with people she doesn't like?"

Margaret sat back, confused by the question. "I don't get involved with those kinds of situations. I see patients, that's all."

"What was your relationship with Dr. Michael?"

"He was our psychiatrist."

"Yours?"

"No of course not. Our clinic psychiatrist. He worked with all of us, as we treated shared patients."

"Do you have a psychiatrist? Personally, I mean."

Margaret hesitated. "I don't think I have to answer that, but no not now." She looked down sharply.

Nick leaned in again. "Not now?"

Margaret leveled her eyes at him. "Not since early college. I had some...some problems. With a boyfriend. We broke up. It was hard for me."

"Which psychiatrist?"

"Dr. Mark Bando. At UCSD. I was under stress and he gave me a mild sedative for sleeping."

"Are you an addict?"

"God, no." She shrank back. "I took the pills for a couple of months and then stopped. I drink herbals now when I can't sleep. Chamomile, valerian. That kind of thing."

"Did Dr. Michael drink tea or coffee?"

"Um...Both, I guess. He seemed to switch to tea later in the day. Sometimes we'd share a chai."

"Did you make tea for him last night?"

"What?"

"Did you fix his tea?"

"Heavens no. I'm his colleague not his Geisha," Margaret retorted. Her eyes narrowed and her lips thinned. "Sorry. I apologize for getting snippy. This is difficult."

"OK. What else did Dr. Michael drink?"

"You mean alcohol? Not that I saw. I would have smelled it. I have an acute sense of smell."

"What do you smell around here now?"

"Death. The smell of death." Margaret reached for her purse. She pulled out a tissue and blew her nose. "Both my parents are doctors. Sometimes I'd go to hospitals with them as a kid. I saw, smelled stuff, sometimes, you know, when I was little."

"So you know a lot about death?"

"No, I...I wouldn't say that. I've just—kind of been around it." She spun the watch round and around on her wrist.

"So who do you think wanted Dr. Michael dead?"

For a moment Margaret's eyes fluttered, then she looked at Nick and breathed out. "There were lots of patients with illnesses around here. Psychotics. People who are...deranged...who might possibly do this..."

She looked genuinely frightened, Nick thought. "Anyone in particular?"

"No." She blushed. "No one wanted to harm him that I know but...but...he might have not always been...er...ethical. It's not really my place to say."

"Why isn't it? If you know something that could help this investigation you need to spill it, Ms. Tanaka." Nick and Gail sat up.

"I'm sorry. I need to confer with my supervisor first. I'm speculating on some things that I'm not sure would be appropriate to talk about."

"OK, Dr. Davis, right?" Nick studied her intently. This could be the crack he was looking for. "OK, we'll come back to that," Nick paused for emphasis. "Who would you say Dr. Michael was close to?"

"Well...he and...Thomas spent a lot of time together."

"Doing what?"

"Talking medication. Diagnosis. Differentials. Treatment. Stuff."
She looked down again sharply.

Nick pushed the opening. "Do you like this Thomas guy?"

"I like him...well enough. He's a fellow intern. We work together, that's all." Nick cocked his head. "We don't date, if that's what you're wondering."

"Why not?"

"We would never date. I mean...because...he's...Korean, for one thing, and I'm Japanese American...it just wouldn't work. Besides," Margaret's dark eyes narrowed to a slit like a cat watching a bulldog, "he's gay." She leaned back, pursed her lips, and folded her pale hands in her lap.

Nick cocked his head to the right. "How do you know that?"

"I just know," Margaret replied, cocking her head to match Nick's.

"Was Ed gay?"

"Dunno."

"Did he hang out with Thomas, outside of work?"

"Sometimes." Margaret blinked several times. "OK, I saw them once at Jake's at the beach. I was out for dinner with friends. Seemed casual, nothing intense or anything."

Nick tapped his pen on his pad. Margaret looked down at the noise, then up quickly, waiting.

"Do you think Thomas killed Dr. Michael?"

"You're asking me to read into someone's motives. I don't know, honestly." She was wringing her hands in her lap now. And looking a little green.

"So what about the Hustons? Do you think they killed him? Lovers' triangle? Caught him sleeping with a patient?"

Shaking her head rapidly, Margaret blurted, "I honestly can't say. But I would really be shocked if that were the case."

"How about Ms. Davis? Ms. Carlisle? The other female intern... what's her name?"

"Sandra. Amanda wouldn't hurt anyone."

"And Sandra? Ms. Davis? Gary?" Nick said, consulting his list of names.

"Dunno. I really dunno." Margaret's eyes darted back and forth between Gail and Nick.

"OK, how about this ethics thing. Go back to that."

"I really have to talk to Nancy first. I am happy to talk with you again when I know...what I am supposed to say...uh, allowed to say..." The girl began hyperventilating. Gail handed her the tissue box from the middle of the table but she pushed it away. Margaret pulled a tic tac from her handbag instead.

"OK, OK, we'll leave it for now. When did you say you left here last night?"

"Between six thirty and seven."

"Where did you go?"

"Shopping. At Nordies...Nordstrom. UTC."

"Buy anything?"

"No, just looked. Got home around nine thirty. My roommate, Kelly, was asleep."

Nick made a decision. "OK you can go—for now—Ms. Tanaka. Just one last question. What were you drinking last night?"

"You mean here at the clinic just before I left? Hmm...chai. New package." Margaret looked Nick straight in the eyes, and then dropped her eyes to her lap in deference.

"OK, that's all," he said.

Margaret left, picking up her iPhone from the table.

"Hey," Nick called out to her, suddenly friendly. "How do you like that thing?"

"Works great," Margaret said, turning in the doorway. "Terrific pictures. Great video, surfing, phone contact."

"Anyone else here have one?"

"Hmm...they're not too sophisticated here technically...but Ed...I guess Ed had one."

"For?"

"The usual stuff." Nick waited. "You know. Downloading songs, videos, e-mailing, surfing, photos." Margaret's face suddenly flushed crimson.

"OK, that's all," Nick said slowly. "Nothing leaves the clinic, you understand, except your purse and keys. Can we hold on to your iPhone for a bit?"

"No problem." Margaret nodded and placed her phone on the table.

Gail spoke first once the girl cleared the door. "She's an interesting one. Clearly hiding something."

"Yeah. Plus that ethics thing. Nancy Davis didn't mention it. We'll have to find out what that's about. iPhone may have something on it."

"Check," Gail said making notes.

"OK, we'll see Sandra Daniels next," he said to Boyd. A thin young woman with green eyes and straight brown hair stood in the doorway seconds later.

"Please come in." Nick signaled the chair across from him. "Ms. Daniels, right?"

"Yes. Sandra." She sat quietly, then turned to Gail and smiled. She placed one hand over the other on the table and waited, returning her gaze to Nick.

Sandra was dressed in a gray suit, white shirt, no jewelry. Her flat, bangless hair lay plastered against her head, falling in strands past her shoulders. No makeup. Dark eyebrows, thin lips, midtwenties, Nick guessed. "What do you know about what's happened?"

"Ed is dead," she said flatly. "I guess it was horrible. I heard all the screaming, but I was in session when he was found." She looked down at the table, then stared at Nick's hands resting casually on the table.

"Do you have any idea who did this?" Nick asked, fanning his fingers out in front of him. Sandra's eyes followed.

"I...I...don't really know."

"You're one of the students, right?"

"Yes, I've been here nearly two years. Work with Amanda. She supervises Gary and me."

"How late did you work last night?"

"Until...after five. I finished up with my four o'clock, did some notes, and went on to my exercise class at the Y."

"And then?"

"Then stopped back by to pick up a file I'd left, then home right after. Fed my cat, put in a load of laundry. Watched an old movie. Then went to bed. I got in here about seven thirty this morning, heard all the noise and had to close my session. Walked my patients out. They were terrified."

"What time did you come back last night?"

"I don't know. Six thirty or seven. In and out. Don't watch the clock much if I don't have sessions."

"Who else was here last night?"

"Oh, almost everyone. Monday is usually a late night since it's the start of the week."

"And while you were 'in and out,' did you kill Dr. Michael?"

"No," she smiled, shaking her head. "I don't hurt people."

"You don't?"

"I mean I'm a therapist. I do the best thing I can for people. I might hurt someone's feelings sometimes but I try scrupulously never to hurt anyone otherwise."

"So who do you think did this to Ed?"

The young woman hesitated. "I don't know, detective. I just... don't know. It's incomprehensible to me. It seems...sad to me. So sad." She looked over at Gail, then back down at Nick's hands.

"What time did you finally leave last night?"

"I told you I didn't really pay attention. A little after seven maybe?"

"Anyone see you?"

"Not sure. Gary maybe? Barbara? Ed? Can't really remember..."

"Did you like Ed, Ms. Daniels?"

"Ed? Oh sure. He's a brilliant man. Learned a lot. Did I like him? I didn't really know him personally too much. I liked some of his jokes. He was funny."

"I understand you and the other interns spent a lot of time with him."

She looked at Nick, puzzled for a moment then finally answered. "We conferred about medication and diagnosis. He liked teaching us the lingo, what to look for."

"What was he into...in your opinion?"

"Into?" She looked at him, squinting her eyes. "Well, he liked anything psychological—the twisted mind. I don't know what he did in his off time. Did a lot of reading, I think."

Nick watched her. There was something vulnerable, almost pathetic about her but he couldn't decide whether it was an act or her normal demeanor. He changed tack.

"Do you have any weapons, Ms. Daniels?"

Her eyes drilled into him. "No way."

"Boyfriend?"

"No, not now."

"Not now?"

"Jeff and I broke up about two years ago, before I came here." She stopped for several seconds, lost in thought. "Sorry. No one serious since then. I sometimes go over to the Belly Up Tavern with friends and meet some people there, but no one special."

"Anyone who would follow you here and harm someone you worked with?"

"No, not really. Jeff wasn't like that. And no one since has...has been that close." The woman's eyes drifted to the windows behind Barbara's desk and stayed there.

"Ms. Daniels, are you OK?" Gail asked after a moment.

Suddenly Sandra looked at them. Nick saw a flash of annoyance in her eyes, then she relaxed and smiled. "Sorry, sorry. This is a terrible thing to happen here. I...I'm just...a little in shock, I guess."

"Have you seen a murder before?"

"I...I...saw someone murdered next door once. Back in South Carolina where I grew up."

"Who was it?"

"A...a...child. Thrown against the wall...by his father."

"How old were you?"

"Ten."

"OK, so this brings back some memories?"

"Maybe." Her voice grew small. Even her body seemed to shrink.

"What happened to the father?"

"Went to jail, as far as I know. It was a long time ago."

"What else do you remember about it?"

"Oh, my father knew him, and the family. Said he deserved what he got."

"How did you feel about it?"

"Sad. Cried a lot, I think. Had nightmares, but I got over it. We moved away later. I went to school to help people with psychological problems like that. Seems like most of us have childhood stories to tell." She looked at Gail, but Gail stayed blank.

"Ed worked with children, didn't he?" Nick drew the girl's attention back.

"Yes. We all did. He seemed good with them, I guess. He mostly talked with the parents. We did more of the face-to-face therapy."

"Would any of the parents want to harm Ed?"

"Well I really can't say specifically due to confidentiality but sometimes the parents would get upset if the ADHD medication didn't work right, for example, and their kid was still out of control. Oh, come to think of it, Carl's mother is probably really mad right now."

"Why?"

"'Cause he had to be 5150ed yesterday."

"You're his counselor, right? Where is he now, by the way?"

"Mesa Vista or county jail. Not sure."

"OK, we'll check it out. Anybody on staff have it in for Ed?"

"There was some arguing about Carl's blowup." She blushed. "I can...hear the executive staff meeting through the wall sometimes... they were discussing it, but it got resolved, as far as I can tell."

"So you've got pretty good ears. Did you hear anything else in the past few days you want to tell us about?"

"Oh...no. I guess now you think I eavesdrop all the time." She picked up a strand of hair and began twisting it around her finger. "I just keep my ears open, that's all. I really haven't heard anything else about Ed. Just the usual stuff. Until he got killed of course." She looked down at the table, embarrassed.

Nick waited. The girl seemed to take up very little space in the room. He watched her for another moment. "OK, Ms. Daniels. You can go for now. Leave everything but your keys and purse. We need to search you on the way out."

Nick thought he saw a flash of anger sweep over the girl's face, but suddenly her face relaxed and she smiled. "Thank you. It was nice meeting you both. " She paused as if she were going to say something more, but then turned and went on out.

Gail turned to Nick. "Now that's a strange one. Fuzzy or something. Shock?"

"Yeah, dazed maybe. We'll have to get more information on her. Check out her background from the files, see if there were any parent problems with Ed."

"Odd duck. Doesn't read like the violent type."

"Yeah, but you never know."

"Nope."

Nick studied his list one more time. "OK, two more of the core people. Both guys. Thomas Wong is first."

"Goody. Let's see what the boys have to say."

Nick nodded at Boyd, and Boyd called in the next suspect.

Chapter Sixteen

Girl Talk

When Sandra exited the building downstairs, she found Margaret waiting for her by her car. "My God, Sandra, I can't believe this happened! I heard them whispering that he'd been stabbed and strangled." Margaret was practically shouting.

"Yeah, I guess it's really bad."

"It must have been one of those felons Ed treated last year. Remember? There were a couple of hard-core addicts he saw around Christmas. Ugly guys, lots of tattoos, remember? Oh, and there was that Jesus guy who came in here with a bottle of water, saying he wanted all of us to drink from it. You remember...the 'water of life'? He'd just been released from Aurora's psych ward."

"Yup. God. It might have been one of them. But how'd they get back there without anyone seeing? Why didn't Ed hit his panic button?"

"I don't know. I don't know why he didn't use that stun gun he keeps in his desk. He showed it to me once, so I know he had it."

"Dunno, Gary and I saw it too. Maybe somebody was after drugs? He has a bunch of stuff in there..."

"What if somebody was in there stealing drugs and Ed caught them?" Margaret gasped.

"What if Ed's really a narc?"

"What if somebody was in there stealing drugs and it was a friend of Ed's AND they killed him?" They pondered the visual for a moment, and then Margaret pressed her. "What did you tell the cops exactly, Sandra?"

Sandra peered at her. "I told them exactly what I knew about last night. That most of us were here later since it was Monday but that we left. Like always." She paused. "That is, unless you didn't leave?"

Margaret could have smacked her. "What are you spraying?"

"You mean 'saying'?"

"Yeah, yeah, yeah, Freudian slip. Just what are you SAYING, Sandra?"

"I don't know. What did YOU say?"

"That I left at my usual time and people were still there. That Thomas was in there and some other people. Ed's office was busy. I think you were there..."

"I wouldn't hurt a fly," Sandra cut her off.

"Me neither."

The young women studied each other for several seconds then Sandra broke the moment. "OK, well I guess I'm going to go now. Talk to you tomorrow if you like."

"Yeah, catch you later."

The women eyed each other for a second longer, then turned to their respective cars. Sandra backed out right away, but Margaret sat in her front seat fiddling with her purse, actually watching Sandra.

"Bitch," Margaret said into the rearview mirror as Sandra drove away.

Sandra didn't see it, but the hairs on the back of her neck stood up. "You're paranoid, Margaret," Sandra murmured into her own rearview mirror as she peeled out after a black Jag passing south. "Get a grip."

Chapter Seventeen

Thomas and Gary

A n obsidian-haired Asian man slouched in the doorway eyeing Nick and Gail. The twenty-something man wore black pants, a rumpled slate-blue dress shirt, and a skinny black tie. Nick motioned him to sit.

Wiry little guy, Nick decided. The man's pupils were black as globs of oil. He had his phone in his left hand and his car keys in the other.

"I'm Thomas Wong."

Nick made the introductions and took a breath to continue but Thomas jumped in. "I know you have to ask a lot of questions. I feel really bad about Ed, uh, Dr. Michael. He was a really great guy."

"What do you know about what happened?"

"I was just coming up the stairs when I heard the screams."

"Do you always take the stairs?"

"Mostly. Exercise, you know." Thomas looked back and forth between the officers, eyes wide, leaning forward. "I heard the screaming, then all the running around. Thought it was a patient going off at first. Got stuck trying to get up to the second floor 'cause this guy came running down the stairs and practically shoved me out of the way. Going real fast, you know?"

"Did you know this guy?"

"I'd seen him in the lobby, usually with a girlfriend, I think. Gary's patients I think. I just saw him going by...really traumatized. No girlfriend though." Thomas sat back.

"And then?"

He sat up again. "And then I hauled up the stairs, saw the commotion at the back. Dr. Huston waved me to stay up front, so I stayed in the lobby since no one was covering the desk. God, I finally realized it was Lila and Jackie crying or something. And Barbara hollering. Hung out until Nancy came and had us clear the waiting area. Then the police showed up. Nancy had me go back into the kitchen. Lila was having a full-on panic attack and Barbara was talking her down. Nancy ran in and told me to go to room four and calm down an elderly couple. I stayed with them until the guy's blood pressure went down. Finally got 'em out of there about twenty minutes later, and walked them to their car. Jetted back up here as soon as I could, but by then the cops were all over the place and Nancy had me go to the big conference room where I've been ever since."

"What do you think happened?"

"Dunno exactly. I hear it's real bad. Stabbing and stuff." Thomas looked bleakly from Gail to Nick. "Lila blabbed some stuff. Some kind of knife or something? I heard Mark whisper to Barbara...Dr. Huston...something about mutilation." He grimaced and dropped his keys on the table.

"OK, so you've all been talking. Who do you think did this?"

"Man, it's hard to say. Pretty rad for a sleepy little clinic like this. At UCSD—I did an internship there too—we had some big cases and some weird stuff...you know, a delusional patient jumped out the window once...couple of schizophrenics went at it. Some ODs—one croaked onsite. But this is vicious, man. He didn't deserve it. No matter what."

"What do you mean 'no matter what'?"

"I mean the guy was definitely in charge of psychiatry here. Really knew his stuff, you know. But, like, he didn't put up with stupid people, you know what I mean? And didn't like backstabbing."

"Backstabbing?"

Thomas made a decision. "OK, some people thought maybe I talked to Ed too much."

"Did you?"

"I needed to know stuff. Nancy thought I relied on him a little too much. But I liked the guy; he was great."

"OK, so fill us in on your whereabouts last night."

"I finished my last patient at five o'clock, then met with Nancy for a while. I was doing my notes, and then got some coffee. Talked with Ed about some patient issues."

"What patient issues?"

"Can't say. Confidentiality and all." He began playing with the purple thumb drive hanging from his key chain.

"This is a murder investigation, remember." Nick thought he saw a hardness set in around the young man's eyes.

"Yeah, OK, man," he said with some effort, his lips curling back ever so slightly. "We had a meds discussion, and he...kind of like reprimanded me...about suggesting a medication for my three o'clock cancer patient. Said I was overstepping. I'm not an MD, of course. He was right—I'm not supposed to give medical advice—even though he knows I know what I'm talking about."

"You're not supposed to pretend to be a doctor?"

"Naw. Assess, diagnose, treat. Stupid. Can't prescribe but we do everything else."

"So did you decide to kill him because you were mad?" Nick suggested.

"Kill him? Don't even joke about it, man. Not me, no way. But somebody, man. Somebody who really wanted to get Ed." Thomas jabbed the thumb drive into his palm.

"Who?"

"Well...could have been a patient." He tapped the thumb drive on the table, emphasizing his points. "He'd hospitalized at least three people since January. Couple of felons got out this year after being convicted of robbery and drug abuse with Ed's help. There was Carl of course. And Sarah Nugent who'd stabbed her boyfriend. A couple more..." He paused.

"And?"

"OK, OK. Some of the clinic people didn't always get the guy. Ed was friendly—to certain people. He and I had coffee sometimes. Margaret saw us once. And Ed did Hillcrest sometimes."

"Gay bar scene?" Nick sat forward.

"I think he got around some."

"With you?"

"No, I said coffee. Well, and a couple of beers. But that's it, detective." Thomas sat back.

"Did the staff dislike him?"

He palmed the thumb drive again. "Some. Tension around here off and on, you know, people get snarky. The Hustons have a tough time sometimes. Nancy's pretty strong...great supervisor...don't get me wrong. Gary's cool. Sandra, Margaret...they're OK. Sometimes in my face. I poached one of Sandra's clients once...didn't like it much. Told me off."

"And Margaret?"

"Margaret is Margaret. I just let her have her space, man. I'm here to finish my final hours. Sit for the boards next year, so I am almost done, thank God."

"What time did you leave last night?"

"Ed and I finished up around six, then I headed out. Went home. UTC. On downtown later."

"Downtown? What time?"

"Around nine. Just hangin' out."

"Anyone see you?"

"Uh. Some guys I know. You can check it out." Thomas's Jimi Hendrix ringer blared. He flipped his phone open, and focused on the distraction. Putting the caller on hold, he said to Nick and Gail, "Sorry, I need to take this. I've got a hospitalized minor and I've got to deal with these parents."

"OK, that's all for now. Officer Fredrick will show you out. No conferring with others. Oh, and leave your cell please when you finish that call if you will. And everything else stays except your keys and wallet. Hey, do you mind if we take a look at that thumb drive?"

He hesitated, but nodded. Back on the phone, he jotted down the number so he could return the call from a landline. "I hope you catch the guy, detective. Nice talking to you." He got up, handing his phone and thumb drive to Boyd as he went out. "Take care of this, man." Boyd nodded and showed him out.

Gail got up, stretching her back. Nick got up and sat on the table. "He's a cool one. Need to check out his alibi."

"So our shrink maybe was bi," Gail smirked. "Wonder what else?"

"Bet that kid knows. Maybe he did it?"

"Could be him. Had motive, strength. Lots of emotion. OK, let's move on to the last intern and see what we get."

Nick flagged Boyd once more. Dressed in khakis and paisley shirt, ashen-faced Gary Bowman stood in the doorway moments later. Nick gestured for him to sit. The two officers introduced themselves while Gary nervously clasped and unclasped his hands before him on the table.

"Mr. Bowman..." Nick started.

"Um, Gary, please," Gary corrected, smiling.

"OK, Gary," Nick replied, noticing the guy's fingers shaking and sweating, leaving smudges of sweat everywhere he touched. "What do you know about what happened?"

"Well, I gather that Dr. Michael has been killed, uh, t-a-a-a-erribly killed..." Under duress, Gary's childhood stutter surfaced. "Sorry, detectives. I have this little s-s-s-speech thing that happens sometimes. Some water may h-h-h-help." He reached into his valise and pulled out a water bottle.

"That's OK, take your time. Were you here last night?"

"Yes, yes, I was," he nodded as he drank. "Saw my last p-p-patient at five o'clock and ended about six. Finished up my notes, talked with Sandra about some referrals in the intern room and... and...talked with-with-with Ed a little after that."

"Were you the last person to see him alive?"

"Uh, uh, I don't think so. There were lots of people around..."

"Like?"

"Like...like...well, Sandra. And Margaret—she was trying to get a report from Ed. Um, the Hustons were here. Um, N-n-n-ancy left sometime during that hour or so I think...I thought I saw her walk down the hall. Amanda left too, I think."

"Anything else? Anything else you saw? Or heard?"

"Ummmm...well...I guess I sort of...sort of," Gary hands gripped the table. "I heard something that was...out of the ordinary..."

"Yes?"

"Arguing...voices...coming from the end of the hallway in one of the offices."

"Which office...?"

"I think it was Ed's."

"What kind of voices?"

"Ummm...a w-w-w-oman's voice..." Gary's eyes darted back and forth between the officers. He snatched a tissue from the box and started wiping his hands, then his face.

"Who?"

"Hmmm, I hesitate to say this, but since I saw Nancy leave a little earlier, and Margaret...oh...and Amanda...were gone, and Sandra had gone to her workout class...that only leaves...umm...Barbara...or possibly a patient I didn't recognize..."

"Which is it?"

"I'm pretty sure I heard Barbara go in and start to come out... that's when I heard them...um...arguing...something about Ed...what he w-w-w-was doing...come to think of it, it must have been Barbara...can't miss the accent...I thought I heard her say, 'If you do that I'll fire you.' Then the door slammed; she must have gone back

inside, I think, because the voices were still arguing, but muffled."
Gary winced. "God, I hope I don't get fired for telling you."

"What did you hear next?"

"It got quiet. I did some more notes, picked up my stuff and...
left." He swiped some more tissue and blew his nose.

"What time?"

"Around seven fifteen or so by the time I got down to my car, I
think."

"Were there other cars in the lot?"

"Yeah, I think so. Sometimes people park there and go across the
street...especially after hours..."

"Where did you go?"

"Down to UCSD to the library...needed to do some research." He
stopped and sat back.

"OK, Mr. Bowman, is there anything else you can tell us?"

"I guess...I should say I came back..." His eyes darted back and
forth.

"What do you mean you came back? To the office...?"

"Uh, yes...no...I came back by on my way home to Solana Beach...
after nine o'clock. I like the coast route. And I saw..." he hesitated "...
Dr. Huston, er Mark...p-p-p-pulling out of the parking lot. It struck
me because I thought it was really late...but then I know they work
really hard...and sometimes do things in Del Mar during the evening."

"What time was that?

"After nine fifteen or so."

"Did he see you? Was he alone?"

"I don't think so. He pulled out pretty fast and turned north.
I was at a stop sign one block back. But it was him. Can't miss the
plates on the SUV: SHRNKME. Looked like he was alone."

"Did you go into the building here?"

"Oh no, just passed by. I have an apartment up the road. My
building manager can vouch for me. We talked about my lease."

"What's his name?"

"Gordon Moore. Sand Dunes Apartments. Here's the number." Gary read it out from his cell.

"OK. Anything else?" Nick asked. "We really appreciate your candor."

"Not that I can recall right now. I hope I haven't hurt anyone...I really love working here...and this is such a tragic thing to have happened...especially..." his voice trailed off.

"Especially?"

"Especially with us trying to get some new grants. One of the committees was due for an inspection this week...so we were all trying to put our best f-f-foot forward." He paused and looked down at his lap.

"OK, Mr. Bowman," Nick finally said. "You've been a great help. You can leave after you've given your phone and files to the officers at the door, if you would please. Call us if you remember anything else." Gary picked up one of Nick's card and dashed out. "Well, that was fruitful."

"Absolutely," Gail agreed, fiddling with her empty coffee cup. "Now we've got an argument, Mark Huston leaving stuff out and coming back here, and Barbara Huston lying perhaps...and having a fight with Ed..."

"If this Gary kid can be believed. OK, let's split up the rest. If you take the three patients, I'll take the three support people: Al, Lila, and that Jackie woman. Let's check back when we're done."

By late afternoon, all the interviews were complete. Nick and Gail and the rest of the team agreed to reconvene the next morning at headquarters; Nick made sure the cell phones would be returned first thing in the morning. The clinic was emptied of all personnel and sealed, and all the security camera tapes were confiscated. A night guard was called in to stand watch and the police team finally headed south. Nick was glad to be going home for the night; the good news is the traffic on I-5 south had thinned a bit. Just then his phone went.

"Daddy?" a young girl asked.

"Baby? How are you?" Nick said, thrilled to hear his daughter, Tracy's, voice.

"I'm fine, Daddy. We had a nice vacation in Hawaii and we went snorkeling and we saw lots of fish and we saw a volcano and everything. Oh and I learned how to hula." She giggled. "I wish you'd been there!"

"That's sounds like a lot of fun, sweetheart. When do I get to see you?" Nick asked plaintively.

"I don't know, Daddy, but maybe this weekend. Here's Mom. You two can work it out." She disappeared from the line.

"Great," Nick said to himself. It took ten minutes to negotiate a hand-off with Tracy's mother for the weekend. Finally Tracy came back on the line.

"Sorry, Daddy. I wish I could talk longer but I have to go feed Candy. You know how she is. She can't stand it when I'm away."

He blurted "me neither" but she was already gone. The life of a divorced detective. Nick sighed. But this weekend would be different. "Even if I have to share it with that damn horse," Nick said aloud. With that, he cranked up some classic rock and headed downtown, putting Seaside out of his mind. The dead shrink would still be dead come morning.

Chapter Eighteen

Sifting Suspects

Murder!

Word quickly spread through Del Mar's tiny downtown. Shops buzzed with rumors and Seaside Clinic, now cordoned off with yellow tape, drew a crowd. Within hours, news people clogged the parking lot, making breathless reports about an alleged murder inside. Local businesses were terrified that a psycho ran loose, but they managed to bury their fear long enough to service the influx of lookie loos with ready cash. For a quiet beach town, Del Mar had suddenly become Murder Mecca.

At seven o'clock sharp the next morning, Nick and Gail picked up coffee then headed over to headquarters where they buried themselves in suspect and evidence detail. By noon, they had every white board in the second-floor homicide conference room covered with names and bullet points.

"OK," Nick said to Gail, yawning despite two more shots of espresso at eleven o'clock. "Let's see what we've got. Four senior people: Huston, wife Barbara, supervisors Nancy Davis and Amanda Carlisle. Then there's four junior people: Gary and Sandra, who go with Amanda, right? And Margaret and Thomas who report to the Davis woman."

"Yup. Three support staff: Jackie Forrest, Al Naylor, Lila Judd—Lila, she's the one who found the vic."

"Plus three patients. Gabe Owen. Sylvia Allen. Darla Sanchez. Let's look at motive. Start with the three patients." Nick scanned the board on the south wall where Gail stood, red marker in hand.

Gail checked off points as she reviewed each suspect. "OK, when I interviewed these three, they were freaked to say the least. The boy—Gabe Owen—is seventeen and one of those...what's it called? Not retarded, but..."

"Autistic? Asperger's?" Nick suggested, unsure of the term.

"Yeah, one of those. In my opinion, this guy seems incapable of doing something like this. Probably has trouble wiping himself, poor kid. Kept asking for his monkey—some toy, we realized. Boyd found it in the waiting area. Kid calmed down some after that. Parents had to come in for him before the interview was over though 'cause he started screaming when Boyd popped in with his walkie-talkie going. Mom laid into me about interrogating her kid, but they said they'd come back with him if we needed them to."

"That brings us to Sylvia Allen, nineteen. She's a cutter," Gail went on. "Maybe a possibility if she wanted to off herself...?"

"And if she's seductive, and if she came on to Dr. Ed, and maybe he rejected her, then she killed him for it," Nick reasoned.

"Yeah, maybe. But she says she wasn't at the clinic Monday night...claims she was at an Overeater's Anonymous meeting." Gail consulted her notes.

"Doesn't mean she didn't slip in later. Let's check her alibi and flag her as a possible."

"OK, that leaves Darla Sanchez. She's thirty-eight, a mother of three, married, depressed. Nearly had a breakdown while I questioned her, cried nonstop. Terrified for her kids, she said."

"Might be a possible. If she walked in the night before, saw the shrink and the child porn, could've gone berserk. Alibi?"

"Dinner with the in-laws."

"Check out her story and flag her too. What about any other patients that were around last night?"

"Well, as far as I can tell, they were all out of the building by seven or so. Unless they were hiding, of course. But there were lots of staff people around...and the vic, of course."

"OK, let's move on to the support people."

"What'd ya get on them?" Gail scribed as Nick read from his notes.

"Al Naylor. Security guard. Says he's been there four years. Left yesterday at six o'clock, usual time. Told me he'd had a good relationship with the doc. Didn't often go into the offices at the back much unless called upon. Hung out in the kitchen a lot, though, I gather."

"Strong guy, must be 240. Could have done it. What's his alibi?"

"At his boy's baseball game that night. Says there are lots of people who'll vouch for him. I'd flag him until we know for sure."

"That leaves two more, right?"

"Yeah, Jackie Forrest, the office manager and...Lila...the girl who found the stiff. Forrest seems unlikely. She was still hyperventilating about the whole thing three hours later."

"Could be a good actress," Gail added cynically.

"Oh, yeah, and we've seen 'em."

"Half a check there. Need to alibi 'er."

"That leaves Lila...uh, Judd. That girl was a scared rabbit when I talked to her. Doesn't seem like the type to me, really. Slight. Could have been on drugs, though, that night. PCP could have helped her do it."

"Motive?"

"Nothing I could find."

"Where was she that night?"

"Uh, Mira Costa College she says, after she left at five o'clock. We'll check it out. Let's move on to the four students." Nick tore open a bag of Rollo pretzels and popped three in his mouth.

Gail reached over, pulled a pretzel from the bag, and started munching. After a moment, she made a face. "Too salty. Don't know how you eat these things."

"Practice," he shot back and waved her on. "Start with that Thomas kid. Korean, right? Calculating, smart."

"Bucks the system. Strong too, seems pretty agile. Tech savvy. Something going on between the shrink and that kid."

"Alibi's vague too," Nick agreed, popping two more pretzels in his mouth. "Lying about something. How about motive?"

"Jealous of the guy? Remember he talked about the medication thing...feeling restricted. There's the gay angle. Maybe he was in love with the guy...and the shrink was into kids instead."

"Crime of passion maybe. Double flag him. How about the other guy, Gary Bowman. Pretty much of a wimp, but you never know."

"Told us he was doing research at UCSD and checked in at the library. We can check the records..." Gail murmured, making notes.

"Of course he could have snuck out, doubled back. Motive?"

"Didn't like the doc? Theft? Rejection?"

"Umm, half a flag until we can check him out."

"OK, the two women. Sandra Daniel...er, Daniels, right? What do you make of her?"

Nick paused for a moment. "Kind of..."

"Vanilla?" Gail offered.

"Vanilla...with something else..."

"Weird. Where'd she say she was?"

"Gym, then home...no...I'm wrong...said she came back by. Have to check out witnesses who saw her—and when she left. Motive?"

"Angry at the guy. Father figure? Porn hater? Sexually involved with him?"

"Could be all of the above. I'd flag her."

"OK, the other girl, Margaret Tanaka. She was pretty straight-forward, I thought." Gail remembered she had a bit more bagel in her bag, so she reached in and snagged the last two bites of bread and tomato cream cheese.

"Withheld some info, didn't she? Said she had to talk to..."

"...Nancy Davis."

"Before she could say...? Say what...?"

"Dunno," Gail answered.

"Maybe she knew some deep dark secret about the doc and killed him for it. Not too fond of that Thomas kid. The doc and Thomas were close so maybe she offed him for it?"

"Jealous?"

"Maybe. Says she left at five thirty or so. We'll have to check out her alibi."

"OK, that leaves the four top people." Nick moved over to the white board to the west. Gail sat down and grabbed an apple, took a few bites, then pitched it in the trashcan. It was better than the pretzels, but still not right.

"Let's start with the Hustons. Both really touchy about the good doctor. Doc could have been screwing around, jeopardizing the clinic. Maybe he...or she...iced him."

"Maybe both together?" Gail said brightly.

"I like that. A killer couple. One to stab, one to strangle."

Gail smiled but didn't laugh. The possibilities were too real. "She definitely had motive. Didn't like the guy...even though she was political about it...*and* she didn't tell us about threatening to fire him..."

"Provided Bowman's telling the truth..."

Gail nodded, going on, "There's the Jewish thing."

"Maybe. A little farfetched, though." Nick knew where she was going. Racial conflict was everywhere these days. Hispanics attacking African-Americans. And vice versa. But the German-Jewish thing seemed old school. "I don't know. The haughty Mrs. Huston..." Nick pictured the blond German woman sweeping down the street in a fur coat and high-heeled snow boots.

"Wow...haughty...big word for you, Caswell..."

"I do read occasionally, you know," Nick shot back. "Anyway, the snippy Mrs. Huston seems like an iceberg for sure...but Dr. Mengele? Could fit. Double flag her."

Gail marked the board, and then turned back to Nick. "OK, that leaves her husband. Pretty calculating, that one," Gail suggested, wrinkling her nose. "Mark Huston reminds me of that stockbroker guy last year. The one who murdered his wife and kids, remember? Slick, cold as stone. Money in offshore accounts. Mistress in Mexico. Psychopath to the core."

Nick nodded, pointing a pretzel at her. "If you ask me, Mr. Huston could take our shrink without even breathing heavy. When we get the tox and autopsy reports back, we'll get a better idea. Definitely think he's a top candidate."

Gail double flagged Mark's name. "OK, that leaves the two senior women."

"Nancy Davis. What'd you make of her?"

"Knows more than she's saying. Might have done it...aggressive enough...but..." Gail's voice trailed off.

"But?"

"I don't know...Seems like a straight shooter...no pun...but she definitely loathed the guy."

"Question mark her. OK, that leaves Carlisle. Amanda."

"Yeah, your frie-e-e-e-nd." Gail stretched out the word like a taffy pull.

"OK, OK," Nick waved her off, "we know I've worked with her before, but she's still a suspect. What do you think?"

"A possible...still have to check her alibi."

"What do you make of that creepy note she got? Maybe 'D' is out to get them both...the doc and Ms. Carlisle."

"Maybe they were peddling drugs or scamming Medicare together? Somebody found out, killed him, and she's next."

"Check her out and let's work the connection angle," Nick said soberly. "We may need to consider some protection for her, if things get ugly. For now, let's send Larry out to do the alibis."

Gail opened up another avenue. "What about someone else? What if there's a doc hater out there who got into the building late or even hid in there for a few hours so they could slip into the doc's office, murder the guy, and slip out without any of the others knowing. Maybe they were even doing sex games late at night..."

"We may be nowhere near finding this perp."

"Or perps. What about the security tapes?"

"We can take a look at 'em and you can check with the Hustons about who has keys to the place. That may help us narrow it down some. For right now, it could be anybody." Nick's phone went.

Gail checked her laptop while he grunted into the phone and scribbled notes. He finally ended the call. "Wuz up?"

"Double homicide. Clairemont," Nick told her. Squaremont, as it was affectionately known, was a rabbit warren of suburban homes where tempers flared fast and people dumped their angst onto their neighbors pretty regularly

"Goody," Gail joked, "close to home."

"Must be a full moon." Nick winked at her. Gail grabbed her gun and her bag, and Nick tossed five empty coffee cups in the trash along with assorted bagel and pretzel paraphernalia. The two hurried down the backstairs and out to the Crown Vic, the dead shrink on hold for now.

"Yup, a full moon: when the loonies loom," Gail quipped as they drove off. Gail had no way of knowing how truly prescient she was— not just about Squaremont, but about Del Mar just to the north where Amanda Carlisle was about to come face to face with a loony of her own.

Chapter Nineteen

Mind-walk

Two miles north of where psychiatrist Ed Michael breathed his last, Amanda Carlisle sat sunning on the deck of her townhouse. Her Olympus digital camera sat on the table next to her and her cell, returned earlier by the police, was nearby. The Del Mar surf was pounding the shore a few streets away, and she could just make out the sounds of traffic crawling along PCH.

Her arms felt warm. Craning her neck, Amanda saw that the noon sun had moved directly overhead. It dappled through the acacia trees spreading above her in a steady flicker of sunlight. Catching movement off her deck, she watched as two hummingbirds hung at the mouths of some honeysuckle blossoms, supping. Amanda grabbed her camera and snapped a couple of stills of the delicate, hyperactive creatures. Checking the shots, she noticed the flowers were clear but the birds were a complete blur; the little buggers were too fast. Sighing, Amanda put down the camera and watched them, distracted.

The delicate little creatures seemed busy but content. For them, fulfillment was just a bloom away. She breathed deeply and the scent of the birds' tropical flowers wafted over her. It all was a very seductive setting for languishing the day away. But the world inside Amanda's head was anything but serene. Visions of blood popped in and out. The memory of Ed, trussed up, impaled, gasping for his final breath, flashed over and over in her mind. Like some horror movie she couldn't turn off, the images churned in her brain in a kind of Technicolor re-loop.

From a clinical place, she knew posttraumatic stress well. She knew how it forced the mind to relive life-threatening horrors again and again. She could name the experience. Easy. But from a very human place, Amanda cowered. Cowered unspeakably in the brutal glare of Ed's tortured demise.

What must he have felt? Who was with him in those moments, exacting this vicious revenge? What kind of demon brought hell to a sanctuary of hope? This was not some CSI episode. She cringed. This was real. This was home, professional home, emotional home. Where she'd celebrated birthdays and anniversaries. Where she and Ed gleefully devoured fruitcake at the clinic last Christmas since nobody else could stand the stuff. Now...Ed was no more. Brutally dispatched. The searing memory burned so brightly, she could barely see the here-and-now before her. The iridescent hummingbirds floated alive in front of her, but she could only glimpse them through a murky film of death and destruction.

Amanda knew it would take time. Time to process the horrific experience, the images, the shock, the awful finality of it, to get it out of her psyche once and for all. She had the techniques. To clear herself. To get it all out of her mind—and heart. But it would take time. Distance. On some level she was grateful for the time to heal while the clinic would be closed. She also knew many of the patients would be traumatized for weeks, months to come. Most had already gone on to other clinics. She'd been in touch with the interns, of course. Counseled them to take some time away. But the healing was difficult when there was still a murderer to be found. So they were stuck, for now, in the web of murder, until the police could out the monster.

As she reached for her iced tea turning watery in the sun, her mind wandered to the detectives. It had been interesting to see Nick Caswell again. That was a bright spot. He'd been promoted since then but she remembered him—fair, compassionate, dogged until he solved his crime, a man who parsed his words, especially when you crossed him. Her dad was like that. Or at least that's how Amanda saw him. To criminals, Nick was probably an irascible SOB. *Just like my dad*, she thought.

Swiftly, Amanda sat upright. "I feel like a swim," she said to the hummingbirds. Minutes later, in tankini and cover-up, she made her way down the hill from her condo into the foot traffic sandaling across PCH to the beach. Feeling the warm grains as she sank into the sand, she dumped her towel, bag, and camera at water's edge. Seconds later she disappeared into the wet crowd playing in the waves north of the Poseidon restaurant.

As the water licked her torso, Amanda registered the chill. The raw power of the swells. The liquid, salty, sudsiness. The crash in her ears. It made her feel alive. The cold pinpricks brought her back into her body. Sea spray and salt hit her nostrils. Seagulls screamed. Kids shouted. Rock music cut against the sounds of the sea. The atmosphere was alive. She was alive. The ocean pummeled her with wet, insistent life. And gradually the horror film of death in her brain dimmed.

Amanda swam a bit then she leaned back and floated. Gazing beachward, she chuckled. At the shore, several kids slid on their boogie boards into the surf over and over though it knocked them into the drink every time. Down they'd go, then up again, chasing their boards, then jumping on fast, gliding into the never-ending waves, hollering as they went.

Gazing out to sea, she watched the surfers paddling out, their lanky bodies hugging their surfboards. Suddenly they were aloft, catching the Pacific swells, riding them in until they pooped out near the boogie board kids at shoreline. Leaning back, Amanda treaded water, lazy. She could just make out a few sailboats tacking south. Several motorboats gunned along toward La Jolla, probably headed toward lunch or cocktails or both.

Suddenly, something raked her leg. Amanda jerked, gulping salt water. Looking down, she saw: seaweed. Thank God. Only seaweed. Not a sand shark. Or worse. "God, I really am jumpy. Girl, get hold of yourself," she blurted. Nobody heard. Paddling in, she fell on her towel and lay there, soaking up sun. Observing the boogie board kids, she grinned and reached for her Olympus. She snapped fast, getting wipeouts, the kids dripping sand and seaweed, lunging for their boards, feet flailing, having a ball. She eyed a seagull swooping down nearby. The gray bird stopped to poke at shells tangled under some seaweed a few feet from her towel. She focused and snapped, catching the bird in foreground, beak raised like a trumpet as a massive wave rushed to engulf it. Snapping again, she caught the smart bird as it rose up, prize in beak, an instant before the wave hit, the fowl escaping its wet pursuer, gulping as it climbed.

Amanda had an eye for the moment, a knack for catching life midstream. She won a prize once for best novice sequence. It showed a little girl bending to sniff a golden tulip. The spring flower arched upward as the curly haired toddler bent into it. Soon, the child's nose collided with the pollen-laden flower, and Amanda snapped as the child's face contorted, mid sneeze, stunned by an onslaught of sticky dust when she inhaled. The next shot caught the stunned girl in mid wail, her face covered in yellow pollen like she'd been smeared with an egg.

Amanda loved her photos. Loved taking them, framing them, sending them out to friends. But sometimes she wondered if she was too much the observer. If maybe she was so intent on watching, she was too busy to live. Likewise, the danger of being a psychotherapist is that it kept her apart. Isolated, insulated. She wanted to be part of life—her life—but Amanda was cautious. Demure even. If nothing else, she realized that Ed's death had shocked her into some new feelings, jolted her into violent proximity with Ed *and* his killer. A killer intimately assaulting Ed, limb violating limb, excruciating acts of brutality evolving moment to moment. Passion engulfed the killer—and then most surely, his victim as well.

It reminded Amanda of a Robert Mapplethorpe exhibit she'd seen once in Cincinnati years ago. Mapplethorpe's infamous flower erotica was there. It was shocking, beautiful, controversial. Many condemned it; others flocked in hordes to see it. Amanda couldn't stay away. It was the XYZ collection—sequestered off to the side for the faint of heart—where the shocking pictures of sadomasochism and black men and crosses and castration made her truly gasp. Exquisite depictions of pain so vivid Amanda could almost see the blood dripping off the prints onto the floor.

She wanted to feel deeply, it was true. But certainly not in that way. Still, there was something visceral, hypnotic, in that level of emotion. Amanda admitted that her photos of flowers and birds and beach scenes and children lacked that blood-pumping immediacy, reflecting, undoubtedly, something benignly safe in her psyche— or something in her needing to feel that way. Her tender images of Helen in the months before she died captured Amanda's mother living, connecting, breathing life. Helen, in the garden in a bright red bandana and long blue skirt, bending over her tomatoes, cleaning off mites, cutting dead leaves, all the while being eaten, devoured by her own infestation, an unrelenting cancer that would take her life when Amanda turned sixteen.

That's when Amanda began taking pictures. When Helen got ill. Snapping with abandon, she evolved an eye for pathos. Like the shots of Helen enjoying the last months of life. Helen, scooping up a green hornworm with a cry of horror and glee, dropping the intruder into a paper sack, relocating the ghastly thing to the vacant lot nearby, alive but out of her garden. Amanda captured Helen's half grimace, half smirk. A look that said: "You can't live in my garden, you ugly little thing, but you have the right to live elsewhere." A life-giving gesture, playing God for the worm but bereft of the power to play God for herself. As Helen lay dying later in a medicated stupor, her visage became transcendent, flickering between this world and the next. But Amanda had been too raw to capture it, Helen's ephemeral death face seared in her memory but not on film.

A boy screamed at his buddy down the beach, cutting Amanda's reverie. Startled, she felt wet on her feet as the incoming tide drenched her. Sighing, Amanda picked up her things and trudged back across the sand, then up the hill toward home, thinking. Consciously distancing from the images. Putting aside the violence in art—and life—coming back again into the feel of her feet slapping the pavement, grit between her toes, sweaty, hot, real.

Entering her living room and dumping her things, she gazed out at the deck. "I feel like a Jacuzzi," she said to Emily, the cat, who sauntered in from the office. Amanda grabbed bottled water from the cooler, and then strolled out to the balcony where the hot tub waited. Cranking up the heat, she dropped her wet towel and climbed inside, not caring if the water was cool or her body was still plastered with sand.

Like a glorious lobster I am just going to sit here until it heats up, and I'm totally cooked, she told herself. Amanda lay back, head on the headrest, willing her muscles to relax, willing her psyche to rest. Plenty of time to deal with Mom and life and Seaside later. Instead, she focused on the bubbles. The luxurious sensation of gentle bubbles and warm water. Safe. Secure. Unhurried. Unstressed.

After an hour or so, Amanda climbed out. The soak had helped and her mind seemed clear. After a quick shower, she dressed in shorts and top then wandered back out on the deck with new iced tea. Knowing how her mind worked, she returned inside for pad and pen, then sat back outside to watch the sunset and think.

OK. I'm ready now. Ready to deal.

Amanda had a method. She called it a *mind-walk.* A true empath, Amanda had a special ability. That ability allowed her to enter the psychological world of another. It was different from photography where she captured life images in the objective. In a mind-walk, Amanda accompanied her subject in the person's experiences from the subjective. The goal: not to stand outside the person, but to walk with him or her toward healing.

It was an art. A psychological art perfected from hour after hour of gut-wrenching therapy with people over the years. It helped her to reach out to them, to engage therapeutically in a healthy way, not to encroach, but to connect. To feel her way emotionally into someone else's world in order to guide the person toward a healthier future. It worked with therapy. Now she hoped it would work with murder.

First, she set her own psyche aside. That is, she safely parked it for a time in a soothing, imaginary place until she could come and reclaim it. For Amanda that place was an imaginary English tearoom. She visualized lovely chintz and delicate porcelain, familiar people chatting amiably, the warm smell of tea steeping and hot scones and butter. Settling her psyche-self there on a cozy couch, she gently allowed another part of herself to peel away. To float in her mind's eye back to Seaside. Then, as that peeled-off-self, to stand before Ed's door, ready to enter the world of the killer that tumultuous night, in the then and there, as if it were the here and now.

Safely, slowly, her mind's eye focused as she reached out, turned the knob, and entered the room with the killer. Her aim: not to interfere, but to observe. To walk where they'd walked, know what they knew when they knew it, not as a voyeur, but as a companion traveler.

Once in *the Space* Amanda picked up the pen and paper from her lap and began to sketch. She allowed her peeled-off self to report through her fingers. Images flitted in and out appearing in strokes on the page. The killer's face was fuzzy but Ed Michael's was sharp and alive. As she watched, she drew. The no-sense lines swirled up, around, connecting, breaking, reconnecting again, drawing nothing in order, but nothing particularly at random. Soon, the swirls became images and the images spoke words. Gradually a story emerged. Beginning, middle, and end.

She looked on from the killer's side. She could *see* Ed. At his desk. Smiling, teasing, laughing. Intelligent conversation. Verbal badminton. Then something...something went wrong. He looked up, and the figure before him altered the game. A new tit for tat, where Ed became the prey. Ed, at his desk, in his lair, so to speak, sitting, talking, doing the normal things, perhaps the abnormal things.

At his desk, Amanda's peeled-off self observed him. What was Ed doing? Writing? Downloading? Gently, she allowed her mind to wander through the progression. How one minute Ed was working, chatting, in charge, then gradually—or suddenly—he was bowed and cowed. Stopped. Stooped. Stifled. Snuffed. She gazed upward. Saw how the cord came to be pulled from the shade, the killer deliberate, in control. How carefully it wound round Ed's fleshy neck, then pulled tight, tighter, until Ed sat strangled, erect. Was he willing? Unwilling? Where was Ed's will to live? To fight? To resist? Gone. Gone somehow. Or lulled, perhaps deadened, soon to be dead.

Her mind's eye travelled over the killer's work, past Ed's grimace and fettered neck, down his sinking chest, across the drooping shoulder, down, down the length of his arm, to the right hand, staked savagely, painfully, in place. The weapon must have come down with tremendous force, the vicious implement slicing through tendon and bone, melding the flailing hand and mahogany desk into one. Unlike the beatified saints martyred on the cross, Ed sat impaled on his desk, an earthbound sinner, all redemption lost.

Then slowly, delicately, her eyes drifted downward, locking onto Ed's lap. To the crease of his pants, where the ferocious knife thrust through cloth and flesh, and found its home in Ed's sexual center. Sex, she thought lightly. Sex and violence. Workplace violence.

Office.

Desk.

Neck.

Torso.

Hand.

Lap.

Groin.

Penis.

They were all connected somehow. Linked. Perhaps the images and the atmosphere and the place somehow drove the purpose behind the game, the killer's triumph. Triumph over death. Ed's death. To get...revenge? To seek justice? To find peace? A peace? A piece? Amanda knew from research that gratification looms large in the mind of a sociopath. A sociopath gets an uncontrollable urge—and is hell-bent on satisfying it. In their world, there is no still, small voice of social or psychological conscience. No inner guidance to temper the actions of a mad, impulse-driven mind. There is only: I see, I want, I do. I kill you if you get in my way because I get everything. No matter what. No matter who. In the mind of a sociopathic killer, there is no WE. There is only ME. A ME in this case perhaps so enraged, so ID-engorged it dispatched Ed in a simple moment. Perhaps as casual as a chef snapping a hen's neck for supper, then ripping her corpse apart to stuff in the pot for stew. In the mind of this ME, Ed was perhaps a carcass, flesh to be used, abused, the killer hungry, hungry for vengeance. Not one, but two corporeal thrusts to the body.

Was it sexual? Sexist? Was the ME reacting to sex? Experiencing sex? Getting off while offing Ed? Ed's body, languishing, just so much dross. To be disposed of? To be dispossessed of? To possess? To devour? To dispatch.

Eyes open he went.

Trussed.

Pegged.

Agog.

Fouling his own nest? And perhaps that's part of it. Invading Ed at his core, where he laid, where he lived. Killing him in his nest most foul? The images twisted together and oozed out on the page. But there must be more. Something missing. Something that made the place a key to the act. Something triggering. Something unspeakable that drove the ME to the point of Ed's no return.

And then it happened.

The phone rang. Shrill and loud. Amanda jumped in her deck chair. "God," she said aloud, and watched as the pad and pen spilled to the deck below, the pen cascading farther through the cracks to the ground two floors below.

Freud's Revenge

"Damn." She steadied herself, mentally pulling back her peeled off self, reclaiming her own psyche with a snap. Moving quickly in the living room, she grabbed her landline. "Hello? Hello?" she shouted, adrenaline-fueled blood pounding in her ears. God only knew who was on the other end of the line.

Chapter Twenty

One Potato Two

"Amanda? Are you all right? It's Sam."

"Oh...oh...Sam," Amanda said loudly, relieved. "Sorry. I nearly jumped out of my skin when I heard the phone ring."

"Where were you? You sound like you've been running?" Sam Cook, her former fiancé, sounded concerned.

"Oh, just out on the deck. Doing some...thinking. I'm sure you heard about..." She stopped, wondering if Sam had seen the papers.

"Yes. I read everything about it I could find. I was up in Seattle at a conference or I would have called sooner. My God, Amanda, you must be an emotional wreck."

"Yes. It...it was ghastly. I saw the body...and it was...pretty... awful." She sank into the couch, noticing Nick's detective card on the end table where she'd dropped it the day before.

"God, you saw the body? The papers were pretty vague. It was Ed Michael, right?"

"Yes. I don't know how much I'm allowed to say. The whole clinic's under investigation...and the patients are completely traumatized."

"Naturally, you're all very upset."

"Yes..." Her voice trailed off.

"You sound like you're not in a good place. Do you want me to come up there? I can be there in no time."

"Oh...well...I don't know." She was conflicted. She knew Sam could be in Del Mar from La Jolla in minutes if she wanted, but she was torn. Torn between wanting comfort and giving the signal she wanted to start things up again. Amanda and Sam had met in grad school in Los Angeles. He'd been a child psychologist now for about four years. They'd dated, then got engaged, but marriage had been a long way off when her feelings changed and they'd broken up.

"Amanda...? Let me help you...you know I'm here for you no matter what...no matter what's happened in the past," he urged.

"Yes, Sam, I know. It's just that I'm coping with a lot right now and...and I don't want to add to the confusion, honestly."

"Well, OK if that's what you need," Sam said. They talked about ten minutes more, catching up on work, Sam's cousin's marriage, Sam's new passion, tennis. She hung up, promising to meet him for lunch.

She was happy to hear his voice, frankly, but she wasn't sure right now while she was feeling off. She was afraid it would influence her to get sucked back in. Sam had gotten obsessive near the end of their relationship. Emotional trauma probably brought it out in him because of his parents. They'd been killed on an Alaska Airlines holiday flight from Puerto Vallarta a few years ago. Mechanical failure. Once the numbness faded, Sam got morose. Then depressed. Had trouble treating his patients. Then he got obsessive. After a while, her skin crawled when she was around him too long. She'd pulled away slowly, trying not to abandon him. She'd finally broken off their engagement a year ago when he seemed strong. It had been painful. Scenes. Crying. Shouting. Reconciliations. Worse breakup.

She wasn't sure exactly what had happened. But it had been too much. Maybe something to do with Helen. Amanda had known what it was to lose a parent. But when Sam lost both of his, it was too much for her. Maybe she hadn't dealt enough with her own loss. Maybe she couldn't commit. All she knew was that she wasn't ready, and no one, not Sam or anyone else, was going to force her to do otherwise. Remembering it all helped her center; she had her own trauma to deal with now and she needed to deal with it carefully, slowly, with no strings attached.

She headed out to the deck to retrieve her things. "Damn, dark already," she said to Emily who strolled out on the deck watching a bird. She decided to walk down to the village for a light supper. She gathered up Emily and went back inside, closing her slider. Before she headed back to her bedroom to change, she glanced at Nick's card. The images of Ed and the threatening note from "D" intruded once again. She felt unsettled, invaded somehow. Off guard. Her eyes wandered to the tall gray file cabinet in her office.

"Well, if I have to, I have to." Reluctantly, she stepped into the office, reached the cabinet, and then stooped to open the bottom drawer. Far in the back in a black case, she found what she was looking for.

The Taser-X2 was a sleek, red and black model, designed for a woman's grip. It had a replaceable compressed nitrogen cartridge that fired two barbed projectiles attached to the Taser by insulated wires. According to her dad, the thing could penetrate up to two cumulative inches of clothing from a distance of up to fifteen feet. She and Phil had practiced with it a few years ago, but Amanda had always kept it locked away. Now, after she changed into jeans and sneakers, she took out the fanny pack holster, stuffed the Taser into it, and strapped it on. Her wallet, keys and phone went into her back pockets.

By 7:30 p.m., she was walking up PCH to the center of town and the plaza at Fifteenth. Bounding lightly up the stairs, she headed into Harvest Ranch Market. She selected a pasta salad and focaccia bread plus some fizzy water, and then sat watching the ocean as she ate at one of the tables outside. A half hour later, she climbed the second set of steps to the top of the plaza for a decaf cappuccino. Up top, the dark ocean spread out as far as she could see; luckily the coffee bar had no waiting. Minutes later, cup in hand, she plopped into a chair looking out to sea and sipped. The cappuccino was hot, forestalling the night chill that was starting to settle. Enjoying the warmth spreading through her, Amanda drifted back to her mind-walk through the killer's world. Nothing new emerged.

Her eyes wandered over to a little boy nearby. About seven, the kid was bent over an electronic game. The grown-ups near him, his parents she guessed, were talking loudly. They sounded like Canadians from the accents. They were arguing about what to do the next day and Amanda could make out the words "Wild Animal Park" and "Sea World." The boy sat kicking his chair leg, completely absorbed in his Nintendo DS, lights flashing, bells beeping as he jammed the buttons.

"That's it," Amanda sat up suddenly. The couple looked over and Amanda smiled, and then looked away. They went back to arguing. The boy never looked up. "That's it," Amanda said to herself again quietly. "That's what I was missing. "

She remembered she'd seen something when she stood next to Ed's dead body: the computer was on. The screen had flashed when she bumped the desk and crunched Ed's glasses. She'd been in too much of a hurry to get out of the room to truly register what was on the screen. But she was sure now it was two figures, some sort of picture, not just a spreadsheet or e-mail.

I need to tell the detectives about this, Amanda realized. She rose quickly, dumped her empty cup in the receptacle, then scooted down the steps to PCH and turned right. Walking rapidly north, she struggled to recall exactly what she'd seen—and wondered if the police had seen it too.

Suddenly she felt odd. The hairs on the back of her neck ruffled. Then a charge crept over her scalp. Turning to the left to see what or who was around, she didn't register anything unusual. Except for a teenage girl and boy kissing and giggling about a hundred yards behind her, she saw nobody else on her side of the street. Across the street she saw several small groups walking along, so she didn't feel especially alone. Still, something didn't feel right. She placed her hand on the Taser in her pack and trudged on, quickening her pace as she strode down the hill to her condo. She thought about the computer screen. What was there? She focused trying to get the picture in her mind. A few feet more and she passed some overhanging bushes on the right, then she turned a sharp right to head up to her street. A moment later, her scalp tingled again.

God, what is that? Is somebody...following me? Amanda tensed, and then she whipped around. She noticed the bushes about a hundred yards behind her move. She peered into the darkness, but couldn't make out anyone. Turning back, she crossed the street, and then rapidly climbed the hill back up to her place. Near her building she went in the back way, and then turned as if she lived on the east side. Taking the backstairs, she headed up to her floor, then turned toward the ocean again and her condo on the west side. Seconds later, she put the key in the door and ducked inside.

"I don't know, maybe I'm just jumpy," she said to Emily who made an appearance, yawning. "I know what you want," she told Emily as she patted the cat's head. Multitasking, she grabbed some of Emily's treats and her phone at the same time, scooping up Nick's card from the table. She dialed while she poured food into the cat's bowl and Emily lunged at it like she was starving. He answered after four rings.

"Nick Caswell," he breathed into the phone. He'd just gotten into his car after finishing the preliminary on the dead Clairemont couple. Apparently the Sanchezes' domestic dispute over who got the last beer had turned violent. Sometimes domestic violence—DV for short—ended that way. Guns in hand, the husband had gotten off two rounds before his wife plugged him with three to the stomach. At least the arguing had stopped. And the couple was now making their final journey together—to the morgue.

"Hi, Nick. It's...Amanda. Amanda Carlisle...from...from Seaside Clinic?"

Nick had to refocus for a minute. Then he remembered her. "Oh yeah," he replied, trying not to smile. "What can I do for you?"

"I wanted to tell you...uh...is this a good time? I remembered something more. You said to contact you if I did."

"Oh yeah, yeah, of course." Taking up a pen and flipping open a worn notebook from his breast pocket, he said, "Shoot."

"Well, I remembered something in the room...uh, the office, where...Ed, Dr. Michael, was found. The computer was on. I mean the screen...came alive. I must have bumped the desk when I came over to see Ed...uh...the body. I was kind of in shock. But I remember that it flashed on as I moved away. I didn't really get a good look at it. But it looked like a person, uh people. I mean not an e-mail or something." She wasn't sure how to go on.

"OK," Nick sat listening. "Go on...what else?"

"Well it's fuzzy...you know fuzzy in my mind, but the feeling... the feeling, now that I think of it...is...is icky somehow." The words stumbled around as she said them.

"Icky. Hmmm. Not very clinical there, counselor."

"Oh yeah...I know...um...I just have a vague sense that it wasn't...OK...not something OK...in Ed's office...I don't know...was it unseemly? I guess you've seen it," she ventured.

"Yeah, we've seen it," he said noncommittally. After all, she was still a suspect herself. Maybe this was an acting ploy.

Amanda grew flustered. "Oh, well...now I feel kind of stupid..." She blushed. "I was just trying so hard to get into the mind of the...killer...that it sparked a memory that hadn't...surfaced...um... before."

"And why were you trying to get into the mind of the killer?" Nick scrunched up his face. "Are you psychic or something?"

"Well, no," she laughed, self-conscious. "I'm not saying that. It's just that many therapists are...pretty intuitive...can get into the emotions of their patients so they can help them through their troubles. Empaths," she finished, not sure what else to say.

"Well, OK." He fell silent, not sure how much more to reveal. "There *was* something on that computer, something pretty graphic."

"Oh my God," Amanda blurted. In that instant she got it; the gestalt of the image Nick and the others must have seen popped completely into her mind. "I can see it now: one figure was tall. The other was...short...much shorter. A child? Child porn?" she trailed off, sickened. It was one thing to treat patients with perversions. It was another thing to practice with a pervert.

"Did you know that? See that, or...what," Nick pressed her.

"No, I got the...image...from what I saw...remembered...and also from...you...from how you said it. I just got it somehow...from your voice...My God, I can't believe Ed was into pornography, but if he was...that is horrific, horrible..."

"OK, well..." He was still confused. The woman seemed real in her revulsion. "OK, I can't really disclose what we saw, but you were right to come forward. Have you remembered anything else?"

"Um...well...nothing very specific...except the way he was... mutilated...

"Yes?" Nick encouraged her.

"Must be somehow tied together with why he died, I guess I'm thinking," she continued. "I just picked up that there was a progression...a progression of steps...and a kind of intention of action that may point to why the killer did what he did."

"He?"

"Well you know...he, she, I don't know. It's just that there seemed to be some kind of raging emotion. Then a calculated mutilation... that progressed...somehow. I don't know. One person? Two people perhaps?"

Now Nick was really interested. "Why two?"

"It just wasn't...messy. I don't know what I am trying to say... really. It's just that there was a mess...but it didn't seem to happen in a messy way. It was methodical somehow. Two people doing it to keep things under control perhaps? Maybe you can put it all together." She stopped, self-conscious again.

"I can tell you've really been thinking about this. Most people can't get past the blood and guts to think straight, but you seem to be doing it," Nick said appreciatively, really meaning it.

"Well I've had my moments, believe me." For a second, she thought about sharing the creepy feeling she'd had walking home, but she ignored it.

"Well, OK. I really appreciate your calling with this. I...I..." Now Nick paused, torn. "If you think of anything else, feel free to call," he said. "Day or night." He winced; it sounded too personal. *Come on*, he argued in his mind, *you say that all the time. Yeah, but this time it felt different.*

"Right. OK. Well I will do that, Officer Caswell."

"Nick."

"OK, yeah. Nick. If I think of anything else I'll definitely contact you."

"Anytime," he responded and ended the call. He made a few notes, and then called Gail who was already home with her feet up, beer in her hand, watching her husband play catch in the backyard with their two boys. He filled her in on the call. They pledged to take it up again in the morning first thing. With the morgue in charge of the dead DV couple, Nick finally headed home to see if he could catch the last half of the Padres game.

Chapter Twenty-One

Shattered

As Amanda put down her cell, Emily jumped in her lap. Cat hair wafted up—a sure sign of summer: when Emily's coat thinned and the castoff ended up in heaps on Amanda's white carpet. She gave the cat a few strokes anyway then Amanda registered how tired she was. "Time for bed," she said to the fur ball who sat licking her paw. "Don't find any mice tonight," she ordered. "I'm way too tired." Emily blinked at Amanda, bored; suddenly, her eye caught a spider climbing up the kitchen wall and the feline went off to investigate.

Rolling her eyes, Amanda headed to bed. In five minutes she was tucked in, Taser on the nightstand. Picking up the remote, she clicked on the television. News blared. Gas prices were up. Airfares were up even higher. Tomorrow was going to be a scorcher. There had been a double homicide in the city, plus the Padres had lost. Not too cheery, Amanda yawned. Seconds after snapping off the light, she was asleep, dreaming about baseball players swatting DC-10s that were buzzing the bases.

Minutes later she came up out of a heavy sleep. Blinking, she forced her eyes open. Then, she heard it: THUD. Out near the living room. Must be Emily, Amanda thought sleepily. Chasing something. Then she heard it again. THUD.

Suddenly she felt a thwack on the bed. Pinching on the reading light overhead, she saw Emily—stretched out on the end of the bed—slapping her tail hard. Whack. Now they both heard the noise clearly—it was down the hall. The cat's ears pricked up as she leapt up arching her back. A moment later, her ears flattened and she growled as she jumped off the bed.

Carefully, Amanda pulled on her yellow robe and flips, and unsheathed the Taser. Pinching off the lights, she inched toward the bedroom door, pushed it open, and then she slipped through noiselessly. She moved slowly down the hallway toward the living room, Taser in front. There was another soft noise perhaps out near the slider. Detouring slightly into the office nook, she grabbed her phone and flipped it open, and then she crept on toward the living room where it met the kitchen. Peering around the corner toward the deck, Amanda's heart wrenched. Just beyond the slider, a dark figure crouched between the Jacuzzi tub and one of the deck chairs.

Something whizzed past her to the right and Amanda watched as her brazen cat padded straight out to the slider, eyes on her prey. Amanda held her breath. Emily hissed, then let out a long, low growl, and flattened her body to the carpet. Shaking, Amanda pointed the Taser to fire over the cat's head and simultaneously pressed re-dial on her cell. By the second ring, a male voice spoke:

"Caswell."

"Detective Caswell...Nick...it's...Amanda..."

"Amanda...?" Nick said, groggy, having fallen asleep on the couch with Letterman blasting.

"Amanda Carlisle...Nick, there's...there's someone on my deck..." she choked out just as the dark figure stood up. Amanda lifted her arm to fire, but a split second before she squeezed, the figure hurled something at the slider. As it hit, the glass shattered instantly. The crash reverberated as glass flew. Someone screamed. Amanda pulled her hands up to guard her face as the phone dropped to the carpet. Emily screeched and jumped sideways nearly three feet, then she loped back down the hallway with her tail bristling.

Through her fingers, Amanda glimpsed the huddled figure rise up and then back up toward the railing through the pile of splintered glass. In the strange, glistening half-light of the moon, it seemed like it skated backward on ice. Swiftly, the figure turned and leapt to the railing, poised like a panther, ready to spring to the ground beneath.

Then she heard it.

POP.

Sharp, short. Then another. POP. The figure disappeared over the railing and there was a thud a few seconds later as the body hit the grass.

Amanda gasped for air, gaping at the mess before her, crawling forward, oblivious to the danger ahead. Nick screamed from the fallen phone. "Amanda...Amanda...what's happening, what's happening...?

"It's...it's someone..." she choked out and snatched the phone from the floor as she crawled, "on the deck...glass...everywhere... break...in...body...somebody..." Fearless, Amanda stepped toward the deck, crunching on glass.

"Amanda...Amanda? Are you all right?"

She looked through the railing from behind the Jacuzzi tub. "Wait..." she hissed. Peering over, she spotted a crumpled body on the grass. Suddenly it was up, limping over the cement, past the pool, and out toward the parking lot. "Yes...yes...he's...he's hurt... getting away..." Amanda leaned farther over the rail, and then she stopped as the adrenaline ebbed and her rational mind stopped her.

"Oh my God!" She backed up rapidly through the glass, into her living room and finally crouched down in the hallway near the kitchen.

"Amanda...get out of there...I'm calling dispatch. I'm on my way. What's your address?

"Del Mar...2910 Sutton...#31...my condo..." she whispered.

"OK, OK. We are on our way...go to a safe room and stay there. Do you understand?"

"Yes...yes...OK...I'm...moving...now..." Amanda managed as she turned and ran down the hallway to the bedroom. She locked the door, then grabbed a small table and savagely wedged it under the knob. "OK, I'm inside."

"Keep your phone. We're on our way. " Nick jumped in the Vic and sped to North County, siren blaring.

By the time the local beat cops arrived and Nick pulled up a few minutes later, most of the neighbors were out and the complex blazed with light. Nick bounded up the stairs and strode inside. Within minutes, he'd surveyed the scene with the first responders, gotten a blow-by-blow from Amanda then began crunching through broken glass on the hunt for evidence. Down below, cops were tracking a bloody trail out to the street.

Amanda sank into a chair at her dining table. She still had the Taser clinched in her hand. She set it down gently on the table and watched Nick out on the deck, coordinating the cops on the ground and the pair swarming the condo. A few moments later, she ventured out on the deck before she realized most of the neighbors were huddled on their decks, watching her.

"Hey, Amanda!" Mrs. Phillips hollered from next door, clutching Bruiser, her Chinese Crested Hairless. "Holy crap, what's going on over there?! Are you all right, dear?"

Amanda stepped cautiously toward the side railing. "I'm OK, Mrs. Phillips. The police are taking care of...everything."

"God, I thought Mike was going to have a heart attack. Was it a robbery? Are you sure you're OK?"

"Yeah, I'm fine. We don't know yet...they're trying to figure it out."

"Mike can come over if you want."

"Oh, no thanks. The police are taking care of it. Sorry to disturb you."

Nick moved over to Mrs. Phillips and conferred with her quietly. "Let us know if we can help, Amanda dear," the woman called out as she turned and went back inside with the tiny dog. "You've got our number if you need us."

Nick smiled at Amanda, and then he walked to the corner of the deck on the phone again. Amanda watched him for a moment, then she moved inside and sank onto a bar stool. *First Ed, now this? What's going on? What have we done?* She racked her brain, sifting through patients, recent conflicts, past cases, people she knew or worked with, had worked with. Faces and stories flooded her brain, sweeping over her like a psychological tsunami ripping through her psyche, searching for someone, anyone, bent on destruction.

Nick came inside. He noticed the Taser on the table. "Oh god, Nick. This is bad. Really bad." She realized she was shaking. Hard.

He came and sat on the bar stool next to her, quietly waiting for her to focus, nearly reaching out his hand, but stopping himself. She finally calmed and turned to look at him.

"From what we can see, it looks like somebody was snooping around on your deck. Then they threw a brick or something at the slider, I guess, trying to get in. But they got hit, maybe with flying glass, maybe something else. Explains the blood. But we also found a bullet hole in the railing, like somebody shot at the perp—or maybe at you. Do you have a regular gun in here? Did you shoot? I see the Taser."

"What? Me? Oh my god...no...absolutely not...no gun...I had the Taser, but I didn't get a chance to use it. The glass shattered first, then the guy leaped...you heard it all."

"OK, OK. It looks like maybe it came from out by the pool area. Wait a minute..." Nick walked over to confer with one of the other officers, then he came back to her. "OK, we found a second bullet lodged in the support beam farther down. The shooter maybe fired twice from across the pool area and hit the perp as he jumped."

"Yes...I heard popping sounds...maybe two...or three..."

"We're trying to find the guy now. Can't get far with his wounds, we expect."

Amanda sat silent for a moment. "Oh my God...does that mean there were...two people...watching me?"

"Two, maybe more. This guy was on your deck...but somebody else...maybe two or more...were watching as well." He paused, letting it sink in. "Amanda, I think you should get out of her...maybe with police protection. Go stay with a friend...or a family member... while we're finishing up. We'll send an officer with you."

She frowned. "Well, I'll take protection," she considered it very deliberately, "but I'm not leaving. Not right now. Not on your life." She was scared but not cowed. "I'll...go stay in my office...until you... finish," she said firmly to Nick. "I know," she said brightly, "I'll call my dad. Best bodyguard I know. He'll come over."

"Are you sure? I'm not sure that's a good idea."

"You don't know my dad."

"OK." He nodded toward the Taser. "Have you got a holster for that? We need to confiscate it for now."

"Will do." Amanda retrieved the holster and sheathed the Taser. Nick stowed it with one of the beat cops and Amanda went to change into slacks.

Phil Carlisle arrived about a half hour later dressed in jeans, his pajama top, and a black leather jacket. "Hey, Pop," Amanda greeted him after one of the officers frisked him and removed a Glock 22 handgun before they'd let him in the door. He grabbed Amanda and smothered her to his chest, his gray head bent toward her burnished brown one.

"Amanda Jane Carlisle, what the hell is going on in here?" he demanded. He studied his daughter, his eyes moist but his voice brimming with anger. "Who's the creep who did this, Amanda? They got him yet? They're gonna have to give me my gun back, you know. I may have to get the guy myself."

"Yeah, Dad...I...I'm OK." She wobbled a bit on her feet, but she stood straight, frankly embarrassed. She glanced over at Nick and two of the beat cops who were studying them, then back at her dad who was scrutinizing every pore in her face. She hated being a victim.

"Dad," she redirected, waving Nick over. "This is Nick Caswell. Nick, this is my dad, Phil Carlisle. Dad, Nick's investigating the clinic murder...and now...this..."

"Nice to meet you, detective." Phil turned. He studied the younger man as the two shook hands. "Oceanside PD. Retired. I'll need my weapon back, son. Looks like you guys need some help."

"Good to meet you, sir," Nick said formally, feeling a twinge when the older man finally let go of his hand. "I know you by reputation. We'll get to the gun later, if that's all right." Phil's eyes narrowed, but Nick returned the stare, unmoved. He knew Iron Phil had a reputation for bashing green detectives. The old buzzard had the same piercing blue eyes as the stalwart young woman standing next to him, Nick also noticed.

"So what 'ya got so far, officer?" Phil demanded like he was running the show.

"Looks like the guy was B&E when he smashed the glass, maybe nicked himself. Looks like he hightailed it over the balcony."

"Idiot."

"Evidence that shots were fired as well."

"At my daughter or the perp?"

"Not sure yet, sir."

"And the shooter...?"

"Looking for him."

"Bullet holes?"

"At least two...so far. Mr. Carlisle, your daughter needs protection...for now...Is there a safe place the two of you could go?"

"Sure...my place."

Amanda paused, considering it. Frankly, the last place she wanted to be was at her dad's house. However, that was probably her most immediate option.

Nick watched her, concerned. He saw that Amanda's sweatshirt was on backward—maybe on purpose, maybe not. Amanda blushed when she perceived the emotion on his face. Her dad saw it too, but, being her dad, he didn't know what to make of it. Phil grunted.

"OK," Amanda said quickly. "I'll need to pack a few things. Oh, and, Dad, I'll have to bring Emily...if I can find her. She could be halfway to Tijuana by now."

"Oh God. Not that cat." He rolled his eyes. "Well I hope she can get along with Scout or he'll eat her for lunch."

"We'll figure something out."

Phil started in as he trailed her down the hallway to her bedroom where she pulled down a suitcase and began packing. "Punkin, I've always wondered about you and those crazy SOBs you talk to all day long..."

"Dad, I'm OK...I...I...am...angry and frustrated and scared to death right now," she said, trying to modulate her voice, "but my work is OK. Sometimes there are a few bad apples...you know that... that's all."

"Maybe you need to get out of the loony bin business, kid."

"I don't need to change careers, Dad, I just need support." She glared at him over a pile of underwear. "I honestly don't like it when you baby me, Dad."

Phil knew this look. It was the Back-Off-Buddy look. Same look he got when somebody button-holed him. Cop or therapist, the two Carlisles were carved from the same wood when it came to framing their own lives and they made sure everybody else knew it.

"OK, OK, sorry. I'm just concerned. At least the bad guys I know are *after* something. Hell, yours are just loony...who *knows* what they're after!"

She frowned, not giving an inch.

"OK, OK, OK. Probably feels...oh hell, what do you shrinks call it, for Chrissake?"

"Invasive."

"Yeah, that thing." He matched her stare, then turned sheepish and sat down on her bed. He began folding some of her sweaters into the suitcase.

Amanda softened. She couldn't stay mad at him when he was trying. She put her hand on his arm and kissed his cheek. "Chill, Dad." Phil gave her half a smile and kept on folding. "OK, one more small bag, then I'm ready to go."

He got up. "All right. I guess I'll go and try and find that damn cat." Twenty minutes later, they were ready to go, Amanda with a two suitcases, and Phil hefting cat food and the carrier with Emily yowling inside.

Nick came in from the deck to see them off when his phone went again. The voice on the other end said they'd found a bleeding man limping along Camino del Mar. His name was Carl Fellman, according to his ID, the voice said. The man denied having any weapons and confessed to tracking Amanda, but not breaking in. He said he thought something zapped him when he jumped; the officers reported a gunshot wound in the man's thigh. Paramedics were on their way.

Nick sighed as he ended the call. Maybe this is the guy who got the doc. But then who was the shooter? They'd found only two slugs so far embedded in the piling. Carl's wound might have been a pass-through, Nick figured, so one of the slugs should have his blood on it. Somebody else was definitely at the scene, though; after a full search of the complex, the cops had found nothing definitive, certainly nobody with a gun.

Amanda waved at him. "We're going now. Got my phone on all the time. Can I have my Taser back?"

"And my Glock, please?" Phil added.

Nick had the beat cops return the Taser with the cartridge out and the Glock without the clip. Phil grunted, but said nothing. "Can you leave your address with Bob here?" Nick directed. "He'll escort you down. You sure you don't want official protection?"

The old man stood up to his full height and answered for Amanda. "Hey, kid, I got it covered. Fenced perimeter, alarm system, and Scout. He can take down a man in twelve seconds. And I've got plenty of fire power on hand."

Amanda smirked; Nick shook his head. "OK. It's your call, Amanda. I'll be in touch. You let me know if anything comes up, OK?"

"You got it." Father and daughter headed out the door as Nick crunched his way back over broken glass to wrap up the investigation on the deck. His phone went one more time and he buried his head in it again.

Freud's Revenge

Across the street from the complex, the wind from the ocean was whipping up the pines as the kid sat in the Nissan, watching the chaos. Cool. Calm. Unhurried.

Now they're starting to get it, the kid thought, confident. *Now they're getting it.* The kid scrutinized the Carlisles as they loaded Amanda's belongings into Phil's car parked about a block away. When the pair drove off, the kid didn't even bother following them. No hurry. He knew where she and Daddy were going. The kid knew everything. The beauty of it was nobody knew anything about him.

Not even THEM. It was perfect. Here but not here.

Fucking invisible.

Chapter Twenty-Two

A Fine Pair

Several hours before, the kid had stood in the shadows near the pool area for quite some time, waiting. Amanda's condo complex had been quiet except for a young woman doing laps in the pool; the woman left about an hour after sunset, and the kid was alone again. He liked to watch, liked to see where Amanda went, what she did, how she lived. Amanda was off kilter now, the kid knew. *Yeah, now you're getting it. How it feels. How life sucks when people mess with you. Fun to watch you, though. Watch YOU deal. Watch you deal with the shit like the rest of us.*

Trailing Amanda from downtown had been easy. She was cagey sure, but everybody knew where she lived so no prob. The kid had leaned on the wall in the shadows, watching as her lights finally went out. Then it was time. But something weird happened. That idiot arrived. He started climbing the trellis, and then leaped onto

Freud's Revenge

Amanda's patio. "Fuck, this place is Grand Central," the kid cursed. So the kid took charge; no one was going to horn in on his stakeout.

Raising the rifle, he took aim. But before he could get off a shot, the idiot threw something hard at the glass and the thing disintegrated. "Holy shit," the kid mumbled as the stupid prick started running for the railing. That's when he finally got the shot. It hit the wood, and splintered the piling. "Crap." The kid squeezed again and connected. The prick grabbed his leg as he fell to the ground. The kid was about to pump a third round when the lights came on. The next second, the stupid jerk was dragging himself through the bushes.

OK, we're done, the kid decided. He quickly slid the rifle into its case, hoisted it over his shoulder, and slipped out to the Nissan as confusion spread through the complex. The kid was just closing the trunk when a couple of drunk surfers staggered up the hill with their boards.

One of them bellowed: "Hey, you. Wan' some company?" The creep staggered closer, his belching friend lagging.

"Fuck off, asshole," the kid growled, slamming the trunk, feeling for the blade in his pocket, "or I'll cut your dick off up to your armpits."

"Wow...hostile...no need to get like that." The drunk staggered closer, then abruptly puked into the bushes. His friend lurched up behind him and both of them fell into the bushes, laughing.

Disgusted, the kid got into the car. Engine revving, the Nissan eased down the hill. Turning south on PCH, the kid passed a couple of cop cars zooming up the hill, sirens blazing. They passed in a whoosh, taking no notice, and the kid drove on, stopping carefully at each stop sign, heading up the hill to downtown, passing through town, unnoticed.

Chapter Twenty-Three

Alibis and Answers

Gail and Nick stared at each other across the long conference table the following morning. Piles of paperwork, photos, and assorted paraphernalia related to the murder of Dr. Edward Michael formed a sizable mound between them. The late-morning sun streamed through the second-floor conference room window, landing on Ed's waxy face as it stared out from photos splayed across the table. The white boards were covered in notes and Post-its. It had been three days since Ed's murder and the detectives were stumped.

"OK, let's go over it again. We need to find somebody who was there Monday evening—somebody who had the time, the skill, and the motive to murder the doc." Nick gulped some more black coffee from Gil's.

"Why do you go to that skanky Gil's?" Gail goosed him, coddling her Starbucks Frappuccino.

"Cuz I hate friggin' Starbucks," Nick growled, "you know that. Plain, ordinary, black coffee from a guy, not a megacorp. McStarbucks is already makin' enough millions off the rest of you."

"Well then let's hope old Gil cleared out some of the cockroaches I saw the last time I was in there."

"Yeah, yeah." Nick took another defiant swig. He was doing his best to ignore Gail's ribbing as well as the persistent torpedo sandwich heartburn that had started at Amanda Carlisle's last night and was still going strong this morning. "OK, from the top. We've got Carl Fellman from Amanda's break-in booked for now. He could very well be the guy who offed the doc as well."

"That guy certainly seems crazy enough, Nick, but I'm not sure if the killer is actually him 'cuz of how the shrink was murdered. This Carl guy's a schizophrenic mess. Our doc's murder was methodical, well-executed..."

"As far as calculated murders go..."

"As far as calculated murders go. We don't even know yet if crazy Carl was still locked up or free at the time of the incident."

"Should know shortly."

"Right. So now there's another potential perp—your shooter from last night."

"Yup. We pulled the slugs—sabots. Two of them. Didn't find any more."

"Who do you think he was after? Crazy Carl or Carlisle?"

"Dunno. Maybe Carl and he were working together."

The detectives stared at each other, lost in thought. "Seems like the thing's all wrapped up together somehow," Gail ventured. "The shrink's murder, the note, the break-in at Carlisle's place, the shots."

"Could be...maybe not. For now, let's look at the doc's murder alone and see where we are on alibis since we've finally got Larry's report."

Gail flipped through the detail. "OK, Larry's done most of the suspects. Looks like the three patients are clear; they were at the clinic Tuesday morning but there's no evidence any of them were there the night before. Monkey boy was home with his family Monday night, and their minister dropped by with some other people, so he checks out. The teenager, Sylvia Allen, was at an OA meeting. Several people vouched for her. The woman, Darla Sanchez, checks out with family. In-laws say she was there for an early family supper and then she returned home with the kids and her husband at ten o'clock. The family made one stop—at Albertson's—for bicarbonate. Bank receipt checks it out. Guess Mama's cooking wasn't so great."

"OK. Did Larry find any of the Monday late-afternoon patients and find out when they left?"

"Looks like he found the obvious ones reported by the Seaside staff. They vacated the premises by six thirty as far as Larry could tell, leaving only staff people in the building. Of course there could be somebody we don't know about, maybe somebody working with one of the staff people or somebody else. They could have remained hidden until the time of the murder, so there are lots of holes."

"OK, let's look at the three staff people."

"Al Naylor was at a ball game," Gail read from the report. "Several people spoke with him, and Al apparently left the game in a huff with his son when it was over. Seems the kid lost and Naylor was pissed. He returned home about nine forty. Neighbor across the street saw him pull in; they discussed the kid's ball game while Naylor watered the grass until about ten thirty. That leaves the two women: Lila Judd and Jackie Forrest. Judd claimed she was at college. Prof verified she attended for a short time, but then left early at the break about eight fifteen. Judd says she was upset by the ruckus in the morning and had to go home. Roommate says she arrived about nine o'clock and they had a couple of beers together. But there's a gap there."

"She might have come back and killed Ed."

"But, she was the one who found him the next morning and flipped out. Could be a helluva good actress, but Fredrick and Lyle reported the girl threw up several times after the body was found."

"OK. Next?"

"Jackie Forrest. Her boyfriend says she stayed out late with girl-friends and didn't get home until midnight. She finally admitted she went all the way out to Pala Casino—has a bit of a gambling problem, according to Larry. He says the casino checked ID for her around eight o'clock and the security camera shows her and her pals at the slots and later at the bar with a couple of guys until eleven." Gail got up to make notes at the white board. "So, for the most part, the three staffers clear, but Judd's a question. What about that patient running down the stairs? Thomas—the student—talked about him."

Nick studied the report. "Larry was finally able to trace the guy. Guess he's a regular clinic patient with major anxiety or something. Hightailed it out of there when Lila Judd started screaming. The guy's a teacher and he and his wife usually come for marriage counseling together, but she had to work that morning. He says he didn't know the shrink at all. Whereabouts the night before check out: the guy was giving a lecture to thirty people on San Diego hiking trails. Wife was there too."

"OK, how about the interns?"

"Start with what Larry had to say about Thomas Wong," Nick suggested. He handed the report back to Gail.

"According to the phone detail we got back from technical, the guy's phone records show he called Dr. Ed's cell *and* his office phone six or seven times between eight and nine. They found messages from Thomas on both phones asking, 'Where are you, Ed?' or words to that effect."

"OK, so Thomas was waiting for our victim somewhere. Didn't mention it to us."

"His alibi checked out at the Brass Rail on Fifth Avenue." Gail read on. "Hey, this is new. They found some kinky photos on the kid's cell. S&M pix, men on men, neck collars and all."

"OK, there may be a connection to the porn on the doc's computer. Definitely call Thomas back in for a follow-up." Nick started a list. "How about the other guy, Bowman?"

"Background seems clean, alibi checks out with the apartment manager. Says they talked until around ten thirty. Guy's wife was there too."

Nick grunted. "Bowman seems iffy, but he knew a lot. We can come back to him if need be. Who's next?"

"The two women. First, Sandra Daniels. Kind of a mousy type. Not particularly stressed during the interview, it seemed to me."

"Yeah, odd. Says she left the clinic, then came back and left again later that night," Nick added.

"Larry checked out the Y but no one really remembers her being there. You don't sign in or anything so there's no way to be sure she was even there."

"What'd she say she come back for?"

"Some files or something, but who knows. Cross-checked with Bowman who says he saw her come back."

"Yeah, but when did she leave?" Nick asked, perking up.

"She told us around eight o'clock. Said she couldn't really remember but says the others saw her go," Gail read from the notes.

"OK, let's flag her and bring her back in."

Gail stood back up to the board and made notes. "How about the other female student, Tanaka. Margaret."

"She told Larry she's under stress and taking sedatives since the incident," Nick read. "Got pretty twitchy about that Thomas kid when we talked to her. Korean vs. Japanese. No love lost there. Seemed to know about the doc's drinking habits, coffee, tea, whatever..."

"Her parents are doctors too, right?"

"Yeah. If the tox report comes back poison, which I am guessing it will, she'd be a prime candidate for knowing how to dose it. And remember, she saw the doc and Thomas together at Jake's so there's something going on there."

"There was that ethics thing. We still don't know what that's about and she didn't cough up anything new to Larry either. "

"Definitely have to pull her and the supervisor—Nancy—back in."

Gail stood over the report again, reading, and then she let out a loud whistle. "Here's something titillating, Nick. There were sexy photos on *her* phone. An X-rated card in one photo and a graphic picture of a nude man humping a black man from behind in another."

That got Nick's attention. "On Tanaka's phone?"

"Yup. That girl doesn't seem like the type but, then, you never know. Definitely gotta bring her in."

"Alibi?"

"Some holes. Says she left the clinic between six thirty and seven. Went shopping at Nordstrom, but there aren't any purchases we can track her by. Larry says the security cameras don't show her coming or going either but, then, she could have been obscured by other customers or something as she came and went. Roommate can't vouch for when she came home since she was asleep."

"OK, she's a strong possible. If we move on to the four senior people, that brings us to Nancy Davis."

"Dr. Davis made no bones about what she thought. Sure has the body strength to stab, strangle, subdue the shrink..."

"And the motive..."

"To do it," Nick finished the sentence. "Knows more than she's telling. Said she left after seven. Larry corroborated her story as far as her family reports since she came straight home allegedly, but they're vague on the time. Definitely a candidate."

Gail twiddled her coffee cup for a minute while she stared at the dead man's face. A light dawned. "Maybe our vic was a certified woman hater."

"That's good. Maybe there's a pattern," Nick piggybacked. "Maybe the women in the place all hated old Ed. If you put Dr. Davis and Mrs. Huston together, maybe you get the both of them doing the deed."

"Gee. If you mix in *all* the females, you get a whole crew going after the doc." Picking up a muffin and peeling the paper away, Gail speculated. "If you take the porn on the guy's computer screen," she said, licking her fingers, "and add in the way the vic was not only impaled on his desk, but slashed in the genitals and trussed up like a pig as well, my gut tells me...female."

"Particularly if Barbara Huston knew the clinic's future depended on the guy behaving...and if he was being a very bad, very bad shrink, using child porn..."

"Unless somebody planted it, of course..."

"Yeah, yeah but let's run with this. If he was jeopardizing the Hustons' investment, then maybe Mrs. Huston instigated it. And Nancy Davis or the others helped her."

"Tanaka, Daniels, Davis, Huston...and there's Amanda Carlisle too." Gail was unable to say the name without grinning.

Nick shot her a look. "I know you're suspicious, Gail, but Larry says her alibi checked out at the restaurant with her friend. And there *was* the break-in at her place."

"Yeah," Gail said smiling, "but for now I'm reserving judgment. She could have orchestrated that whole thing at her condo."

"Possibly. You're staying objective...that's what we pay you for." Nick nodded, being rational, but in his head he didn't want to believe it. "Hey, I forgot something until now. When she called me last night...Amanda...before the break-in. Said she'd had some brainstorm or something that there were two people who killed the doc. So she's on to the same idea: a twosome—but it could be two men just as easily as two women."

"OK, if we restrict ourselves to pairs, maybe that's where the Doctors Huston come in. Maybe one of them started the job..."

"And the other one finished it?" Nick liked the idea. "We definitely need to get all four senior people back in here, plus some of the interns. This thing's a snake pit. Mark Huston didn't tell us he was back at the clinic after nine, so the guy lied—unless Bowman is implicating him, of course. Mrs. Huston, Barbara, didn't tell us about threatening to fire the shrink..."

"So she lied."

"Nancy and Margaret have that ethics thing going plus the porn on Tanaka's phone..."

"And Thomas has some kind of relationship with Ed and has the rough sex connection as well."

"*And* we haven't gotten the detail from the security tapes, so someone we don't even *know about* could have helped one of them—or all of them—to do it..."

"So where does that leave us?"

"One dead body and lots of suspects."

Gail slumped down in her chair and flipped her ponytail up a few times to clear the heat off her neck. There was a knock at the door and Liz popped in with the toxicology and forensic reports, plus an update on Carl. The two investigators pored over the new paperwork.

"Looks like Crazy Carl was definitely the perp in the break-in at Amanda Carlisle's. Blood samples and fingerprints match. Report says he was off his meds. He's in lockup now for breaking and entering plus attempted assault. The original 5150 detail from Monday is here too and it looks like Carl was locked up for forty-eight hours starting Monday morning and wasn't released until Wednesday long after the shrink was dead."

"So he didn't kill Dr. Ed. Maybe somebody did it for him?"

"Mama maybe? Let's get Larry to check out her alibi plus any friends, relatives, who might have had motive."

"Check. Carl's mom's on the list."

"OK, here's the forensics. This should be good." Nick pulled several inches of paperwork from a manila folder. Nick and Gail read for several minutes and then Nick looked up and sighed heavily. "Better order in lunch. This is going to take time."

"I'm on it." Gail reached for the phone to tell Liz to order in. "No Gil's, please," she said to Nick over her shoulder. He grunted. "How about Chinese?"

"Yeah, OK. No Szechwan. That stuff gives me heartburn—and I've already got a good case going."

"Ah so." Gail turned back to the phone, salivating for the Peking duck before she'd even ordered it.

Chapter Twenty-Four

Bonds

The hot noon sun refracting off PCH distorted Amanda Carlisle's view of the road as she sped up from the fairgrounds with her dad in the passenger seat. She was on her way to lunch with Shelby at L'Auberge, but the hot sun on the tarmac warping her view suddenly triggered a long-forgotten memory.

Amanda was six years old and Daddy Phil was doing the driving that dusty July day. Sweltering in shorts and sleeveless T-shirt, Amanda's hair was slicked back in a stumpy ponytail, her bangs matted with sweat. Phil was at the wheel of their old Pontiac, swearing about the freaks cutting in front of him on Interstate 5. Her mother, Helen, young and vibrant in a red sundress and polka dot sunglasses, hummed along to a Beach Boys' tune on the radio doing her best to ignore Phil. Little Amanda hung her head out the window letting the breeze flick her hair, while she watched the dirt devils swirl along the median as the car plodded up the road.

Freud's Revenge

Phil Carlisle was a beat cop at the time. They were making their way to Del Mar for the county fair where, every summer, the racetrack grounds transformed into a teeming carnival with livestock stables, rickety rides, food-on-a stick, and crowded tents where carnies hawked everything from kitchen knives to backyard spas. After Phil finally found a parking place on the scorching blacktop, the family headed first to the fair's barnyards. Amanda was aghast when she saw a camel wander by. It was a grotesque creature with two exotic humps and a huge, chewing mouth. A skinny girl in an emerald-green harem costume was leading the beast around, selling rides for $10 a pop. Daddy Phil bent down to little Amanda and asked if she wanted a ride.

"Nope," she answered flatly. "Too high up, Daddy. And too stinky."

The Carlisles wandered on through to the main thoroughfare where the food shacks were. People were gorging themselves on bean burritos, barbecued beef sandwiches, and mystery meat on a stick. Amanda particularly liked the candy-sprinkled ice cream in waffle cones that Daddy Phil bought them. She was licking her ice cream and watching the stuff drip down her shirt when it happened.

A deranged man came tearing through the crowd right at them. He was high on something—PCP, her dad explained much later. The guy had robbed one of the game booths at the far end of the park. Phil's instincts took over. He leapt at the guy, making a perfect in-air grab. Hitting the dirt with the thief, Phil whipped out handcuffs and locked the man's wrists behind his back. Face in the dust, the man thrashed around, wild. Little Amanda stood transfixed, fascinated by the seething man in cutoffs and ragged T-shirt. He pulled against his restraints until blood dripped from his hands and bloodied the ground. She remembered looking up at her dad. Phil's face was hard as he jammed his boot into the guy's neck. Amanda had never seen her father look like that.

Phil ground his heel farther into the guy's flesh when he started to squirm again. Finally, the heap stopped moving and Amanda noticed a tiny silver cross from a heavy chain break away from the man's neck and land in the dirt at her feet. The man took no notice, but it made her feel sad. Amanda's mother had suddenly jerked her away, but not before she saw the man's face contort, then spit out a stream of ugly foreign words followed by vomit. Amanda's nostrils curled back at the smell. Vomit. Sweat. And something else. Desperation perhaps, although she didn't know what it was called at the time. She wasn't sure exactly which man it came from.

The crowd surged forward. Sirens blared. Helen pulled her back, back out of the chaos to a safe place at some picnic benches nearby. Later, Daddy Phil joined them and her parents distracted her with a bright pink Slurpee and a green balloon. The memory of her father and that man stayed with her. When she finished her undergraduate work and decided to focus on therapy as a profession, she knew she wanted to help all kinds of people—no matter which side of the law they fell on. During a Padres game a couple of years ago, Phil, long since retired and a widower since Helen's death from cancer, asked Amanda how she could sit there, listening to people's stories day after day.

"Especially the no good ones," Phil said, disgusted. "The creeps. The shitheads. The ones who hurt children. Not just the bored housewives and the bickering married folks. The real scum, I mean. The ones who should be locked up forever, no parole."

"Compassion, I guess, Dad. I don't know that I do it well all the time. But at least they deserve to be heard." It was all she could muster. He looked puzzled and turned away, skeptical. He'd never asked her about it again.

And now Amanda was driving. And doing therapy, still satisfied with her decision to help people face their demons. Just like that man spewing filth all those years ago. "It's just what we do," she said aloud.

Phil looked at her. "What?"

"Nothing, Dad." She looked at him and smiled. "You know, I love you, Pop." She placed her hand on his hand in his lap.

He stared at her. "Love you too, punkin'. But watch the speed limit, will ya? You must be goin' about fifty, girl!"

Freud's Revenge

Amanda turned back to the road and shook her head. He was who he was—and likewise for his daughter. At the crest of the hill, she turned a sharp right into L'Auberge resort in the heart of Del Mar. Cool in coral shorts and top, she braked at the valet stand and got out. Popping her Oakley shades up on her head, she snatched her straw bag from the backseat and handed over the keys to the Audi. Phil got out on the passenger side and waited until Amanda passed into the lobby. He scanned the area and noticed the valet punk ogling Amanda's behind. Phil stared him down until the guy registered the Carlisle burn. Then the punk quickly slid into the driver's seat and drove off into the parking garage. He glanced into the rearview mirror as he went; he saw that the old man was still watching him.

"Prick," Phil grunted and felt for the Glock under his sports coat as the Audi disappeared. He'd agreed to come along to the girls' lunch but only as an onlooker.

"Dad," Amanda had been clear, "Shelby and I want to meet for lunch because I'm going stir crazy, frankly—and I really miss my best friend and doing *normal* things." Phil argued that until the perp was caught she should probably stay home, but Amanda prevailed.

"You can come along and keep an eye out but not too close, please. It's just lunch, Dad. Daylight. L'Auberge. Nothing will happen. Who knows, you might even meet someone!" Phil groaned. He was looking for a killer, not a date.

As Amanda entered the bar off the main lobby to the left, she spotted Shelby's blond hair at the far end of the bar. Max was working as usual, pouring margaritas and shots. She noticed that Shelby was deep in conversation with a man two stools over. Her friend was looking very sleek in a lime green jumpsuit with wooden beads at her throat. The man chatting Shelby up was impossibly tan. He had curly brown hair, a diamond pinky ring on his left hand, and he was very GQ in dark slacks and an open, crisp white shirt. Leaning over he was telling Shelby some story and she threw her head back and laughed as Amanda passed behind them. The man had a slightly foreign accent and Amanda spotted a mass of dark, curly chest hair peeking out of his shirt.

As Amanda slid onto the stool next to Shelby and deposited her bag on the floor, Phil paused at the restaurant entrance. He then swung into a booth near the door, watching but pretending to study the menu.

"Hey look at you, girlfriend. Shorts, sandals, summer. Lucky you."

"Yeah—but it's a forced vacation. Wish I were enjoying it more."

"Sweetie, I am so sorry about all the crapola you're going through. What a nightmare!"

"Yeah, I can cope. Of course I've got my pit bull over there," Amanda laughed, glancing at Phil.

Shelby looked in Phil's direction but knew she wasn't supposed to be obvious. "God, Amanda, I'm no good at all this cops and bad guys stuff. How are the repairs on your place going?"

"They're replacing the slider now. I broke down and got an alarm system installed. It even extends to the perimeter of the deck. I might be able to go home tomorrow if all goes well."

"How are you holding up? You know you can come to my place anytime, Mandy. You must be going out of your mind. I mean your dad is great and all...but..."

"Definitely has its drawbacks. It's kind of nice to spend time with him, but I wish it were under different circumstances. I see you've made a friend." She nodded in the direction of the handsome man.

Shelby leaned in to Amanda. "Yup, gettin' chatted up pretty good." She giggled, fingering the wooden beads around her neck.

"He's handsome—in a John-Paul Belmondo kind of way. Oops." A redhead in black leather pants suddenly slid onto the stool between the man and Shelby. He deposited kisses on the woman's cheeks and he soon became engrossed with his new seatmate.

"Looks like he's got other plans." Shelby giggled. "Probably a high roller with offshore accounts and a pregnant wife in Milan." A family law attorney, Shelby was often right about people.

Amanda felt playful. "Hey, Shel, remember when we were in here during college and we saw...?"

"Oh, yeah. You almost ran smack into him." On spring break, Amanda and Shelby had been at the beach all afternoon, and then come up for iced coffee at the hotel. Passing through the marble-floored, glass-lined L'Auberge lobby, she and Shelby came upon a stooped, balding man. He was coughing as he shuffled along; a middle-aged woman followed close behind him. He was grumbling loudly. Amanda needed to pass in front of him to get to the café. He'd suddenly stood tall and looked her straight in the eye. As they connected, he seemed familiar. His ancient face then opened up into a brilliant smile and he croaked, "Hello."

In that split second Amanda knew him. Gregory Peck. The rumbling voice was hard to forget. Amanda grinned in recognition. For an instant he seemed pleased, the elegant movie star still. Then he remembered himself, and stooped back into the betrayal of an aging body. He shuffled off, grumbling to the woman behind him. Amanda watched them go. She regretted not having her Olympus with her and the moment passed. She'd never seen him again and he died a few years later.

"Yeah, that was a special moment. Part of the charm of old Del Mar. Haven't seen any movie stars around here today, however— unless Mr. Handsome over there is an actor. Something tells me no. Anyway, we're both coming out of a funk, Mandy, dear. I promise not to talk about my ex today and maybe we can plan something fun to do when all the bad guys are finally locked up!"

Shelby was Amanda's closest friend. They'd met at a football game one fall during college. They were dating brothers at the time. Amanda was slogging her way through abnormal psychology classes and Shelby was navigating cost accounting in the business department. The brothers, who were sports fanatics, seemed more interested in yardage than their dates; ultimately the brothers went by the wayside, but the women's friendship had stuck. She and Shelby had gotten an apartment together in junior year and nursed each other through boyfriends, breakups, a miscarriage, and now Shelby's nasty divorce. Amanda realized she could now add murder to the list.

Hungry, the pair moved to a four-top beyond the bar proper but within view of Phil. They ordered lunch. Amanda noticed Phil was already downing a club sandwich; it looked like two middle-aged matrons with big hair were flirting with him from the next table, however. He looked over their big hair at Amanda and winked. Amanda nodded back, pleased.

"Hey, here's an idea," Shelby said, sipping her iced tea. "How about a trip to Cabo? Remember when we went last time and there were hardly any people and we tried parasailing? We got dunked—and I lost my bathing suit top?"

"Yes. I got some great shots of you flashing! Good thing I had a cover-up."

"You still have those pictures, don't you somewhere?"

"Yup." Amanda laughed. "When you're fifty, you'll be glad to see how foxy you were."

"Well flasher or not, I'd go again. How about you!"

"I'm in. Wish we could go now—especially now."

"How's it going anyway?"

"The detectives are working on it. No answers yet. Nick says it's a complicated case."

"Nick?"

Amanda hesitated. Shelby smiled broadly. "You're blushing, counselor. What gives, girlfriend?"

"Come on, Shel. He's working the case. And yes, he's kind of cute. But it's a murder investigation. It just turns out I knew him before."

"Have I met him?"

"Nope. He's somebody I worked with on a child abduction case a few years ago."

"Oh, nice. Do you think Nick will find the guy who killed your psychiatrist?"

"Hope so. I keep getting visions of the whole thing and my mind is working on it big time. A few nightmares..."

"Well, stay grounded girlfriend. Maybe that's my job...to keep throwing sand in your face to keep it real."

"For that I am grateful." Amanda placed her hand on her friend's arm. "Let's talk Cabo." The women spent the next hour planning an August getaway, while Phil fended off Phyllis and Linda from Dallas and kept an eye out for a killer.

Around two in the afternoon, Phil and Amanda piled back in the Audi and Shelby got into her Toyota to head back to a mediation case in Vista. While Amanda tried to pull out onto PCH, Phil watched as the usual sports cars, SUVs, bikers, and delivery trucks sped by. Nothing unusual. Phil yawned as Amanda pulled out and sped north toward the fairgrounds and Phil's place. Neither noticed the dark Nissan two cars back. To the south, Gail and Nick were just tucking into Chinese food—with a side of forensics.

Chapter Twenty-Five

The Devil in the Details

Nick gulped some cashew chicken as he read, while Gail picked at her duck. When the two had finally digested the whole forensics report and most of the Chinese, they sat back and stared at each other. They had been here before. Between the two of them, they'd solved fourteen murder cases—a pretty good number—*if* you didn't count the dozens more sitting in cold case files up on the fourth floor. Cold and getting colder. Sometimes there was too little evidence. Sometimes there was too much evidence and no suspects. Sometimes there were too many suspects and the case was still never solved. Nick really hoped this one wouldn't be like that. Everybody deserved justice. "Even this guy," Nick murmured under his breath as he reached over Ed's dead face for a fortune cookie.

"Well, there's plenty there." Nick nodded toward the bulky report. "One piece of luck: all these clinical types already have their fingerprints on file with the DOJ. That'll save time."

"Lots of detail, plenty of suspects," Gail added. "How 'bout if I get the forensic stuff up on the board and see if we can get a clearer picture." A half hour or so later, Gail had the key points penned across a free-standing white board Liz had brought in.

"OK, here's the short version," Nick summarized. "Definitely the stiff is Dr. Ed Michael. He died of digoxin poisoning. Based on the stomach contents and the body decomposition, Marcus estimates the guy died between eight and ten at night. Digoxin—isn't that heart medication or something?" Nick looked over at Gail who was fiddling with a marker.

"Yeah," she said walking around and peering over Nick's head at the report. "They found a near empty bottle of Digitek in his top desk drawer. My Gramps takes that—thought I recognized it. It's a brand name for digoxin."

"Yeah Marcus says so down at the bottom of the next page. They found it in the guy's tea. And it was soaked into the mouse pad. Maybe happened when the cup crashed over."

"But I don't get it. If the guy had heart trouble and was taking the Digitek, he'd have it in his system anyway, right?"

"Marcus says the level of digoxin in the shrink's body was *ten times* the normal dosage. Poison level. Also says here the Digitek brand was already under recall by the maker. Looks like the manufacturer goofed and made pills with twice the dosage. People are overdosing all over the place..."

"Including our dead shrink."

"To complicate matters, it looks like Ed also had a mega-dose of Valium in his system."

"So if the killer wanted to use a heart medication overdose to kill the guy, he or she might have slipped in some Valium to loosen the doc up first," Gail speculated.

"Then the shrink, numb on Valium and drinking tea with triple-strength Digitek, probably didn't know what was happening until it was too late."

Gail picked up the report from Nick as she sat down. "Marcus says digoxin toxicity would have slowed the vic's heart at first, causing confusion. Then he would have had difficulty breathing; with all that going on, the killer could have easily trussed up the guy and nailed him to the desk, then simply waited until the vic finally went into cardiac arrest and died."

"Was that before or after his cock was tattooed with an eight-inch blade?"

"Your guess is as good as mine."

"OK, well let's add in the fingerprint and fiber detail and see what comes out of the hopper." Nick read for a moment while Gail scribed. "First, the report says there were all kinds of fingerprints in the doc's office. Most of the core staff's prints were there, along with various patients. Mostly it's senior staff, the students, and the doc's prints on the surfaces in and around the desk itself, however."

"Slow down," Gail said, scribing as fast as she could.

"Looks like they also found black leather fibers on the cord, the vic's neck, his trousers, and on the mouse and mouse pad. They look consistent with leather half gloves."

"Half gloves? Like biker's gloves?" Gail stared at him.

"Yeah. Looks like they've put it together from the print pattern on the shrink's neck. Analysis shows that the fingerprints on each hand stopped halfway up the digits then leather fibers take over. Hence, half gloves. OK, here's the blood section." Nick read further. "The blood splatter pattern plus the angle of the groin wound suggests the perp was medium height, somewhere between five-five and five-ten. The single wound to the groin cuts into the penis, but not across..."

"So the perp wasn't necessarily trying to cut the guy's thing off?"

"Nope. Assume the pose." Gail sat down in a chair and shoved it back from the table. Nick moved in like he was the perp. "More like a straight arm thrust straight into the groin *through* the penis." Nick made a fist at the end of his right arm and pantomimed a thrust into Gail as she sat, stopping short of her crotch.

"Nice." Gail pushed Nick's arm back. "Down, boy. I get it."

Nick collapsed into his chair and continued talking. "So the perp must have had enough upper arm strength to shove a blade in like that. The blood void pattern also shows someone who was probably right-handed."

Gail got up and added some more board notes. "Got it."

"This is interesting." Nick sat up. "There are faint blood spatter footprints that go from the desk toward the hallway door, then into the hall, and on into the kitchen in the break room, where they stop. Smallish foot. Perhaps a man's size shoe, 10 or less, or a woman's size 8–10. Shoes with some kind of tread."

Gail turned toward Nick. "So the perp either took his shoes off in the kitchen and pitched them or he had a change of clothes and took the bloody set with him." Gail riffled through the report. "Looks like no bloody clothes or shoes were found in any of the clinic trash cans, in or out. The vic had desk and leather chair fibers under his fingernails though...where I guess he clawed the surfaces. Looks like he wasn't able to move much once the drugs kicked in."

"Report says there were semen stains on the guy's clothes and carpet."

"Maybe he ejaculated when he was looking at the porn?" Gail offered.

"Or later nearer the point of death? I have no clue about that one."

"Ejaculation not your field of expertise?"

"Funny. We'll come back to that," Nick warned her off. His love life was definitely off limits here. "The medicine cabinet in the shrink's office was apparently wide open. And the keys are missing. Marcus studied the contents in it but he says it's hard to tell if stuff's missing since the shrink didn't seem to keep an inventory anywhere. Plenty of samples in there though."

"Whose fingerprints are on it?"

"Ed, Barbara Huston, Nancy Davis, and the Asian kid, Thomas. Looks like Barbara Huston's prints are on the mouse pad along with the doc's and the mystery guy with the leather half gloves."

"OK, something else to ask in the follow-up interviews." Gail pawed through the piles. "I'm looking for Scotty's technical report." When she found it, she sat down and read for a bit. Nick opened another fortune cookie; chewing, he mulled over the fortune: *Something you lost will soon turn up.*

"This could be good."

"What?"

"My fortune. Says something I lost will turn up."

"Does that mean we'll get our killer?"

"That or the $5 I spent on a lottery ticket this morning will come back to me."

She groaned and went back to reading. "Here's something that's 'turned up.' There were twenty-plus pornographic Web sites on the browser history of the vic's computer. At least ten were child porn."

"So our shrink WAS a scumbag."

"And the guy's landline records show calls to the F Street bookstore downtown..."

"Great. San Diego's hotspot for paraphernalia," Nick offered, having investigated the place about fifteen times.

"As well as a few calls to our boy, Thomas. Looks like Scotty's also given us the guy's computer logs. One of us should wade through these. There's a separate section on building security. Apparently, security locks the building every night at nine and reopens it at six thirty the next morning. Only five people have entry keys: the Hustons, Nancy, Amanda, and the dead guy."

"So the killer was in there before lockup," Nick suggested.

"Or they used a key to come back in after nine. Any cleaning crews?"

Nick searched the report. "Nope. Don't come until Thursdays."

"OK, Nick, I think we need to pull this whole thing together through a timeline. Your turn."

Nick got up and graphed a 7:00 p.m. to 10:00 p.m. timeline. Gail sat down, put her feet up, and opened her own fortune cookie. She read it to Nick "*Every excess becomes a vice.* Well that fits!"

Nick grunted. "OK, if we start at seven, Mark Huston says that's when he left for dinner. Sandra, Amanda, Thomas, and Margaret are supposedly gone by then. Barbara, Nancy, and Gary are still there. Sandra comes back later but we don't know exactly when. Around seven thirty, Nancy and Gary hear voices. Gary says it was Barbara and Ed arguing. So let's say the shrink and Barbara were fighting about that time. A little later, Gary, Nancy, and Sandra supposedly leave, and Barbara finally heads to Bully's for dinner."

"So by eight, that leaves the shrink—alive, we think—sitting at his desk maybe trolling for porn, getting off perhaps..."

"Then somebody finds him...Maybe the killer sees what the doc's doing..."

"Maybe even doing it with him..."

"But something happens. He goes ballistic and sets about killing the doc between eight and ten that night."

Gail leaned into it. "The killer makes tea—or maybe even Ed makes his own tea—but somehow the killer—or even Ed—slips in some Valium and ol' Ed gets looser and looser."

"But then the killer comes back with something else," Nick picked up the thread, "and slips in even more tea but this time with a Digitek chaser..."

"And Ed keeps drinking and drinking, and gets weaker and weaker..."

"And then the killer takes his moment..."

"Oh goody. You play Ed." Gail grabbed Nick's head where he sat, and torqued it back slightly. "Our killer pulls him back, and wraps the cord several times around the guy's neck. The vic's weak by now, so he doesn't fight too much. Then he holds the doc's hand down on the desk and runs the knife clean through, pinning him to the desk." Gail shoved a pen vertically between Nick's fingers, and then she grabbed another pen and continued talking. "So then maybe the perp comes around the back of the chair, spins the doc slightly, and stabs the guy in the groin..."

"I get that part," Nick said, guarding his privates with his free hand.

"And then our killer watches the man die slowly..."

"But then our killer makes a big mistake," Nick interrupted, waving Gail away. "Thinks the doc is dead or dying...But Ed lingers, reaches toward one of the wounds," Nick pantomimed, "finds blood on his left hand, and then discovers he can spell out something in his own blood..."

"F-R-E-splob-splob..."

"And then..."

"He dies..." Nick collapsed forward, and then popped his head back up again. "What, no applause?"

"No Oscar yet, Meryl." Gail reached for the photo of the letters. "So why write this?"

Nick stared at it too. "Amanda Carlisle said she thought it spelled Freud."

"But why that? If Amanda's right, why waste your last moments writing that? Is that the killer? Freud? A dead psychiatrist? And why would the killer leave anyway, give the guy the chance to write this?"

"Maybe he heard something?" Nick popped up to the board, adding names to the timeframes. "Either Huston could have come back after dinner. Barbara says she went home from Bully's but who knows? Mark Huston was seen leaving the lot at nine thirty by Gary, if the guy can be believed. Sandra, Gary, and Nancy were all around some of that time and we're not sure exactly when any of them left."

"The only insider therefore who's completely alibied out is— Amanda Carlisle. That leaves all the others as possible suspects."

The words hung in the room.

"OK." Nick broke the silence. "I'm fried. Let's get interviews set up here for tomorrow morning: we need the Hustons and Nancy Davis and the students. Oh, and Amanda Carlisle. Want to check out a few things."

"Right-o."

"After that, let's see where we are by afternoon."

"Sounds good. Got to pick up my youngest anyway. How's yours, by the way?" Gail asked casually.

"Tracy? Haven't seen her since...gosh, ten days ago. Been on vacation with her mom...and what's his name...in Hawaii. But I *have* heard her voice."

"Well it's nice she got to see Hawaii."

"Yeah. I miss her a lot. Getting some time with her this weekend. May do Sea World—again."

"Whatever you do, keep her safe," Gail said, looking down at the pictures of the dead doc with a rope around his neck.

"You too," Nick echoed. "You never know who's out there."

"Let's get this guy, OK, Nick?"

"Oh yeah." Reaching down, Nick grabbed the computer printouts and Ed's planner. "By the way, did you read through the doc's planner?" Gail shook her head. "Makes no sense. All kinds of gobbledygook in there. I guess I'll take this stuff home for a little bedtime reading. Maybe shed some light on some things."

"Have fun," Gail said, "but..."

"I'd rather be surfing," they chimed in unison.

Gail picked up her bag and left. Nick neatened up a bit, stuffed his briefcase full, and then headed out the door to home, oblivious to the fact that the fortune cookie had been right. Something *had* turned up—it would just take Nick some time to realize it.

Chapter Twenty-Six

Coupling

High up in the Del Mar hills on Pines Lane, Barbara and Mark Huston rested on opposite leather couches in their sunken living room, sipping cocktails. Through the bay windows behind Barbara's silhouette, Mark stared dreamlike at the glistening Pacific Ocean sweeping to the horizon. Barbara watched him, vaguely aware that their massive walnut bookcases filled with psychology tomes perfectly framed Mark's anguished face.

"Mark, I can't believe this has happened." Barbara rolled her mojito glass between her fingers. "Our beautiful clinic. All our hard work. The funding, the plans. Now that damn Edward has ruined it all."

"For God's sake, Barbara, the poor man is dead." Mark swallowed another mouthful of scotch and palmed his empty glass in his lap.

"Good riddance, I say." Barbara reached up and rubbed her neck. "You know as well as I do that he had...issues."

"Yes, yes. But it wasn't the right time, Barbara, to do anything about it. We had to keep things going until..."

"Yes until the funds came through...And now it's all a big mess anyway."

"Yes, it is." Mark reached for the Johnny Walker bottle on the end table. Carefully he added another two ounces to the golden puddle at the bottom of his glass.

"And now we have to go into that nasty police station in the morning," Barbara complained, pushing her hair back with her hand. "Lord, what more do they need to know?" She dropped her head back on the couch and closed her eyes.

"Did you mention the...allegations to the police?"

She sat up. "No. Did you?"

"No. But perhaps someone else did. Nancy?"

"Maybe. She didn't mention whether she said anything. Well, we'll probably have to disclose it all to the authorities even though I don't think it's any of their business since we had no firm proof yet."

"We had a pretty strong rumor, Barbara." Mark got up and paced in front of the empty white brick fireplace with the gold-scrolled Horchow fire screen.

"Nancy was about to present some evidence, right?"

"Yes, now I wished we'd heard it that night. I waved her off since we had dinner with Tom and Mary. We were going to cover it Tuesday morning."

"Oh, Mark, Ed makes me...so angry," Barbara wailed. "He was so arrogant. So flippant, eternally flippant, that nasal voice always demanding, sneering."

"Barbara, my darling, I know you loathed him. You tolerated him for my sake, for all he'd done for me, and my...family."

"Yes, you were beholden to him, I understand that. But look how he used you, Liebling. There were times I wanted to smash his revolting little face in..."

"Would you have, Barbara? I know you didn't like him, but Barbara, how far did it go?"

She took a deep breath. "I despised him...certainly. He wasn't the man you thought he was, my dear. But to even suggest I might have...might have really had the inclination to..." Her eyes, like blue sapphires nestled in cream, searched his face. "Sheisse, Mark. You *do* doubt me. I can see it in your face."

"For God's sake, Barbara, I don't really think you would have..." His voice trailed off as he sat next to her.

"And what about you, Mark?" she cut him off. "What happened to you after dinner? You were gone a long time, my dear. You never said where...and you were vague about it later. I was so sleepy that night after all that wine, I didn't dwell on it. Where were you, Mark? Paying Ed a visit?"

"Come on, Barbara, you know I wouldn't...couldn't do anything to someone like that..."

"No, frankly, I don't know that, Mark. What about the man who killed your wife and child? You were angry then, weren't you, angry enough to find the man...and kill him, you said?"

"Barbara...that didn't happen...you know, I was just ranting, overreacting."

"How do I know, Mark? You were angry with him. He died. Suddenly, mysteriously. I wasn't around then so how do I know? You were angry at Ed too. How do I know you aren't a magnificent liar? And you've duped me all along?" She studied her husband, nearly strangling her mojito glass.

Mark stared at her and put his glass down, willing himself not to react. It was an ugly moment—that moment in some marriages where trust sours in the face of betrayal, and the drive for domination, even annihilation, begins.

"Barbara," he said, his voice so low and grave that she recoiled against the couch, "in my every breathing moment, I think of you. In your greatest vitriol, I love you. Love you past that hateful side of you that so mistrusts, that so wants to hurt. *I* don't want to hurt you. And I don't want to hurt us. I do everything to keep you safe. I would never go so far with another human being as to..."

"And neither would I..."

Freud's Revenge

They stared at each other. But in that moment, each hesitated. There *was* something. Something neither would say, but each sensed. A glint in the pupils that each, as practiced psychologists, could see in the other, but could not, would not, acknowledge in themselves. Finally, Mark leaned into her and embraced her, running his hand over her flaxen hair as she pressed into his body. She dropped her glass on the end table. Her arms rose and wrapped themselves around his back. They held each other. But each knew there was something new between them, something that had never been there until now. And Ed's death was the cause.

* * *

"Nancy, I didn't know what I was supposed to say!" Margaret Tanaka wailed to Nancy Davis on the other end of the line.

"I know, I know. You protected the confidentiality of the family."

"I didn't know what to tell the police. I hope I'm not in trouble. I said I would check with you."

"You did the right thing," Nancy reassured her as she sat folding laundry on her kitchen table.

"But what about my phone? By now they've seen the pictures and the one with the two men."

"Yes, you will simply have to spill it when you go in there tomorrow."

"How much do I say?"

"Say what you saw and when. You don't have to name the family right now. You can just share what you saw and what you did."

"But, Nancy. I am so scared. I don't want to be in trouble. It's so horrible what I saw...what I found...and what the mother said."

"Yes, I know. But you need to be honest. We hadn't filed anything official yet...and..."

"Yes?"

"Never mind. Just tell them what you told me. "

"Nancy?"

"Yes?"

"Have you ever seen this before? Have you ever...seen anyone... like Ed...killed this way?"

"Yes, Margaret. Sometimes it happens. Sometimes people do bad things and bad people get things done to them."

"But it's...so...horrible!"

"You're learning that human nature isn't always pretty. You'll get through this. I'm here to help you. Go in there and tell the truth. Do you hear me?"

"Yes. I will. Can we meet afterward?"

"Absolutely."

"Will Thomas be there?"

"Maybe. I'll let you know tomorrow. Good luck." Nancy hung up. She wandered out on her front porch and plopped down on the worn, brown rocking chair that had been her great-grandma Bertie's favorite. She reached inside a small table to her left and pulled out an old package of camels. She pulled one out and lit it.

Her husband Merle happened to look out the window. He rapped on the glass to get her attention. "Hey, Nancy girl, are you smokin' again? After six years?"

"Yup. Just this one."

"What are you thinking about?"

"Chickens."

"Chickens?"

"Yup. Chickens."

"Eaten 'um?"

"No. Killin' um." She took a long drag, casting her eyes out across the front lawn to the twinkling lights of the border communities to the south. "How they come home to roost," she murmured, "yes siree."

Nancy sat smoking for a while. After one last, glorious puff, she stubbed out the butt. Then she got up and went inside where Merle was waiting.

* * *

Sandra Daniels picked up the phone after three rings. "Hello?" She put down the adolescent and child therapy tome she was reading.

"Hi, Sandra? It's Thomas. Thomas Wong." Thomas had decided to see if Sandra had been called back in by the police as well. "How are you, anyway?"

"Oh I'm good. Getting lots of studying done. Weird to have so much downtime, though. Where are you—I can hear the noise?"

"Peet's. Yeah, pretty weird. Do you have to...go in there tomorrow...to talk to the police again?"

"I...guess. They called me. I talked to Amanda. She said just go in there and answer every question as best I can. How about you?"

"Yeah, me too. 'A Person of Interest.' Uh, Sandra, did you say anything...about me?"

"What do you mean?"

"I mean, did you talk about me...and Ed?"

"Does it matter? I answered their questions; that's all."

"But what did you tell them about Ed and me?"

"Do you mean that you and Ed were pretty tight?"

"Uh, yeah."

"Look. I told them we all worked with Ed. We had to. I said we shared information and we saw patients that Ed prescribed for and that we all conferred with him. I don't really remember saying anything specific...or disparaging about you. What are you torqued about?"

"Well I just don't want to be on the hook, that's all."

"For what, Thomas? Have you done something?"

"Come on, Sandra. You're a big girl. Ed was murdered, for God's sake. Get a clue. They think one of us did it. That's why we have to go back and talk to them. It's just that I..."

"Yes?"

"You know...I sometimes talked to Ed about personal stuff..."

"Yeah. I heard a rumor to that effect. That you and Ed had a thing..."

"Come on, Sandra, we were friends, that's all. Shared some drinks a couple of times."

"If you were just friends, what are you worried about?"

"I'm not worried. I just need to finish my hours and take my boards, man. I'm almost done. Don't want any problems. Not from you...or anyone."

"Thomas, I'll tell the truth. That's all I can do. If you didn't do anything, then you can chill out and tell them the truth too."

"OK, OK. I'm cool. I'm not the guy, OK?"

"Whatever. I'm going now." She ended the call. She sat for a moment twisting a clump of her straight brown hair around her fingers. He certainly sounded worried, she thought. Where there's smoke there's fire, her mother used to say. With that she got up and headed into the kitchen for a cold Coke.

* * *

Phil Carlisle coughed as he came in from the garage.

"Dad?" Amanda Carlisle jumped up from the couch where she was watching a reality show on television. "Are you wheezing again?"

"It's nothing. Just fiddling in the garage."

"Dad, were you also cleaning your guns, by any chance? You should have let me help you."

"Hey I'm not infirm, child. I worked on my guns a little—got to keep them in condition. Might go huntin' in a couple of months with Bill Leaderer. Did you hear from those detectives today? They catch the creep who plugged your shrink yet?"

"Dad, he wasn't plugged. No, they haven't found him yet but I have to go back in there tomorrow."

"Why you?"

"Standard operating procedure, I guess. I'm doing my best to help them."

"Mark my words Amanda Jane Carlisle. This perp is some angry SOB."

"What'd you find out last night from your buddies?" She knew Phil had put out the word for the dirt.

"That your doc's killer had a vicious streak."

"Did one of the papers talk about..."

"Mutilation? Naw. Somebody leaked it."

"Great. I am sure the police love that."

"All in the course of justice. You never know when somebody or something will lead ya to your perp. In my book, this guy's particular signature, murder plus mutilation, means revenge. Revenge is a real strong emotion. Look for that and you'll find your killer. Tell that to that Caswell kid."

"Oh my goodness, Dad, you're actually talking about feelings."

"Yeah, yeah, OK, murderous feelings. Does that count? Now those feelings I understand. Not that free-floating anxiety stuff or whatever the hell you call that crap. Murder is murder. Motive, action, payoff. Remember: perps always leave traces of themselves. If not physical, then psychological. That's what I know about the psychology end of things. Traces. Can't avoid it. Remember that, daughter."

"Yeah, OK, Dad. By the way, I'm going down to San Diego on my own tomorrow, to meet with the detectives. I'm going over to the townhouse first to check on the work since they called and said everything's done. You can come over and check on it with me if you like, but I'm going downtown on my own. Then I'm meeting Shelby later that evening. After that, I'm going on home to move back into my place."

"You're playing with fire, girl." He glared at her until she caved.

"Well, OK, if you really insist—God, you're tough." He smiled, satisfied. "You can follow me in your own car to the police station, but after that, Shel and I are going on."

"You'll never know I'm there. I just worry about you, punkin, that's all. Right now, you need protection—no denying it. Maybe you should get rid of that worthless cat and get a dog, a *real* dog. My golf buddy Ken has some pit bull puppies..."

"No, Dad. No pit bulls...not in a townhouse."

"OK, OK. Anything else I can do for you?"

"Nope. I'm good. Oh, you could take me to a Padres game, I guess?"

"You're on. I'll get tickets for next week."

"OK, thanks, Dad." She headed for the kitchen. "I'm going to pull out something for dinner. Lasagna, OK?"

"Sure. You know I love the stuff."

"Yes, Dad, I know."

Phil sat down on the couch, gazing at a picture on the end table of Amanda, Helen, and him; Amanda was about thirteen years old. "We'll get him, Helen, if it's the last thing we do," he told his dead wife, "nobody's gonna hurt our little girl. I promise."

* * *

In a small, crumbling white house in a sixties-style development east of Torrey Pines, the kid sat on an old picnic table bench in the backyard, cleaning a hunting rifle. Some of the neighborhood kids were screaming and hollering beyond the fence. They were at the end of the cul-de-sac trying out new skateboard moves. The kid could hear the wheels rolling along the pavement then crack and crash as the kids jumped old tires they'd set up for jump practice. Most of the parents were hard at work trying to make their middle incomes stretch beyond next week.

The rifle gleamed in the bright sunlight. He stroked the long, thin barrel slowly, loving the hard feel of the steel. He glanced up to see a bird poking around in the flowerbed across the way, and then looked back down at the barrel, thinking.

She doesn't get it. Doesn't know I do the best I can for us. Do what needs to be done, dammit. She should know that—but I doubt She does. Sure thing she doesn't. She goes on Her way, busy little bitch, doing Her thing. But I'm the one. The ONE. Don't sit around saying, oh please, just let me be. Oh please, just let me be my own little self. Don't hurt me; I'm good. Look how good I am. I listen. Really listen.

Stupid joke. People don't care about you, you stupid dimwit. Not him for sure. Not nobody. They only understand one thing: when I say, 'This is the end of the line, creep. No more, scumbag." Then I fix it. Fix it for Her. For her. For the three of us. We help each other, see? Crap, neither of them helps me much though, that's for sure.

Freud's Revenge

*Why does that stupid bitch bring it on? Doing that slinky dinky crap.
Showing her tits like a goddam slut. Does she really think it'll get her somewhere? Get real. She piles that crap on her face, parades butt-naked, 'til their
dicks are hangin' out of their zippers.*

Then I have to show up and take care of things.

*Like that dick, the shrink. You can have as many degrees as you want,
ol' buddy, but you don't get a free pass. Yeah, you learned it. You don't get a
free pass. So She does it Her way, and I do it mine. No one walks on me. On
us. Not ever.*

With that, the kid lifted the gun to shoulder height, aimed carefully at the bird still rooting in the flowers, and squeezed the trigger.

* * *

Nick Caswell, in jeans and a sweatshirt, sat in his downtown
high-rise at the kitchen table poring over paperwork. He gulped
back some Coors and tilted back his chair to think. His quasi office
was cluttered with files. Bits of napkins and tiny pieces of paper with
phone numbers and suspect info peeked out from under his laptop
and his old green banker's lamp. An old Quizno's wrapper poked out
from under a stack of crime photos about to topple over.

In the background, the Food Network was blaring on his big
screen. Emeril bammed spices into some Cajun shrimp recipe and the
TV audience applauded, hungry. Nick liked watching the TV chefs
do their thing with food. Once in a while he even cooked himself,
trying a pasta dish or a braised lamb recipe. His deck barbecue stood
at the ready, though he hadn't been using it much lately.

Once in a while he'd look over to the window and out over Petco
Park where his Padres played. He could see the top of the stands
from where he sat. He loved baseball, but he wasn't getting around
to the games much despite living close enough to walk. The Padres
were having an up-and-down season; some said it was the coaching,
others thought the talent wasn't there. Right now, the fans were getting restless, wanting results. Sometimes murder's like baseball, he
realized, as he gulped the last of his beer. Inning after inning with no

results. The hits are what keep you going, he reminded himself. Same for homicide. The problem with the shrink's case, however, was that it felt like he was up to bat blindfolded with one hand in his belt. He had no idea who was pitching.

He scratched his two-day stubble but got no new answers. His eyes fell on Dr. Ed Michael's appointment book lying on his stone and glass coffee table a few feet away. Nick walked over, picked it up, and thumbed through the pages for the fourth time this week. Odd how the guy wrote all his appointment stuff by hand, rather than on computer—especially since he was such a Web troll.

The planner had all sorts of shorthand and acronyms scribbled across the appointment times and along the margins. A couple of cartoons slipped out when Nick flipped back a few months. One read: *Better Living Through Chemistry.* Another one showed a cop pulling over an elderly couple after they'd driven over a stop sign and a fire hydrant when they turned the corner. The ancient man at the wheel explained, "Well, I thought I felt something, officer, but I guess I just thought it was gas." Nick laughed in spite of himself.

Studying the appointments for the weeks just before his death, Ed had written a lot of detail, but most of it didn't make sense. *Frankl football, Dreikurs coffee, Skinner POW wow, Enns eruption, Perls meltdown, Jung on LM.* Then there were initials and a bunch of abbreviations. *A.B. – MDD. F.L. – ANX, NOS. M.M. – DID. K.R. – PPD. L.T. – IED.* There were also entries for *Glaxo, Merck, and Wyeth*—drug reps or something Nick surmised, mostly at lunchtime—followed by lists of what looked to him like abbreviations for medication: *Klon, Hal, Thor, Lam, Zyp, Bus, Pam, Pax, Ati.*

Sometimes Ed would write a phrase or two after some of the abbreviations. *A.L. + G.V. = Bord + Nar = pure bliss. M.J. ADHD pyro – come on baby light my fire. O.P. PS – Jesus freak. P.L. TIC – call hairclub.com.*

Nick scratched his chin. "Gibberish," he finally said aloud. A black crow out on the deck rail jumped. Nick watched the bird flap away as he turned back to the planner. Must be some clues here. Who the doc met, where he went, what he was thinking. Nick needed help. He reached for his phone and punched some numbers.

She answered after two rings. "Amanda Carlisle."

"Oh, Amanda? This is Nick. Caswell."

"Oh hi, Nick. Any news yet?"

"Nope...none that I can report. But I'm going to need some help."

"Help? What kind of help?"

"I need to run some things by you. Can we change the time you come down to the station tomorrow afternoon to three thirty or so?"

"Am I still being investigated?"

"I can't really answer that, but this is really more of a...consult."

"OK. Anything I should bring with me?"

"Nothing special. See you tomorrow."

"OK," she answered.

He hesitated two beats, and then he repeated: "Uh yeah, see you then." He flicked his phone shut and sank into the couch. On screen, Emeril had given way to Paula Deen. She was trussing a chicken, southern style.

"I hate that woman," Nick muttered. "Her drawl is so thick it makes me wanna chew gravel." He punched the remote and the screen flashed off. Stretching out on the couch, he was snoring in minutes, dreaming of a fang-toothed chef in a clown suit called Bezelda who overdoses her vics with cyanide-laced coconut cake.

Chapter Twenty-Seven

Mark

Nick had had a restless night. He was just getting back to sleep around 5:00 a.m. when a commuter jet slammed through the sky on its way to Lindbergh field. He gave in and sat up. Looking around his living room overflowing with evidence, Nick wondered if the stuff had seeped into his pores as he slept. God knows he felt grimy enough.

He got up, stripped, jumped in the shower, and decided not to shave—again. He dressed and sat down in his kitchenette for breakfast. Mulling the evidence over toast and coffee, he felt sure there was a marker in there somewhere. Between computers, phones, and forensic evidence, there was an avalanche of detail; it would just take some savvy analysis to pop out the right answer. The thing about killers, Nick knew, is that they had a hard time thinking of everything. It was the rigidity that made them kill in the first place, but it was usually the impulsiveness that got them in the end. Find an impulse, get a killer.

This case, Nick reasoned as he reached for a slice of smoked salmon, seemed impulsive in its inception, but pretty methodical in execution. If it was linked to the Carlisle break-in, it pointed to a vendetta directed at authority. If not, the murder stood alone. The fact that the shrink was murdered at his place of work rather than his home, a bar, or some other setting, suggested it was most likely work related. That is, unless a frenemy thought getting away with it at the clinic was easier. A patient-based attack was also a high probability. On the other hand, the torture foreplay suggested an inside job by someone with enough time and proximity to commit the crime. In the questioning today, Nick knew he was looking hard for motive, means, and impulse. Even if the people he and Gail saw today were not directly responsible, their individual penchant for observation could point the way toward the perp. Especially Amanda Carlisle.

His brain fuzzed for a moment. There was something about her... her face. Her high forehead. The cornflower blue eyes under dark eyebrows. Her sweatshirt turned inside out. A kind of sound in her voice when she said his name. Nick...kind of drawing out the i. Ni-i-ck.

"Shut up, Caswell." He snapped to; he had to get to work for crap's sake. In ten minutes, he'd crammed everything into his car and was pulling into the station twenty minutes later. Gail arrived ten minutes behind him with coffee and Danish. By 9:00 a.m., they were in the conference room, ready.

Liz, dressed today in blue jeans and a green turtleneck since it was Friday, came in through the open door and announced that the Hustons were in the lobby. "OK, thanks. We'll buzz when we want you to send them up." Nick said to her. He took a swig of coffee and watched Gail plowing into her Danish. Gail had her hair in a bun this morning, all business. "Any last thoughts as we head into this?"

"We may get something out of this lot, but we'll probably end up having to find those missing shoes and half gloves before we can finally nail down the perp. We could search the homes of all the suspects, I guess."

"That could take days."

"Need a bunch of warrants. By now all that stuff could be gone."

"Yeah. Maybe we'll find out enough today."

"Oh, this was in our box." Gail handed him a short report. "It's the results of the search of the vic's home. More child porn on the doc's home computer. Some S&M paraphernalia, a few personal letters, nothing too incriminating. A little Valium but nothing heavier. No weapons."

"OK, let's see what we can dredge up this morning."

Gail sighed. They'd been here before. Sometimes they broke a case in the second go-rounds. Sometimes it just got more convoluted, especially with multiple liars.

"You know the drill: we want to get a confession today if we can."

"Yeah, but don't be too tough, Nick. You know how you can get." Nick smirked. He had a rep for going for the jugular, but he knew he'd have to finesse it, especially with these psych types. Gail fiddled with the in-room camera for a time then she sat down. Her eyes drifted over to Ed Michael's planner. Nick had been poring over it again before Liz came in. "Get anything more out of that thing?"

"Don't know. All sorts of stuff in there—codes, acronyms, people's names, meeting notes, cartoons, weird stuff. Most of it only a shrink could understand, I guess."

"Are you going to ask Doc Huston? Or should I say Mr. and Mrs. Doc Huston?" She reached for her mocha Frappuccino to wash down the Danish.

"I'd like to see if they notice it first. Maybe they'll flag us if there's anything incriminating in there."

"Righto."

"OK, you good?" Gail signaled she was set. Nick picked up the COM line. "OK, Liz, we're ready for Mark Huston." Seconds later Mark, dressed in tan khakis, black Hawaiian shirt and caramel deck shoes, came through the door. He sat down heavily at the end of the table where Nick indicated. "Good morning, Dr. Huston," Nick greeted him brightly.

Mark nodded and echoed the greeting, matching Nick's tone. He smiled at Gail. She nodded in response.

"We've called you back in here," Nick began, watching Mark's face, "to try to get a handle on a couple of things. Is there any reason you can think of why someone would name you a suspect in the killing of Dr. Ed Michael?"

Mark's eyebrows folded in. This wasn't the question he was expecting. "Me? Are you telling me someone named me? That sounds rather...farfetched." He looked indignant. Then he caught the mood in the room. "OK, I think I get it." Mark had watched a few *Law & Order* episodes himself. "You're planting a seed. Goosing some kind of paranoia." The man cocked his head slightly to one side, and then he smiled broadly, first at Nick, then at Gail. "I can tell you with all confidence that I doubt anyone has implicated me. I've done nothing to Ed."

"So why did you lie?"

"Excuse me?"

"You told us you left the clinic on Monday night, went for dinner in downtown Del Mar, then went home. But you stopped somewhere first, right?"

Mark cleared his throat. "After I left Bully's I...I...hadn't recalled it when we first talked, but I stopped back by the clinic before I went home."

"Yes, we know. You were seen."

"Seen? By whom?"

"Witnesses. We also got a read off that fax machine in your office. Says a fax was received, then another couple were sent at 9:45 and 9:47."

"I'm not clear what that shows."

"Nothing, particularly since you or someone else could have picked up the fax anytime over the next twelve hours, and sent the outgoing ones automatically."

"So what's the issue?"

"We know you were there, Doctor. The summary report gave you away. You ran one, didn't you?"

"Look," Mark shook his head. "I did stop by. I had some business to check on, but that doesn't mean it had anything to do with Ed's death." His gaze was steady.

"Why hide it, then?"

"Technically, officers, I guess I omitted it. It had nothing to do with Ed. I guess I spaced it or I thought it was...irrelevant."

"Which is it?"

"I honestly don't know. I stopped in there for only a minute or two...no more."

"You realize you could either *be* the killer or have *passed* the killer when you came and went?"

"I see that now."

"You also could have been victim number two."

"Oh. I...hadn't considered that."

"Interesting. It makes you all the more suspicious. Come on Dr. Huston, what else are you hiding?"

Mark looked at them and sighed heavily. "I guess I didn't feel it was relevant to mention that we...are...about to be sued."

"For?"

"A drug death related to one of Ed's patients."

"Tell us more."

"Ed had prescribed multiple medications for a patient and neglected to check some cross prescriptions from another physician. The mix of drugs killed the woman. She was elderly. Her family has launched a lawsuit. I wasn't trying to hide it from you. I was trying to contain it...from..."

Gail picked up on something. "Your wife?"

"How did you know that?"

"Experience," Gail said. "Do you regularly keep things from Mrs. Huston?"

Mark pursed his lips. "She gets a little upset. Upset about Ed's and my...relationship. And when things threaten the stability of the clinic."

"What *was* Ed's and your relationship?" Nick asked quietly. He smelled a stinker.

"Nothing sexual or devious, I can assure you," Mark empha-sized, reading the innuendo. "Ed and I went back a long way. He was instrumental at the time of...the deaths of my wife and son. He helped me as a colleague...and friend."

"Were you his patient?"

"No. He set up a...group. A specialized group for psychologists dealing with...trauma. He had a colleague facilitate. He was an infor-mal grief buddy for me, I guess you could say, and he...he saved my life, frankly. I would never have harmed Ed, I can tell you that. I cared for the man."

Gail piped up. "What about Barbara? What if Ed had harmed her?" Mark looked at her, his eyes glinting. Gail knew she'd found a crack and kept going. "You might not have harmed him for your own sake...but your wife is special to you, isn't she?" He was silent. "You might cross the line for her, right, Doc?"

"No."

"You might do what had to be done, wouldn't you?"

"No I would never go that far and I don't like what you're imply-ing."

"I'm sorry if this is painful, but I'm certain you want us to get to the bottom of this. You'd already lost one wife, we know, but now you are remarried and happy again, right? Did Ed get in the way of that?"

"I...I..."

"You are married to a brilliant, captivating woman who you love and who you cherish and who you'd maybe die for. Or kill someone else for...

"I...I...would never..."

Gail bore down. "I'm guessing Ed used it...used you...the rela-tionship...to be...cavalier...to maybe practice badly...make mistakes... serious mistakes...and it endangered your work and the new life you'd built. It pushed you to the breaking point, didn't it?"

"No, that's not true..."

"Are you saying you didn't do it, then?"

Mark sat sullen in his chair. When he spoke, his voice was grave. "Ms. Burton, I *do* love my wife a great deal. You are astute about that. I also loved my previous wife, Lorinda, very much. And my son. But I can tell you here and now with utmost clarity, I did not hurt Ed. I admit I was angry with him. I wish he and Barbara got along better and that he weren't so maddeningly juvenile. But I would never have done that to him—I can't tell you more plainly than that."

There was silence. The officers waited. "All right, who else do you think should be eliminated as a suspect?" Nick asked, taking a different tack.

Mark sighed deeply. "I don't know really. Surely the students... the interns would not have..."

"Why?"

"Well they're transitory...not part of the core...and not part of his caseload...I can't see them having a vested interest in...seeing Ed... dead."

"Why not?"

"Why in the hell would they? Could he have done something to one of them to warrant such a response? I'd find that hard to believe. They've been vetted, interviewed, background checked by all of us as senior staff and the DOJ."

"And you're infallible?" Nick asked quietly.

"I am not infallible." Mark leaned forward, placing his hands flat on the table. "Obviously I've made mistakes in my life...I just don't think one of our students had the wherewithal to do this."

"Which ones would you eliminate specifically?"

"All four of them."

"And the rest of the core staff? What about them?"

"Well, Amanda wouldn't hurt a fly."

"Nancy?"

"Frankly, not sure. I like Nancy a lot, respect her immensely. But I'm not sure. I hope not. "

"You've left someone out, haven't you?" Gail interjected. There was a beat.

"Barbara," he said her name quietly. "I don't believe Barbara did this...

"But you're not sure."

He paused, taking a breath. "Honestly, officers, I am not entirely, 100 percent sure. I'm not objective, for heaven's sake. You know that."

Gail almost felt sorry for him. "She lied to you, you know."

"What?" Mark frowned. He noticed the camera for the first time in the corner of the room.

"About Ed. She was about to fire him." Mark's jaw tightened. "She must have kept it from you. She threatened to fire him the night he died." Gail watched Mark's reaction. Nick sat back, watching her work.

"I...I...didn't know about this."

"It's possible she *did* fire him, Dr. Huston...and he went for her."

"Yeah, it's possible he went for her and someone...maybe you... stepped in to stop him," Nick piggybacked.

Mark's face crinkled. "I am shocked, frankly, by this revelation. My wife didn't...must have forgotten..." He stopped, bewildered.

"So you see, she did have motive. If she lied about firing Ed, she could have lied about killing him."

Mark's eyes darted from Gail to Nick. His face paled. Nick studied him for a while longer. "OK, Doc. Just a few more things. Are you right- or left-handed?"

"Right."

"Height?"

"Five-ten."

"Do you recognize this?" Nick indicated Ed's planner on the desk.

"Ed's calendar? I recognize it because all the rest of us logged our appointments electronically. He was a stickler for paper and pen for appointments. Carried the thing everywhere with him. I think he gets those from the American Psych Association. Logo probably there on the cover somewhere..."

"Are you saying he was computer phobic?"

"Oh no. He surfed the Web a lot. He was on various clinical list servs because he would send me links, messages, and such." Mark paused, studying both investigators. A lightbulb went on. "You found something..."

"Found what?"

"Some pictures or..."

"Or...?

"Pornography?" he said slowly, searching their faces. "In his planner? His computer? Oh God. That's it." He closed his eyes.

"What do you know about 'it'?"

"I know there were some allegations, but I personally hadn't seen any evidence yet. Nancy—Nancy Davis—was about to present some findings...but of course Ed was killed...and we hadn't had time to pursue it."

"And so does your high opinion of the good Dr. Michael extend to him using porn in your own clinic?"

"Of course not. I would have taken the appropriate steps if that had been proven. It's just that there wasn't time."

"And what about children?"

"Children?"

"Oh my god, was it child pornography!" He read the answer in their faces. "Good Lord. I didn't know. I swear to you. I should have pushed it up...the investigation...I didn't want to upset Barbara...the lawsuit and pornography in one day...God I still should have done it..."

"OK, Dr. Huston, is there anything else you want to tell us?"

"My wife...doesn't know about the lawsuit."

"You're lying to *her*?"

"I just hadn't told her yet...so many others things were going on..."

"Anything else?" Mark shook his head. "OK, that's all for now. We're going to sequester you in a room down the hall," Nick directed, "until we interview your wife."

"I understand."

Nick buzzed Liz and she popped open the door to take Mark Huston down the hallway. Standing, Mark said to Nick, "Please know I want to help in any way I can. I'm sorry I omitted...some things. I'm deeply embarrassed that I didn't pick up on...whatever you've found out about Ed." He looked at Gail and added, "You sensed that my wife is very important to me. She is. I love her very much. Please know, however, that I wouldn't go that far for her—or anyone else."

"We will take that under advisement, Dr. Huston," Gail said.

"You went for it," Nick said to Gail once they were alone.

"Yup."

"How'd you know?"

"For a psychologist type, he doesn't hide his feelings very well. Not used to lying, I think."

"Maybe you should go into the shrink biz someday."

"Are you kidding? I'd rather sit in a room full of ax murderers than deal with a bunch of sniveling psychotics every day. I'm not that crazy!" They laughed. It was a good tension breaker. "So what'd you think?" Gail lobbed it back.

"Trying hard to convince us. Could he have been that dumb?"

"Or that smart?"

"Implicated his wife."

"Yup. Let's see what she has to say. Remember we found her prints—and she downplayed the argument."

"Right." Nick reached for the phone. He told Liz to cue up Barbara Huston. "You ready for Madam Shrink?"

"Ya vull," Gail saluted as they eyed the door.

Chapter Twenty-Eight

Barbara

Gail snuck a sip of water, and then readied a clean page in her notebook. There was a tap at the door. Barbara Huston entered. The slim blond sat down where Nick indicated. She wore a matching cream blouse and slacks, accessorized with Gucci. Expensive, Gail thought, noting the belt, which alone must have cost $400. Gail made sure the camera was running.

"How are you, Mrs. Huston?" Nick said.

"Well I've been better, detective, frankly." Barbara smoothed her top over her flat stomach. "Our clinic is closed. Our psychiatrist is...dead. Most of the staff has signs of posttraumatic stress, not to mention our poor patients who are barely keeping mind and body together through telephone counseling and emergency referrals. Other than that, I wish you all would do your jobs and find the person who did this so we can get back to some level of normalcy." Suddenly she looked up. "Oh," she blurted. "I...I just realized...you're probably taping this, aren't you?" Her gold bracelets clanked as she twisted in her chair seeking the camera.

"Yes," Gail replied, trying not to smile.

"Well, I have nothing to hide, so if you have me venting on tape, so be it. Please just find this maniacal killer and let's be done with this."

"What do you think should happen to this maniacal killer?" Nick asked casually.

"That's an odd question, detective. It's not for me to decide. That's what we have a court of law for."

"Yes, but what do you think should happen?"

"Leniency, of course."

"You know this is a capital punishment state, don't you Mrs. Huston?"

"I'm aware of that. I thought capital punishment was for first-degree murder. That's premeditated, right?"

"Sometimes. Are you saying this was not first-degree murder?"

"I am not saying anything of the sort. I am just having a discussion, posed by you, of what punishment should be meted out."

"Why leniency?"

"Because...Ed may have caused...hum...let me rephrase that. Ed may have incurred the wrath of whoever ended his life, but conceivably they may have acted in the heat of the moment. A moment of insanity. That's second-degree murder, correct, detective?"

"Sounds like you've been studying."

"I don't know that for a certainty, but I do watch television occasionally."

"OK, so tell us," Nick went on, "regardless of whether it was premeditated or not, why would someone implicate you in Ed's murder?"

"Implicate me?" Her eyes narrowed. Glancing first at Gail then Nick, she pressed, "I can't see why anyone would implicate me. That's ridiculous."

"You already told us you didn't like the man. Other people knew that."

"I told you we didn't always get along. I didn't wish him dead."

"Didn't you?"

"No."

"Is there anything you want to tell us now, Mrs. Huston?" Gail asked.

Barbara clasped her hands on the table, the bracelets punctuating her first words. "I hadn't wanted to bring this up before, but it sounds like you may have found..."

"Found what?" Nick asked

"God this feels like cat and mouse. I guess you found something...in Ed's office, on his computer..."

"What specifically?"

"Well I can't really say for sure what *you've* found...but..."

"You can't? We found your fingerprints, Mrs. Huston."

"My fingerprints?"

"I can't see why that would be relevant since we all used each other's computers from time to time..."

"But your prints are very clear."

"Look. I did use Ed's mouse inadvertently on that Monday evening. He was showing me a spreadsheet and I was moving the mouse around while he was...on the phone. That's when I saw..."

"What?"

She clucked her tongue. "The photos."

"The photos of..."

"The children." She paused wondering the extent of what they'd seen. "OK, the pornographic images of adults and children. There. I've said it."

"Why didn't you share this before?"

"Because Ed promised me he'd get rid of it. And never do it again. I was absolutely infuriated. I told him if I saw any of it again, I'd..."

"Kill him?"

"Don't be idiotic. Fire him. I told him I would fire him despite his cozy relationship with my husband, and that I would ruin his career with the psychiatric board once and for all."

"Once and for all?"

"I knew there had been...an incident." The detectives waited for the bomb to drop. "He'd molested a young boy five years ago at a clinic in Canada, while he was on a speaking engagement. That's why he came to us. Mark agreed to take him on for the sake of their history. He swore he would never participate in anything immoral again."

"Why didn't you tell us earlier about the computer porn?"

"Because I was trying to..."

"Protect yourself?"

"Lord no. Protect my husband. It would have meant...an investigation. It could have potentially cost us our clinic, our grants, our reputation. Ed had promised Mark..."

"...but he lied."

"Yes, he lied."

"So you thought about it and then you came back after dinner that night and killed him?" Nick leaned in, trolling. "He deserved it didn't he, Mrs. Huston? He liked porn. Kiddy porn. No need to fire him. Murder was better."

"No. I tell you again, I did not harm him. I feel badgered when you do this, detective. I have told you everything I know."

"Mrs. Huston, Nick is just trying to find out who did this. I am sorry if it seems harsh, but murder is harsh." Gail inserted herself, good cop bad cop. "Who *did* do this, then? Your husband?"

"Mark isn't like that..."

Gail continued gently. "But he had the physical power to do it. If your husband knew what Ed was doing, that it would cause a scandal, he might have had a 'moment of insanity' and murdered his old friend. You said it yourself..."

She slumped back against her chair and rubbed her forehead. "I don't believe Mark did this. What more can I say to you?"

"He lied to you." Nick dropped the other bomb.

"Who?"

"Your husband."

She stilled, not breathing, the mask in place.

"He lied to you about a lawsuit against Ed and the clinic that was about to hit."

Her jaw tightened, but after a moment she regained control and smiled. "OK, detective. You're trying to split us apart, create doubt. I understand that. If my husband kept something from me, he must have had a good reason. I trust him."

"Mrs. Huston, do you have any children?" Gail said very quietly.

"No. Not now." Her eyes dropped for a second.

"Not now?"

"I had a young child. Many years ago."

"Go on."

"But...he died. Leukemia. When he was four." Barbara sat forward at the table, one arm resting on her chin, holding her head up.

"May I ask his name?"

"Hans."

"Would you have done anything you could to protect Hans?"

"I did do everything I could to protect Hans." Barbara's eyes looked old, full of pain.

"Would you have protected Hans from someone like Ed Michael?"

"Of course. Of course." Barbara's eyes grew moist. "I didn't... do...the right thing. I see it now. From the beginning."

"What right thing?"

"I should have stopped Mark from hiring him. I should have reported Ed the moment I saw it again. To protect others, other children, ourselves. I can't believe I was so hell-bent on protecting him." She began weeping quietly.

"Ed?"

"Mark."

"...that you put more children at risk?"

"Yes. I'm guilty."

"Guilty of murder?" Nick chimed in.

"Of neglect," Barbara said flatly. "Of neglecting my principles. Of retreating into anger instead of action. I should have fired the man, on the spot. The murderer saved me the trouble."

"So you're glad he's dead?"

"I didn't kill him, but I can say I'm not sorry to see him gone."

"Dr. Huston," Nick asked casually, "how tall are you?"

"Five-seven." Why?"

He suddenly tossed his pen toward her. She caught it with her right hand. She put it down on the table in front of him, puzzled.

"Do you drink tea?"

"These are odd questions, but no, I detest the stuff. I'm a coffee drinker."

"What else do you drink?"

"Are you probing for alcohol abuse?"

"No, trying to understand your lifestyle."

"I enjoy a good wine, a stiff cocktail. A good ale."

"German?"

"No, Belgian."

"Any chemical expertise?"

"Short of bug spray, no."

"What would Sigmund Freud say about people who like child pornography or...sex with children?"

"Freud? Interesting you should ask. Freud would say it was... an obsession. A genital fixation, perhaps. Sometimes the individual might be a regressed offender."

"Regressed offender?

"An offender who grows into adulthood with normal sexual orientations, but in the absence of a marital partner or in the presence of other high stress, regresses to sexual involvement with...children."

"And if Ed were in that state of mind, were there any children around the clinic on that Monday night?"

"That is a painful thought under the circumstances, but, no... none that I can recall..."

"In your opinion, could Ed have been regressing just before his death...and found whatever method he could to satisfy himself?"

"Maybe," Barbara replied, about to add more but stopped. "Detectives, I am sorry if I have been difficult. I understand you're trying to figure this out. I will try to think about the pornographic implications for you if you like. I am just a little fuzzy right now...

stressed. Thank you, Ms. Burton, for helping me...see myself a little better today. I hadn't realized I had...been...complicit in...standing by when I should have stepped up."

Nick looked over at Gail, uncomfortable. Damn. These psychological types had a way of turning interrogations into group therapy.

"OK, Dr. Huston. You can go for now. Thanks for your patience. Liz will take you to a secure room for now. If you're willing, can you stay available in case we need to call on you after that?"

"Of course." Barbara got up, shook hands with them both, and left.

Nick leaned back in his chair and sighed once Gail shut off the recorder.

"Jesus, I feel like I've been at an AA meeting."

Gail laughed. "She seemed pretty sincere at the end."

"Maybe. I'm not sure if the two of them are for real or if they're the world's greatest sociopaths. Both had motive. I'm no shrink, but they sure sound fucked up to me. Maybe not homicidal, but definitely screwed up."

"I'll make a note of that in the log." Gail grinned. "Hey, let's grab some more coffee before we do our next ones. These psych types wear me out." They sent out for caffeine and croissants from Gil's. "Does Gil's actually have croissants?"

"Gil's has some class, for God's sake, it's not a gas station," Nick defended.

"Close."

After the caffeine arrived and they'd each downed a croissant slathered in butter, Liz fetched their next suspect, Nancy Davis. Gail stood near the north side of the room and did some yoga stretches while they waited for Nancy to come up from downstairs.

"Hey, what does that do for you, anyway?" Nick asked her, yawning.

"Gets the energy flowing. Keeps everything from coagulating in my butt. You should try it."

"I like my butt."

Freud's Revenge

Gail burst out laughing. "I am not even going there...I'd never dream of getting between you and your butt."

"Good. Some things I like to keep to myself."

The door opened and Gail sat down, back in the mood for murder.

Chapter Twenty-Nine

Duality

The tall, dark-skinned southern woman entered the room and smiled grandly at Nick and Gail. Nancy was casual in jeans, a navy sweater, and black pumps today. Her hair was twisted up in back in a twist.

"Ms. Davis."

"Officers." Nancy nodded and sat. She plopped her oversize black handbag onto the seat next to her, and slid her left foot onto the chair base oblique to her, getting comfortable.

"We've invited you here today to help us clarify a few things about Dr. Michael's death."

"OK."

"Do you think the final results of the investigation will clear you, by the way?"

She considered her answer. "Of course."

"Can you say why?"

"Because I didn't kill the man, that's why."

"Nevertheless, we've found that you're one of several people who had access to the victim and the motive for harming him."

"I might have had access, but I didn't need to kill him."

"All right. Then is there anyone you think who could eliminate you from suspicion?"

"That's an odd question, detective. Who would eliminate me? Most everyone, I guess. I was open with you before about what I thought of the man. I don't have anything to hide, then or now."

"So what's the reason someone named you a suspect?"

Nancy paused for a moment to reflect. "Well, that's an interesting angle, detective. However, I've worked in the prison system and I know that's a typical approach you use to get to a confession."

"So what made you kill him?"

"Nothing, since I didn't." Nancy said sharply.

"You sound annoyed, Ms. Davis."

"It's Dr. Davis, and yes, I get cranky when people waste my time. Cut to the chase, will you, detective? I came down here of my own free will, let's not forget."

"Point taken. But we're puzzled why you didn't tell us about the investigation you were launching into Dr. Michael's behavior."

"So that's in the goulash, is it? I can tell you that I had evidence of him using pornography onsite plus there were some allegations of child abuse by the esteemed Dr. Michael. I was about to present the evidence but the guy turned up dead."

"Why didn't you mention this?"

"Because, detective, I know the difference between truth and hearsay. I didn't bring it forward for two reasons: First, I had to present the hard evidence to the proper channels, the clinic directors. Second, I had a duty to protect the family until the allegations had gone through a child abuse investigation."

"But it was a potential motive for murder, Dr. Davis, and you withheld it. You've killed before. You must understand how we might think you had 'the steel in your belly' to do it again."

"Good memory. But I was investigating the guy, not stalking him, detective."

"Can you tell us about Tommy Ray Carson? New Orleans, 1995."

Nancy sat back, contemplating her answer. "Yes, I shot him. It's in the records, obviously. I was working in a clinic in the Seventh Ward off Esplanade. We were treating a family and the youngest daughter—a ten-year-old—spilled the beans that her father had raped her regularly since she was five. We reported Tommy Ray and he got put in jail."

"And after that?"

"He got out and came after me and the treating counselor. Walked into the clinic one day with a machete and went for us in the lunchroom. I pulled out my gun and shot him. Twice. Died later in the hospital. Ruled self-defense."

"What about PTSD?"

"What about it?"

"Dr. Davis, I'm sure you know all about posttraumatic stress and what it can do to somebody. How it shows up in delusions and flashbacks after the fact?" Nick said expertly.

"Yup."

"So in the days leading up to Dr. Michael's murder, you were quietly gathering evidence against him, weren't you? Potentially another child abuser."

"Yup."

"And involving one of your students, weren't you?"

She sighed. "Yes. Margaret Tanaka. She had some pictures. Plus there was a report from a family about inappropriate touching by Ed during a child eval. I was about to deliver the details to the Hustons, but they were tied up."

"And that frustrated you?"

"Sure."

"So you were working late that night, sitting with the evidence. And you heard voices. Loud arguing. The voice of a woman, and a man threatening her."

"It wasn't decipherable..."

"And you moved into action, didn't you? It was Margaret, wasn't it? Margaret and Ed having an argument, either about what she saw him doing or what he caught her taking pictures of. And he was trying to stop her maybe? And you sprang into action, didn't you, Dr. Davis?"

"No, not true."

"Like last time. Another disgusting, filthy pervert, and a psychiatrist at that...not a blue-collar guy working in a factory...but an educated, professional man who denigrated you."

"That's your interpretation..."

"Who, despite all his training and stature, was still just a pervert. Margaret was in trouble, so you jumped on it, maybe you even thought it was Tommy in some posttraumatic stress delusion..."

"That's ridiculous."

"Only this time you didn't have your gun. So you found something else. There were plenty of meds around Ed's office. Your fingerprints are even on the medicine cabinet. You knew you could get the young girl—Margaret—out of there, and then give Ed something to immobilize him. Maybe she even helped you. Then once he was comatose, you did it."

"Nope."

"It fits though, doesn't it? Who could blame you? One *more* less pervert in the world, isn't that right?" Nick stopped, watching her.

Nancy smiled, and studied him. "Wow. That was really good, detective. You worked hard on pulling all that together. Quite a fantasy. Only it's *your* fantasy."

"How so?"

"Because none of that happened. I finished up in my office like I told you, heard some voices. Had a chat with Ed and the interns about a case and things were calm. Went back in the kitchen for my lunch bag then into my office for my things, heard some loud talking in Ed's office, but then I went home. Plain and simple."

"What about your fingerprints?"

"I bet there are at least seven or eight identifiable prints on that cabinet. Ed was so lazy sometimes he'd sit at his conference table and have the interns grab the samples for him. Or one of us. We all got into that cabinet from time to time. And for your information, I dealt with my posttraumatic stress years ago. Now do you have anything relevant you need from me? If you don't, I think I'll be on my way."

Nancy sat back and rummaged in her bag for Juicy Fruit. She popped a fresh stick in her mouth and offered some to the detectives. Suddenly she looked around the room, spotted the camera, then raised her hand and waved.

Nick leaned back and clasped his hands on top of his head. Gail took up the slack. "Dr. Davis, I'm sorry about all this, but we really would appreciate your help. Who do *you* think did this?"

Nancy raised her eyebrows and cocked her head to the side, chewing. "Somebody real mad. Somebody strong. Probably male."

"Why male?"

"Don't know. Just smells male."

"OK, just a couple more things."

"Sure," she said popping her gum.

"How tall are you?"

"Five-ten and a half."

"Right- or left-handed?"

"Left."

"Do you drink tea?"

"Tea, coffee, chai, lemonade, scotch, and now and then a little hooch." She laughed, the throaty sound echoing off the walls. "Anything else, officers?"

"That'll be all for now," Nick said finally. "We really do appreciate your cooperation." Nancy leveled a look at him like he was a naughty four-year-old. "We're going to show you to a separate waiting room until we interview the rest of your colleagues, if that's all right. There's coffee and food in there."

"OK, I'll be around if you need me," she directed her comment to Gail. To Nick she said, "You, not so much." Liz came to the door after Nick buzzed her and Nancy picked up her bag and left.

"Good try," Gail said turning to Nick. "I thought you had her going there, but she didn't bite."

"Appears so. I still think she could have done it."

"Maybe."

"Definitely had motive." Nick tapped his pen on the yellow pad in front of him. "One thing I will say, she knew what we were talking about. Even seemed to be considering the scenario."

"Maybe we're right. Right scenario, wrong killer."

"She thinks it's a man."

"Could be a way to throw us off," Gail reached into her back pocket for lipstick.

"Setting us up?"

"Could fit into the dual killer thing," she said as she applied some coral splash. "Maybe she did the drug part, and the killer did the rest of it. Who's likely?"

"Margaret? Thomas? Gary?"

"How about her and Helga...Barbara Huston?"

"Well I sure wouldn't mess with those two in a dark alley."

"Who's left for today?"

Nick studied the roster. "Margaret Tanaka, Thomas Wong, Sandra Daniels. Oh, and Amanda Carlisle." Gail smiled but didn't comment. "OK, let's do one more then we'll break for lunch." Talking quietly into the phone, Nick said, "Liz, send in Margaret Tanaka and have the others take a lunch break, back at 1:30."

A few moments later, Margaret entered the room tentatively. Dressed in black jeans and lime-green sweater, Margaret sat down at the end of the table and clutched her purse in her lap. Gail noticed she had pink kitten earrings dangling from her ears today.

"Good morning, officers."

"Ms. Tanaka."

"Please. Margaret."

"Margaret. Thanks for coming back in. We have a few more questions," Nick began.

"I understand."

"When we talked to you before, you indicated there were some things you couldn't reveal until you talked to your boss."

"My supervisor. Nancy," Margaret replied, twisting the handles of her purse.

"Can you share that information now?"

"Has she told you what it was?"

"Why, are you working together?"

"No...not in the way you mean." The girl blushed. "I mean we're under strict ethical parameters when revealing certain information."

"Like the fact that you and Nancy killed Dr. Michael?"

"What? For heaven's sake, no! We didn't murder Ed!"

"So then, Nancy did, right?"

"No. I mean I don't think so...I mean she, we couldn't have done anything like that."

"But you could have. You were implicated as a suspect."

"Me? Implicated? In Ed's death?" The girl's eyes darted around the room. "I didn't do anything to Ed. I simply took a picture—from his computer screen." Her eyes dropped to her lap.

"Of what?"

"Of...well if you have scanned my iPhone, you've probably seen it. Two men...um...having...sex. Anal sex."

"How do we know that wasn't *your* photo?"

"Oh my God, that is *not* mine. I took that photo when I was in Ed's office last week. I showed it to Nancy. She must have told you that. I had to report it because it was inappropriate, especially in the office and because someone else..."

"Someone else what?"

"Someone else had reported that Ed had touched a child sexually during an assessment last week."

"Tell us more."

"He fondled a nine-year-old boy. Supposedly. In his office. The boy told his mother and she told me. I reported it to Nancy."

"Did you report it to the authorities?"

"I...she...told me to wait..."

"To wait? You're a mandated reporter. You should have reported child sex abuse immediately."

"Yes, of course," she fidgeted with her purse, leaning over it like it was a baby in her lap. "It's just that it happened on a Friday...last Friday...very late. Nancy thought we should be sure first and investigate Monday."

"Be sure first of what?"

"The mother. She's histrionic."

"Histrionic?"

"Dramatic. Makes things up sometimes. We needed to have a reasonable suspicion. So we were going to investigate it with Ed on Monday...and the Hustons of course. We kept the family separate from him of course—Ed. But things got messed up because of Carl and it wasn't the right time. Nancy talked to Ed late Monday about it a little in her office before their staff meeting. While they were in there, I had to go into Ed's office for something and I saw the sex photos...and another...Web site...open."

"So you were Nancy's spy?"

"Oh no, it's not like that. I was doing what I was supposed to do: investigate."

"So when you were in Ed's office spying and you saw the stuff on screen, you shot some photos to make your case?"

"It corroborated that he was using pornography in the office, but it didn't corroborate the mother's allegations."

"So what was the sexy card you also took a picture of?"

"Oh. That."

"Yes. What did it say?"

She blushed. "'I want to...blow you.'"

"Was it from you to your boyfriend?"

"God, no. It was from...Thomas."

"Thomas?"

"From Thomas to...Ed."

Nick and Gail looked at each other. "OK, Margaret. Where did you find this card?"

"On Ed's desk."

"On the day of the murder?"

"Yes. It was on his desk that afternoon. Carl had a breakdown in the lobby on Monday morning, and then we were talking about it later in the kitchen. I saw Thomas go into Ed's office after that and I went on into session. Then, after lunch, I happened to go into Ed's office. I saw the card sitting there...actually, on his chair."

"So you picked it up?"

Margaret looked down at her lap. "Yes."

"You tampered with Ed's personal correspondence, and then took a picture of it?"

"Yes. I feel bad about that. But what I saw creeped me out."

"Surely you've seen the phrase, 'I want to blow you,' before?"

"Yeah, but not in a card from Thomas to Ed."

"Thomas had a thing for Ed?"

"I guess."

"What do you think about it?"

"It's...disgusting. Maybe they were consenting adults and that makes it OK...except..."

"Except it was in the office, in the clinic, right? And it was getting very clear to you that Dr. Michael liked...

"Men."

"Men and...maybe...boys?"

"Yes, boys."

"What do you think of that, counselor?"

"It's reprehensible."

"...Horrible for a man with degrees in child psychiatry."

"Yes."

"...Who preyed on people for sex..."

"Yes."

"...And brought sex into a clinical office..."

"Yes." She reached into her purse, pulled out a tissue, and rubbed her eyes.

"So you were happy when Ed turned up dead?"

"Huh?" She wadded up the tissue in her fists and held them in front of her mouth. "It makes me uncomfortable when you say that..."

"So you—or you and Nancy—set it up to get rid of the man?"

"No. No!"

"You knew the doc liked tea, didn't you?" Nick pushed. "You shared chai, you said. You drank with him. And you know all about poisons, don't you, Ms. Tanaka?"

"No, I don't..."

"But your parents are doctors, you said. And you and Nancy Davis, between you, know a lot about drugging somebody, slowing them down, then murdering them."

"My God, we didn't do that. I swear! I took some pictures that's all. I didn't kill him! We didn't kill him!"

"So if you didn't, then Nancy did?"

"No, no."

"You realize, Margaret, that if you tell us everything you know about Nancy Davis doing it, you'll get off? If you're protecting a killer, however, you'll be charged as an accessory."

"Oh my God. I don't know, I don't know," she wailed, holding her head. "I didn't hurt Ed. I don't think Nancy did either."

"But someone killed him." Gail moved it along. "That mother? Or the kid? The father? The Hustons? Sandra? Gary? Thomas? Who would have done it, Margaret?"

"I don't know..."

"I think you have an idea and I have faith in you to do the right thing and tell us."

"I don't know...maybe...Thomas?"

Nick paused just a beat for emphasis. "Why him?"

"Because...maybe Thomas got...rejected?"

"Rejected? By Ed? You saw Thomas cozy up to Ed for months? You'd seen them drinking together, and maybe Thomas didn't get what he wanted."

She stared at Nick, wide eyed again, her mouth open.

"Maybe Ed rejected him," Nick went on. "And maybe Thomas came back to the office that night and killed him for it."

"I don't know, I don't know." Margaret burst into tears and covered her face with her hands, sobbing.

Gail looked over at Nick. He shrugged. Finally, after Margaret wept for nearly a minute, Gail reached over to the corner table, opened a drawer, and took out a large box of tissues. She pushed the box toward the pathetic girl. Margaret dabbed her cheeks where black mascara was dripping like sludge all the way down to her chin. Finally, she looked up, eyes swollen.

Gail asked Margaret quietly, "Margaret, are you left- or right-handed?"

"Right."

"How tall."

"Five-two. Why do you ask?"

"Just checking on some details," Gail said, making a note.

Nick made a decision for both of them. "OK, Ms. Tanaka, uh, Margaret, that's enough for today. Liz will escort you out. By the way, could you leave the name and number of the family that filed the complaint? We will have to investigate that. Stay in town this weekend in case we need you further, please. We really appreciate your candor. I know it wasn't easy but you're doing the right thing."

"Oh, thank you," she said, relieved. "I'm so sorry, officers. For everything. For all of us. For Dr. Michael." She hiccupped then burst into tears again.

Nick pushed the COM line and Liz took the blubbering girl out. Nick sat back and rubbed the back of his neck. Gail pulled out some tic tacs and the two sat there, staring at the empty chair.

"So."

"So." Nick echoed. "OK, no confessions so far."

"Gave it our best shot."

"Yup."

"That kid was a weep fest." Gail rolled her eyes.

"Yup."

"Think she and Doc Davis did it together?"

"Possibly. But if they did, Davis would have probably had her hands full keeping Tanaka from coming unglued while they did it."

"Yeah, unless she was drugged too. Or terrified. Or hypnotized."

"Lots of possibilities. Right now, I feel like lunch."

"Yeah I know. Interrogations always make you hungry."

Nick smiled for the first time in two hours.

"Willing to brave the cafeteria?"

"If I have to. Guess it would save time." The two officers locked the room, and then headed down to the backstairs to the second floor where the line was short for fast cop fare. Trays in hand, the two spied a window table and Gail and Nick sat down with their torpedoes.

Marv Hendricks, a balding fifteen-year veteran of homicide wandered by as the two tucked into their sandwiches and chips. "How many live ones ya got on the books right now? Or should I say dead ones."

Nick smirked at the joke. "Four."

Marv whistled, rubbing his sweaty, nearly-bald head with his hand. "Could keep you busy, dude. Ya got that shrink case, right?"

"Yeah, wuz up?" Gail asked, licking mustard off her fingers.

"Sounds like one we had about ten years ago. South Bay. Psychiatrist murdered by a dealer. He was doing shrooms at home on weekends. Got paid a visit when his credit card bounced."

"How'd you find the perp?"

"Stupid guy sat down, did some shrooms with the shrink, *then* murdered him just before the perp vomited all over the couch. DNA everywhere. Maybe you'll get so lucky."

"Maybe. Thanks."

Marv went on his way.

"We gotta crack this case soon, Nick, so we can get on to that homicide in National City. Plus that murder-robbery in PB," Gail reminded him as she munched her dill pickle. Nick handed her his.

"Yeah, yeah." He took a swig of Mountain Dew after he ate the last of his torpedo. "My gut tells me our shrink killer is around today."

"Sure it's not gas?"

"Funny. Strikes me that all these psych people are really torqued about their work and seem pretty tangled up emotionally."

"I see your point. Stands to reason that somebody with an emotional ax to grind could find several reasons to decide to off this guy..."

"And take the extra time to truss him up, stab him, and torture him before they finished the job."

"Sounds like maybe he deserved it."

"Whose side are you on?"

"Ours."

"So let's see what the other ones cough up after lunch."

The two officers picked up some more caffeine and headed back upstairs in time for their one thirty with the next name on the list: Thomas Wong.

Chapter Thirty

Desire

At 1:30 p.m. sharp, Liz knocked on the door and entered. Thomas Wong sauntered in after her. Black shades wrapped around his head, the young man wore jeans, a white T-shirt, and tennis shoes. He sat where Nick pointed as Liz left.

"Mr. Wong. Thanks for coming."

"No problem. Good to see you again, officers." He removed his shades, and then hung them off his shirt pocket.

Gail noticed his hair was slicked with gel, spiky toward the ceiling like a comic book character. "We have a few questions."

"Sure." Thomas's dark eyes watched them, waiting.

Nick saw him spot the camera in the corner of the ceiling. "Mr. Wong..."

"Thomas."

"Thomas," Nick continued, "we're wondering if you've thought of anything else you'd like to tell us about Ed Michael's murder?"

"Not sure what you mean."

"What exactly was your relationship to Dr. Ed Michael?"

"We were friends."

"Lovers?"

Thomas snorted. "I liked Ed. We had some fun. Nothing serious."

"Explain that, please."

"Well like I said at Seaside, we had a lot in common. I learned a lot from the guy, liked spending time with him."

"What else?"

"I wanted there to be more, I guess."

"Were you having sex?"

"Nah. I liked him, but he...was kind of...cagey."

"He rebuffed you, then. Perhaps you murdered him out of revenge?"

"What? Nah, that's bogus, man. Things were moving along but nothing serious. I had no reason to harm the guy. Come on, man."

"Why does everyone think you murdered him?"

"Everyone? Who do you mean 'everyone'? Did Margaret say something? She's a bitch, man."

"Strong words from a therapist."

"Psych assistant, really. She didn't like me. I'm sure she told you. Margaret's incompetent, man, screwed up so many times. Hated me for knowing more than her. Resented Ed and me...our...friendship."

"Tell us about this." Nick showed him the photo of the pornographic card.

"I wondered what happened to that. Ed must have left it out somewhere...and you found it."

"So are you a pervert?"

"What do you mean by that? That's harassing."

"You're working in a mental health clinic. You're around children, minors. Were you bringing sexual literature in there?"

"Hey, man, you're barking up the wrong tree. I gave Ed something *personal*. Not meant for other people to see."

"What about the phone calls?"

"Yeah, OK. I called him."

"Several times the night he died, on both his cell and his land-line."

The young man began drumming his fingers on the table. "He was supposed to meet me."

"So why did you stop calling him?"

"Why did I stop?"

"Yes, your calls stopped around eight fifteen that night."

"Did they?"

"Did they stop because you weren't getting what you wanted so you drove back to Seaside and killed him?"

"I told you before it wasn't me."

"Why are your fingerprints everywhere?"

"I don't know what you mean but I was in there nearly every day. Lots of us were."

"Why are your fingerprints all over his desk and cabinet?"

"The cabinet? You mean the meds cabinet? Look. I don't know what you found but I cleared that up with Ed last year."

Nick hid the fact that he had no idea what Thomas was referring to. "Yeah, tell us about that."

"Hey, man, it was only some Vicodin. Ed caught me taking it out. Reprimanded me but said he wouldn't tell anyone about it."

"But he did."

"Oh, man, the bastard. Uh, sorry. Who did he tell? The Hustons? Nancy? Oh, man, I'm screwed."

"That's why you came back and killed him."

"No, I am telling you I didn't come back. I liked the guy. Maybe he slipped up about ratting on me, but I know he liked me. He knew what a tight ass Nancy is; neither of us liked the place. Ed tolerated it better than I did, I guess. Barbara was friggin' paranoid. Margaret was always following me around the little cun...er, creep."

"Why were they watching you?"

"Other than Margaret, I don't think anyone was watching *me* particularly. But Barbara was paranoid about anything going wrong. There was that Nazi thing last year. Stupid really. Ed laughed about the Jew-German thing. Didn't bother him a bit but he knew it really amped Barbara. He razzed her."

"Sounds like you don't like the women there very much?" Gail asked pointedly.

"Hey don't get me wrong, ma'am. I have nothing against women in general. Nancy is usually pretty cool, does things by the book of course. Generally she's OK to work for. But I have to watch out for myself, you know. No one's gonna give me a free ride."

"Speaking of rides, do you own a motorcycle?" Gail asked.

"Yeah, why?"

"Wear gloves, helmet?"

"Of course. You can't arrest me for not wearing a helmet." Thomas laughed.

"Do you ride your bike to the clinic?"

"Off and on. Sometimes I take my car."

"How about the night of the murder?"

"Can't remember...oh wait, I guess I was on my hog."

"But you came back to the clinic from downtown and killed Ed, didn't you?"

"No, I didn't. I was downtown and stayed."

"We checked you out. You were at the Rail that night, then you left around nine. You went somewhere, and then showed up around eleven at Croce's. It gave you enough time to drive back to Del Mar, do the deed, set the evidence, and then be back downtown before midnight."

"You're smoking crack, man."

"So you are telling us you didn't come back to Seaside and you didn't murder Dr. Michael?"

"Yes. I mean no, I mean yes—I didn't kill him." The young man sunk his face in his hands.

"Why are you confused? Because you can't keep your story straight? Nancy, Margaret, Amanda, Dr. Huston, Barbara, Sandra, Gary...they all think you did it."

"I don't believe that. I've made some mistakes, but I didn't do this. I liked the guy...loved him kind of, I guess. He made the rest of 'em look like idiots. Somebody was, like, jealous of us. Maybe they're trying to frame me—have you thought of that?"

"Who would frame you?"

"How about Sandra? Or Gary? Now those two are pretty freaky."

"'Freaky'? How?"

"Mouse and mousy. Give me the creeps, that's all I know. Maybe they had it in for Ed. Sandra was always...around. She knew about..."

"About what?"

"She overheard about the Vicodin thing. Always watching stuff... people...hanging around. Said she'd keep it under her belt since I'd cleared it up with Ed. And Gary...he's a mouse. Check out those two."

"How tall are you, Thomas, by the way?"

"Five-nine. Why?"

"Right- or left-handed?"

"Left. Why?"

"You seem like a pretty smart guy, Thomas. You know a lot about how things got done at Seaside."

"Yup," Thomas said, flattered.

"Who do you think did this to Ed?"

"Some schizo, for sure," he blurted, glad to be off the spot.

"Schizo?"

"Somebody out of their fuckin' mind. If I were you I'd look for a truly psychotic individual..."

"Who hated Ed?"

"Or what he stood for."

"Do you know what this is?" Nick said suddenly, pointing to Ed's planner.

"It's a planner. Oh. Is that Ed's planner?"

"Yes. What do you know about it?"

"I know Ed had it with him most of the time. Logged everything."

"Why not use the computer?"

"He was a big computer guy, but he liked to log his personal notes in that thing. Maybe he was gonna write a book?"

"What did he use the computer for?"

"Hey, man, you seem to be digging. We used to do research on his computer, list serves, articles, stuff like that."

"What else?"

Thomas stared at Nick, searching. "You're looking for porn, aren't you, detective?"

"How would you know that?"

For the first time, Thomas smiled. "Because you've been up my butt...sorry, you've asked...about that card I gave Ed...about my sexual preferences. And you don't hide stuff very well, frankly, detective, with all due respect. Remember, I am a therapist, man."

Nick ignored the comment. "Did the two of you use porn in the office?"

"Not me, man. Not on clinic time. Never."

"Ed?"

"Ed may have looked at some stuff at night...late...a couple of times."

"With you?"

"Maybe once."

"Probably more." Thomas fell silent. "What kind of porn?" Nick pressed on.

"What are you driving at, man? Oh, I get it. You must have found kid porn." Thomas focused hard on Nick. "That's not my scene, man. I like grown-ups, not kids."

"And Ed?"

"Can't answer for him. You would know more than me, by the sound of it."

"Aren't you ethically bound to do and not do certain things in your profession?"

"Yes. I do my best to toe the line, man."

"But your ethics sometimes run thin, don't they, Thomas?"

"Hey, man, there's no need to insult me. I screwed up. I admit it. But I didn't kill Ed." The young man sat back and laid his hands flat on the table.

Nick leaned back. He glanced at Gail. "OK, you can go for now. Liz will show you. We may need you over the next few days so remain available, please. Thanks for the information."

"OK, right, OK. Thanks."

Nick buzzed Liz and she collected Thomas to escort him to the sequester room. Gail spoke first once the door slammed. "OK, I think we got somewhere on that. This guy seems like he had the motive and means no matter how much he denies it."

"Could be. No confession, though. We're going to have to prove it. How about the redirects?"

"He's been the most upfront about the others. Still think we're missing something big."

"Probably right. OK, let's see Sandra Daniels." Nick signaled Liz to bring in the young woman.

Sandra Daniels stood in the doorway thirty seconds later. As before, she was dressed in a plain, tailored blouse, modest gray skirt, and dark loafers. No belt. Her hair was parted in the middle and pulled back in a flat ponytail with a scrunchie. Tiny silver hoops hung from her ears.

"Ms. Daniels, uh, Sandra, have a seat." As she sat and folded her legs underneath her, Nick kept on talking. "We need some further information from you."

"All right." She carefully hung her navy shoulder bag off the side of her chair. Then she clasped her hands together on the table in front of her and waited.

"You detailed your whereabouts on the night of Ed Michael's death, but you were vague about the exact times. Several people have flagged you as a suspect since you were there at least twice the evening Ed died."

She stared at him, barely moving an eyebrow. "Me, a suspect? That seems so...weird."

"Why weird?"

"Well, I just wouldn't...couldn't have done...that. I don't know exactly what happened to Dr. Michael, but from the rumors, I gather it was pretty awful. I'm pretty squeamish...about blood...and stuff."

"Why would that stop you? Haven't you done difficult things before, Ms. Daniels? You treat felons, don't you? Your father was in the military. You probably learned about weapons and self defense..."

"Well...maybe..."

"Something might have set you off about Ed Michael, and you came back to the clinic and decided to kill him."

She stared at him, silent.

"Was this the first time you've murdered somebody in a fit of rage?"

She stared at Nick, then Gail. "I don't kill people, sir. I didn't hurt Dr. Michael. I had nothing to do with it, believe me."

"You said you left just after five."

"Yes."

"Then you worked out, and then you came back."

"Yes, to pick up a couple of files."

"Why?"

"Why? Because...they weren't finished."

"Why did they need to be finished?"

"Because I had case notes to write and they had to get done." She gave Nick a stern look, and then abruptly averted her eyes.

"How long were you there...the second time, I mean?"

"I...I...it's a little fuzzy."

"Fuzzy?"

"Well...I don't know, I was at the gym, worked up a good sweat... endorphins going, you know...then I came back by and wrote some notes...my mind was kind of on other things..."

"When did you leave?"

"Like I said, I think it was about eight or so."

"When did you get home?"

"I wish I could be more specific, but it had been an exhausting day. I just sort of came home, crawled into bed, you know..."

"Ms. Daniels, you seem spacey."

She snapped upright at the mention of the word. "I am *not* spacey. I was under stress that day. I wasn't watching the clock is all. I don't like being grilled like this, as if I should know everything about everything and everyone. I don't know who would have done this to Ed but it wasn't me and I wish you would just get off my back." She looked down at her fingernails.

"You sound defensive."

"I don't like being cornered. I feel like you're forcing me to say things, do things, that I can't...be sure about...can't remember..."

"Who else forces you?"

"Forces me? No one. I take care of myself. Nobody makes me do things."

"How about Amanda, your boss?"

"She supervises my therapy work."

"Does she make you murder people for her?"

Sandra burst out laughing. "Amanda? Amanda wouldn't ask me to help her hurt anyone."

"So who would hurt Ed?"

"Hmm. I don't like to point fingers."

"Point a finger."

"You want me to implicate someone else? Can't help you."

"Ms. Daniels, were you in love with Ed Michael?"

"What?" She smiled suddenly. Nick noticed her teeth were gray and tiny. "No way."

"But you liked him a lot, you said."

"I learned a ton from him. Sometimes it was over my head...but I learned a lot. He was always good to me."

"When was he bad?" Gail leaned in toward the girl.

"Bad?" Sandra looked blankly at Gail. "Can't answer that."

"Did you know he used pornography? In the office?"

Sandra tensed in her chair. "Ed? Pornography. I...I didn't know..." She looked down at her fingernails again and sighed.

"Does that disappoint you?"

"Oh yeah. That means he was not...fit."

"Not fit?"

"If he didn't know any better than to do that. He was so smart about other things. Not about that, I guess." She stared down at her nails again.

"You don't seem surprised."

"Once you've been in the therapy business for a while not a whole lot surprises you."

"It doesn't bother you?"

"It bothers me that Ed made bad choices."

"Is that all? Is that what Ed's murderer did—made bad choices?"

"No, no, that's clearly wrong. Pornography in the workplace is clearly wrong. Murder is wrong."

"How about child pornography?"

"Child pornography?" She looked like he'd punched her in the stomach.

"You knew all about that, didn't you?"

"No, I didn't know Ed was into...that..." Her lips curled in disgust.

"You talked to Ed that night didn't you?"

"Only in passing."

"You probably went in to talk to Ed...or saw him in the kitchen... discussed a client or two."

"Maybe in passing..."

"Something set you off, right? Something he said or did set you off?"

"I don't know what you mean."

"Something set you off and you got angry. You got so enraged you killed the man..."

"No, I didn't."

"You poisoned him, then stabbed him, then trussed him up so he could see you while you finished him off, right?"

"No I did not." Her eyes grew moist.

"Maybe you got Thomas to help you. Or Margaret. Or Nancy. Or even Barbara Huston, but you did the stabbing yourself, didn't you?"

"Oh my God, I couldn't do that..."

"You realized the man was a pervert. You found out he uses, abuses children, and you'd seen that before, hadn't you? You said you saw a neighbor child brutally murdered by his pervert father."

"Some of that is partially true..."

"When you came in and saw Ed that night, you went berserk, didn't you?"

"No." She was crying hard now, her pale face blotching like sunburn. After several seconds, Nick reached for the tissue box and slid it toward Sandra. She took a few moments to register what was in front of her. She shuddered convulsively, and slowly reached out to grab some tissues. She mopped her face and her breathing became normal. For a moment, the girl closed her eyes, and slowly swirled her neck around, relaxing. After a moment, she opened her eyes, and then reached around to her shoulder bag, and carefully took out a tube of lipstick and a tiny mirror.

Looking at herself, she blurted, "God this looks awful. May I?"

Nick nodded.

She pulled the scrunchie off her ponytail and shook out her hair, which fell in waves to her shoulders. She carefully opened the lipstick and applied a thick coat of pink. When she was done, she put the tube and mirror away. Reaching out once more to the tissue box, she took a single sheet. Carefully, she placed it between her lips and pressed. Wadding up the tissue in her lap, she looked up at Nick and smiled, composed. "You really can be kind when you want to, officer," she smiled, her lips bright against the dingy teeth.

"Ms. Daniels, how are you feeling now?"

"Wonderful, officer. A good cry always helps me clear my head." She flipped her hair out over her shoulder, beamed at Gail, then turned back to Nick as she perched her elbow on the table and plopped her chin into her hand.

Nick leaned forward, considering. "Ms. Daniels. How tall are you?"

"Five-seven."

"Right- or left-handed?"

"Ambidextrous actually. But I favor my left," she answered, stretching out the fingers on her left hand slowly, and then flipping the hand over to study her palm.

"Drive a motorcycle?"

"Lord, no. But I've ridden one." She smiled again. Then she winked.

Nick watched her for a moment. "OK, Ms. Daniels we may need you later on. Don't leave the county, OK?"

"Wouldn't think of it. I wish I could have helped you more." She smiled at the two officers as she got up and flung her shoulder bag across her chest so the strap separated her two breasts. As she turned to go, she glanced back at Nick and said, "Bye. Let me know if there's anything else I can do."

Nick nodded, and then looked away as he buzzed Liz. Sandra left the room when the admin opened it. "OK, so she's another sniveler," Nick said, reaching over to the tic tacs.

"Yeah, and something else."

"What?"

"She's spacey or something. What is that?"

"Could be lying."

"Drug user?"

"Maybe. Nothing comes up on her record. Amnesiac?"

"PTSD from childhood?"

"Maybe she murdered the guy..."

"And can't remember?"

"Could be. How about the teeth? Ugly."

"Probably bulimic. That's teeth rot from the throw-up." Gail had experience with bulimics from some of the county juvenile offender programs.

"She coulda done it. She and someone else."

"Maybe. Kinda skinny. But with help...Oh well, we should find out some more about her from Amanda Carlisle. She's coming in next, right?"

"Yeah. OK, no confession from Ms. Space Cadet but another likely perp."

Just then Nick's phone went. He talked for a few minutes, and then turned to Gail. "Larry's been out investigating friends of Ed's. Nobody in particular comes up with motive at this point. The shrink's ex lives in Ohio and she's married again with two kids. Ol' Ed doesn't show any unusual bank account activity although he had a few porn parties. Not much detail on that, but Larry's digging. Crazy

Carl's mother was down at the county jail trying to get him sprung during the murder window, so she's out too."

"Someone else might have done it for her."

"Maybe. OK, that only leaves one more. Amanda Carlisle. Our clinical expert."

"Is that we're calling her?" Gail stifled a laugh.

"Yup." He punched the COM line and said, "Liz can you send in Amanda Carlisle now? Oh, and maybe get some Cokes...for three?"

Cokes for three, Gail said in her head. She started to speak, but stuffed it. Nick was being Nick and there was no way around it. *Maybe I should be a shrink someday*, Gail thought. *Naw*, she reconsidered. *Talking to these kinds of people all day would drive me nuts!*

Chapter Thirty-One

Splitting

Amanda stood in the open door for a moment, surveying the interrogation room and the two detectives inside. Gail and Nick looked like they had been holed up for a week. Papers and files piled up in half a dozen stacks on the table. Photos were strewn in front of the pair. Coffee cups spilled out of the trashcan. Amanda came into the room and settled into the chair opposite Nick. An assistant came through the door with a new tray of drinks, plus some potato chips and mints. Amanda laughed when Nick pushed aside old coffee paraphernalia to make room for the new snacks.

"Thanks, Liz," Nick said as he offered Amanda a soft drink. He noticed Amanda was wearing a long skirt and a peach-colored blouse; she had an evening wrap with her. As she poured some Diet Coke into a cup, Nick noticed how the afternoon sun streaming in from the west window burnished her auburn hair. He turned in his chair. The sun was already dipping toward the harbor. She must be dressed to go out for the evening, Nick realized. She looked rested. Dangling crystal earrings grazed her cheeks, casting sparks like fire against her skin.

To Amanda, Nick looked bushed. His button-down shirt opened unevenly at the throat. His rumpled khakis had ketchup—or blood—splashed across one knee. His day-old beard was closer to week old, but he still looked attractive. Despite fatigue lines around the corners, Nick's eyes gleamed with life. She smiled and tried to keep her color even.

Gail watched Nick watching Amanda. She spied a flush moving up the back of Nick's neck. His index finger lightly tapped his right thigh and he was staring, transfixed. Since her partner was distracted, Gail dove in. "Thanks, Ms. Carlisle, for coming in again." Nick snapped out of his trance. He reached for a Coke and poured it into a cup while he listened to the two women.

"Oh, call me Amanda, please. I haven't talked to you since that first day, but you must have been very busy since then."

"You have too, it sounds like. You had the break-in..."

"Yes."

"Hopefully you're recovered. Sometimes it happens." Amanda nodded. "We need your insight on a couple of things," Gail continued. "We really want to crack this thing..."

"OK, first of all, Amanda," Nick said authoritatively, "we want to talk some more about that vision thing. You thought there might be two people involved."

"How do you do that, by the way?" Gail asked.

"Well it's not a psychic trick or anything. It's sort of an imaginary stroll, a mind-walk, alongside another person's psyche."

"OK, so you kind of watch?"

"Observe. In this case, in hindsight. Since I saw it firsthand that day, I tried to revisit the murder scenario in my memory, looking at the details and feeling my way through the killer's process. Kind of entering the space with them, so to speak."

"Walking around inside the mind of the perp?"

Amanda nodded. Gail looked at Nick who was nodding like Amanda's perp stroll was run of the mill. "OK," she continued. "Why the idea of two killers?"

"Well, what Nick and I talked about was that there seemed to be a progression of steps in Ed's, uh, the murder."

"Yes we're thinking that too. Did you know drugs were involved?"

"No, but that would make sense somehow." She sipped her Coke. "Why?"

"Because it seemed like he was immobilized, then..."

"Mutilated?"

"And then murdered." Amanda shuddered. "If he had been administered some chemicals that relaxed him, he would still have been alive to..."

"Torment," Gail added cheerfully, "before he died."

"Why *two* people?" Nick asked.

"Well you would know better than I what the probable sequence of events was, but it seems to me that it took time to do it all. And maybe it took two people to do it that way, to control Ed, to manage the environment, to complete all the tasks until Ed was finally dead."

"We found Valium and lethal levels of Digitek in the Doc's system."

"Oh, I forgot that Ed had a heart condition. That explains the Digitek. Do you think Valium was for sedation?"

"Probably. A Digitek overdose eventually killed him." Nick added.

"How much was there?"

"Three times the normal amount."

"Wow." Amanda sunk in the chair.

"What about the mutilations? Did you notice them specifically?" Gail asked, leaning over and popping open a sparkling water.

"Well I saw the cord, of course. And his hand on the desk. I guess I realized there was a knife or something sticking out of his..."

"Groin."

"I only saw the hand and...groin...wounds at first. And the smashed cup. Then I realized later I'd bumped into the desk and the computer had flashed. It came to me later that he had something like pornography on the screen. I got a sense that the mutilation and the pornography were linked somehow. Maybe that the mutilation was in retribution. Or even part of a ritual of some kind."

"Retribution?" Gail asked. "It's possible the killer never even saw it."

"Could be. But the areas of mutilation seemed geared to...sexual retribution."

"Tell us what you know about Ed's using child pornography," Nick pushed on.

"I had no idea he was doing it. It's absolutely verboten in a mental health clinic."

"We found a lot of it in his computer history, both in his home system and at the clinic."

Amanda frowned. "Oh God, I'm shocked. Ed was a brilliant man...but...I guess he had some major problems."

"Seems so. Why would someone like Ed use child porn, especially a psychiatrist who's trained in the psychological and professional reasons to avoid it?"

Amanda closed her eyes for a moment, searching. "Well, if I put my clinical hat on, the research shows that with a typical porn user— if there is such a thing—there's often a progression in pornographic consumption. A user is often a sex addict who seeks sexual stimulation when a partner or paraphernalia is not available. The porn acts as an aphrodisiac. It's then followed by sexual release—masturbation. I have a hard time seeing Ed doing this in his office but I guess if you have the evidence..."

"Go on." Gail looked at Nick. He sat stone-faced, listening.

"In the case of child pornography, the individual eroticizes...children." Amanda had a hard time hiding her disgust. This wasn't some clinical case; this was Ed, for God's sake. "Therefore, merely seeing children, touching them, being with them stimulates the addiction. Often, an active porn addiction requires more and more explicit material. As time progresses, the addict gets desensitized to the shocking images. Child porn, child sexual manipulation, exploitation—they become part of the package—and then there's an increasing tendency to act out the behaviors seen in the pornography."

"So if the doc was using it over a lot of years, he might have forgotten what the limits were?" Nick asked.

"Even in his own office?" Gail queried.

"Yes." Amanda grimaced. "He might have begun acting out, even in the office, seeing children, blending his sexual needs with his clinical responsibilities, taking risks, getting high on the danger."

"Even blatantly approaching clinic children?"

"I can't believe I am saying this about Ed, but yes, he might have lost all sense of boundaries and started doing *anything* to make his sexual fantasies real."

"So if the killer or killers saw him in the act, so to speak, what do you think would happen?"

"Depending on who it or they were, they might get angry..."

"Or snap..."

"Or snap."

"OK, so the motive may coincide with the doc's actions *in the moment.*"

Amanda had to ask. "Was he masturbating when he died?"

"We found semen." The three fell silent for a moment.

"Who, in your opinion, would turn homicidal if they saw the doc doing that?" Nick gently asked. "You know, make him suffer for sport, then kill him?"

"Someone who'd been a victim."

"Now? Before?"

"Could be both."

"Of all the people in the clinic, or friends, or family, or patients or patient families, who does your gut tell you did this to Ed?"

"Someone close."

"How close?"

"Look how intimate the actions were. I sense this is someone able to get close to him—in his office, near his desk, up against him.

Somebody who had drugs or access to them and the weapons handy. Someone who would sink to murder."

"Is it possible it was just S&M?" Gail asked.

"Well I'm really no expert, but this might have been sex play that evolved into murder."

"You mean foreplay with the doc using the restraints as part of sexual bondage?"

"Perhaps. Or maybe this was a sexualized murder from start to finish."

Gail thought about it for a minute. "What's the psychological profile of a killer like this?"

"Perhaps a previous victim driven to the edge. A victim to whom the exercise of sexual power and suffering was essential. That's a major clue my instincts tell me. Someone psychotic perhaps, certainly somebody sex savvy, but also willing to put the man to death. A punisher."

Nick remembered the planner and handed it to her. "Speaking of clues, take a look at this, will you? It's Ed Michael's planner. He wrote all kinds of stuff in here. We're trying to see if there's a link between his notations and the bloody letters on the desk."

Amanda pored over the pages. "Sure. It looks like Ed's planner. He wrote in it a lot. The cartoons are definitely his."

"Can you decipher some of this?" Nick turned to a page two weeks before the murder. "The codes don't mean anything to us. What's this, for example: *N.P. – P.S. (I hate you and you and you, stop following me)*.

Amanda burst out laughing. "Sorry. Gallows humor. N.P. is probably the patient's initials. P.S. is most likely the diagnosis: paranoid schizophrenic. *I hate you and you and you, stop following me* sounds like Ed being sarcastic."

"Huh?" Gail looked puzzled.

"A paranoid schizophrenic hears voices, *bad* voices, and he or she is paranoid about what the voices say, tormenting the patient no matter where he or she goes. Ed's amusing himself, I guess."

"The guy had quite a sense of humor, didn't he?"

"He had a genius IQ; I imagine he got bored. He loved cartoons, puns, clinical humor, making psychological fun of people."

"What a guy."

"How about this," Nick read. "*A.L. + G.V. = Bord + Nar = pure bliss.*"

"Oh. I guess that's a woman—A.L.—and a man—G.V.—and she's a borderline and he's a narcissist. These are severe personality disorder types who often find each other in relationships. They drive each other mad with drama, drama, drama."

"How about this one: *M.J.—ADHD pyro (come on, baby, light my fire).* Oh wait, let me guess. Pyro is a pyromaniac...and ADHD is attention def disorder? So this is a hyperactive kid who also sets things on fire?" Nick was pretty sure he was right.

"Sounds pretty close to me."

"'Come on, baby, light my fire' takes on a certain blue humor in retrospect, though." Gail frowned, studying the pages.

"Was he in the habit of leaving other little messages around?" Nick asked.

"Messages? Not that I saw on a regular basis...except, of course, the letters he scrawled on his desk."

"OK what did your perp walk tell you about that?" Gail leaned in.

"Somehow, I have a feeling that that came after the killer had left the room. I think it was some kind of message for us, you. I'm no expert but it seems to me that if the killer had seen it, he or they would have wiped it..."

"Maybe they were interrupted..."

"And left before the doc expired," Nick finished it for them. "In the final moments, Ed spelled out the letters."

They pondered it for a moment. "OK, counselor," Nick said quickly, "what's the *F-R-E-* message about, in your opinion?"

"The most obvious word to me is *Freud*," Amanda answered.

"Why would he write that?"

"Wow, lots of reasons. Maybe he was recognizing Freudian dynamics in himself as he died. Maybe Freudian aspects in his killer."

"Speak English, counselor."

"Well this might be kind of complicated, but Freud was the father of modern psychiatry and Ed's idol. Ed loved spouting Freudian theory. Freud's view of personality development was that we all pass through key psychosexual stages in the first six years of life. He thought human behavior is determined by a combination of irrational forces, unconscious motivations, and biological and instinctual drives that roll around in our psyches as we grow. These impact our personality development as we grow into adulthood."

"OK," Nick said, scratching his beard, but following it. "Keep going."

"To understand how we pass through these early phases, Freud devised the concept of a personality system."

"Is that the id, ego thing?" Gail jumped in.

"Yes. Freud thought personality was structured around three human energy systems: the id, the biological and instinct component; the ego, the psychological part or traffic cop; and the superego, the social component and judge.

"OK, id, ego, superego. I get it. Go on," Nick said.

"Freud thought that because the amount of energy is limited, one system can gain control at the expense of the other two *if* a person undergoes early childhood experiences that damage the person's ability to evolve into a fully-integrated personality."

"OK, so if I remember this right, the id part likes pleasure, correct?"

"Yes. It does everything to *avoid* pain and anxiety, and *experience* pleasure. The ego deals with the external world of reality and regulates the personality. The superego decides what behavior is bad or good. It strives for perfection. Ed loved cracking id jokes—linking it to people's idiosyncrasies, like overspending, sucking on water bottles, smoking."

"So what would create a whacko who sexually abuses and/or kills people?" Nick asked.

"According to Freud, the integrating personality system also evolves through various stages in childhood. One is the oral stage where suckling, getting nourishment, pleasure and pain are experienced."

Nick pointed to Gail's tic tacs. "A holdover?"

"Maybe, maybe not." Amanda smiled warmly at Gail.

"Go on," Gail commanded, making a face at Nick.

"Another one is the phallic stage, the one where sexual desires pop up and get projected onto mommy or daddy at first, but later are supposed to turn outward into normal healthy sexual behavior with more appropriate partners."

Gail glanced at Nick but he ignored her. "That's where the penis envy thing comes in, right?"

"Yes, you got it!" Amanda smiled at Nick. "And there's the anal stage, etc. So if trauma occurs at one of these stages..."

"Like child abuse or war deprivation or torture or murder..." Gail jumped in.

"Sometimes the individual skews emotionally or gets fixated on say, anal sex."

"Skews?"

"Skews toward one of the energy systems or gets fixated during one of the developmental stages so they don't grow properly into a well-balanced adult personality."

"And then we get em, right?" Nick inferred.

"Sometimes. Not all criminals are personality disordered, but many of them are. If Mack the Knife, for example, was traumatized as a child, say beaten every day or forced to do things no child should have to do, his personality may even splinter into discrete parts, one with memory of the abuse, another with no memory, in order to cope. If Mack is repeatedly molested as a toddler, his child personality may also begin to associate sexual pain with pleasure. The child grows to adulthood and perhaps becomes a serial rapist. In a case like that, the ego and superego systems get sublimated to the id..."

"Shoved in the trunk, so to speak..."

"Yes." Amanda nodded. "They no longer work properly to moderate the person's behavior. That is, to keep them from doing illegal or immoral things to get their needs met. Without treatment, they keep making bad choices."

"They molest or kill people and think it's OK?"

"Yes. To them it's OK within the framework of their skewed personality system. Of course, that doesn't make it moral—or legal. But to them, psychologically, it makes sense."

"So psychiatrist Ed Michael was treating people while he was a screwed up personality himself?" Nick summarized. "How could he do that and get away with it? You didn't know, for example."

"Freud might say that Ed's superego wanted to be a psychiatrist, but his id had more power. Therefore, he was perhaps more and more driven to act out his inappropriate, addictive sexual impulses in order to satisfy his id. He was split. He may have compartmentalized his impulses and that's how he coped with it. When he was around the rest of us clinicians, he must have been able to stay in his superego self for the most part. So we missed it until his id forced his hand."

"The shrink part lost the battle to the pervert part?" Gail asked brightly.

Nick was more direct. "In other words, he was fucked-up big time."

"Seems so."

"Sorry for the language."

"No problem."

"So what does that say about the murderer and Ed's message?" Nick asked.

"Maybe Ed was leaving us some message about himself as a classic case of a Freudian screwup?" Gail guessed.

"Couldn't he just have been telling us who the killer was?" Nick insisted.

"You mean 'Freud' killed him?" Amanda asked.

"Freud getting even?"

"Now that's a thought. Freudian fallout. Id on id. Total war." Amanda played with her cup, lost in thought.

Nick poured himself another Coke and sipped for a moment. "OK, there's got to be something we're missing somewhere in all this. We need a real name and a real person." The group fell silent once again.

"Well, right now, *my* id, ego, and superego definitely need a break." Gail stifled a yawn.

"Me too. I guess that'll do it for now. We appreciate your coming down, Amanda."

"No problem. Glad to help, although I'm not sure if I did. Sorry about all the Freud stuff. Maybe it was too much."

Gail's beeper went off and she left the room to take the call. "Naw," Nick said, "we need to explore every angle so whatever you can offer helps. Not sure about the psychology stuff, but it's grist for the mill."

"Freud also said sometimes a banana is just a banana."

"Yeah, I think I've heard that one." Nick decided to take the plunge. "Hey, you look like you're going out."

"Yes. Meeting a girlfriend down at the US Grant. She dropped me here and I thought I'd walk back. It's just a few blocks and I have my Taser with me, although I really don't think I'd have to use it." She rolled her eyes. "And my dad's trailing me—for safety's sake."

"Oh, well I'm heading out. Can I give you a lift?"

Amanda paused for a second, and then answered. "Sure. If it's not too much trouble...and I don't look like I'm getting hauled off to county jail."

"No problem," Nick laughed. "Unmarked car."

"OK, great."

Nick flagged Gail he was leaving, and then piled some files and Ed's planner in his briefcase while Amanda picked up her wrap and bag. Moments later, the two were in the elevator, heading down to Nick's vehicle waiting below.

Chapter Thirty-Two

Downtown

Nick's car edged toward the water along Broadway straight toward the sun about to melt into San Diego bay like a round pat of butter. Downtown traffic was slow. Businesspeople were getting off work, scurrying to their cars and rapid transit, weaving in and out of the homeless who shuffled along the street. Some of the panhandlers barely missed getting briefcased in the back by people rushing by. Out-of-towners in resort wear milled around, especially as Nick neared the Grant Hotel and Horton Plaza. Downtown was percolating and people poured in to join the brew.

"This whole murder thing must be pretty disturbing for you," Nick said collegially, idling the car at a light and glancing over at Amanda.

"True." She turned back from the window. "It's pretty awful having someone you're close to...gone like that."

"I see it every day so you kind of get used to it."

"What do you do to get your mind off it?"

"Sports, Padres, stuff like that. And Tracy." Nick felt shy about his personal life.

"Oh," Amanda said flatly.

"My little girl."

"Oh," Amanda repeated, upbeat. "How old is she?"

"Seven."

"That's a great age. Still sweet, not teenage yet. You must have fun with her."

"Yeah, I share visitation with my ex, but Tracy and I are cool. Daddy's girl, you know. Seeing her tomorrow, actually."

"Any fun plans?"

"Not sure. She loves to swim. Might do Sea World but we were there a couple of months ago. Penguins are her favorite. How about you? I mean plans for the weekend?"

"No kids of course. Hope to...someday." She blushed. "Playing the weekend by ear. Still at loose ends really with no clinic work and things up in the air."

Around Third Avenue, Nick found a parking spot and pulled in. "Is this close enough?"

"Sure. It's just around the corner." She gathered her things up off her lap and unbuckled her seat belt.

"So you like the Grant, huh?" Nick said, lingering.

"Oh yeah. We like the ambience of the old glamour—I mean at least for a drink! But then we usually head over to Horton Plaza or the Gaslamp for jazz after that."

"They've really done up the old Grant since the renovation. For a hotel built in 1910, it's looking pretty good now."

"Do you like old hotels?"

"Sometimes. Depends on the company," Nick responded, and then wished he hadn't.

Amanda laughed. "I hear you on that one." She waited a moment then reached for the handle to get out. "Um, this may be kind of weird, but would you like to come in for a minute? I mean, for a glass of wine or something?"

"Where's your bodyguard?"

"Behind us." Nick realized the old guy must be watching him too. "He's going to meet a buddy at the bar so Shel and I can chat."

Nick smiled, thinking it through. She was released as a suspect, but he had mixed feelings. He was drawn to her, he admitted, but he didn't quite know what to make of it. Not sure about bumping into Father Phil. He also thought about his empty condo near Petco Park where a stone-cold pizza sat hard as a rock in the freezer waiting for him.

"OK, for a little while." He turned off the engine and got out. Amanda exited the other side and the pair walked around the corner to the hotel. Nick glanced back at Phil who followed at a distance trying to look nonchalant.

The US Grant touted itself as one of San Diego's luxury hotels in the heart of downtown. It was built near the turn of the century by Ulysses S. Grant Jr., the wealthy son of the famous Civil War general and US president. Grant Jr. had become rich from Wall Street, but he needed a better climate for his ailing wife. He and Fannie headed west and bought the old Alonzo Horton Hotel in the booming city by the sea. Later, Grant razed the old hotel to build the luxury US Grant, complete with pictures of the patriarch in the lobby. Various dignitaries stayed there over the years in the two grand presidential suites or one of the elegant rooms. Famous on the National Register of Historic Sites, the hotel also made the six o'clock news in 1969 when a women's protest finally forced the Grant Grill, the hotel lobby eatery, to start admitting women before 3:00 pm.

Seated in that very same Grill, Shelby Dutton, dressed in a shell-pink pantsuit and glittery sandals, was tucked into a booth near the back. She was nursing a white-wine spritzer when Nick and Amanda wandered in. Coldplay blared on the speakers. Several businesspeople bent over their smart phones while they sipped martini specials and noshed on Asian-fusion appetizers.

"Hey," Amanda called to Shelby as they moved through the crowd toward her. Shelby chortled as Amanda and Nick sauntered toward her. She guessed instantly that Amanda's companion must be the famous Detective Caswell. The day-old beard and surfer hair were a dead giveaway. Amanda's cheeky look told the rest.

"Hi. I'm Shelby Dutton." Shelby reached out a hand to Nick after she and Amanda shared a hug.

"Nick Caswell. How are you?"

"Great."

"Nick just stopped in for a minute," Amanda said quickly as she sat. She saw her dad stop at the end of the bar and order a drink. He soon became engrossed in a conversation with an older man but Amanda knew he was keeping an eye on both entrances as well as on her—and Nick. Sure enough, when his beer arrived, he looked up and winked.

Nick motioned for the server to come over and the three ordered cocktails: chardonnay for Amanda, another spritzer for Shelby, Corona for Nick.

"Thanks for waiting for me. Sorry it took so long."

"No prob. I know police work is intense."

Nick grinned, playing with the menu. He had to admit it was kind of nice relaxing in an elegant place with two attractive women who weren't sporting badges or shackles. It wasn't that he didn't get out much. It's just that he was buried in crime. For once, he was going to hang out in the regular world for a half hour. Normal was nice for a change.

"So how's it going?" Shelby asked. "Find out whodunit?"

"Lots of leads. No arrests."

"If I can add something," Amanda said tentatively, "it seems like more things are coming to light, aren't they?" Nick shrugged. "I guess no results is still no results," Amanda went on. "I suppose I should really just enjoy the time off."

"Poor Amanda. You're used to treating victims, not being one, aren't you?" Shelby offered.

"Hard to sit around not doing anything to fix it." Amanda turned to Nick. "I wonder how you do it, day in and day out."

"Kind of fell into it." He popped the menu on the end of the table. "Dad was a cop—I guess you may have figured. Actually I started out wanting to own a sugar shack in Baja."

"So do you still find time to surf?"

"Sometimes. When I have the energy to get my wetsuit on."

"Where's your favorite place?" Shelby was firing questions as fast as she could. Sometimes the lawyer just came out.

"Oh, all along the coast, really."

"Ever been to Tunnels beach? My brother loves that place."

"On Kauai? Yeah that's a great place."

Amanda enjoyed the chance to observe Nick. His face relaxed and the frown between his eyes disappeared while he fielded Shelby's questions.

Nick could feel both women studying him. "So what do you two do for fun?" He took a swig of his Corona that had finally arrived.

Amanda sipped her chardonnay. "We've been friends since college so we've done quite a bit. We were just planning a trip to Cabo over July Fourth, as a matter of fact."

"That's a pretty cool place, I hear. What do you like about it?"

Shelby quipped: "The massages and the margaritas!"

"Sounds like you have some tales to tell."

"Yeah but we're not talking, detective." Shelby dissolved into giggles.

"How about you? Any good stories from your surfing safaris?" Amanda buttonholed Nick.

"You'll have to wait for my memoirs." Everyone laughed. "It's good to relax, frankly. Not much humor in my work these days." Nick tossed back some more beer.

Growing serious, Shelby asked, "Are there a lot of crimes you never solve?"

"Sure."

"How do you deal with it?"

"Do our best. Wring everything we can out of the case, then either solve it or shelve it. Not much more we can do."

"How about this one?" Amanda asked.

"Not sure. Something tells me we're getting closer. Speaking of, I really should get back to it. It's been nice meeting you Shelby...and sharing a drink with you two ladies."

"Likewise," they both said at once.

Nick paused, and then got up. "Have a fun rest of the evening. Amanda, I'll be going over some things between now and Monday. OK to call if I need some assistance?" He dropped a ten dollar bill on the table.

"Anytime. Thanks for helping me out with that break-in nightmare, by the way. You were really on it and I appreciate it."

"No problem." A look passed between them. "OK, I'll be seeing you." Nick strode out of the room, glancing at Phil who subtly tipped his glass at him as he passed. Shelby watched Nick's back until he disappeared around the corner. She looked over at Amanda who sat innocently sipping her wine. Then the two burst out laughing.

* * *

Across the street from the US Grant the kid sat on a long, white bench. The bench stood within splashing distance of the fountain on the square in front of the Horton Plaza entrance. A few steps away, the quirky outdoor Horton Plaza mall fanned up and out, its turrets and towers framed against a sunset sky. People streamed in, heading to the shops, movie theaters, and cafes inside.

The kid had been watching for some time. Observing Nick's Crown Vic as it left the police building. Noting Amanda Carlisle next to him in the passenger seat. Following the Vic as it trekked down Broadway, and then parked near the Grant. Amused that Nick was oblivious to being tailed. The kid had parked down the street, then watched, curious, as Nick and Amanda went inside the lobby. Within minutes Nick had left the hotel sans Amanda.

"Very cozy," the kid said to the pigeons flapping around the bench for food. The day's events had been wearing. But they were still no closer to figuring it out than a few days ago, the kid was certain. "It's not possible," the boy said to a black footed pigeon pecking at his shoe. The kid shifted the windbreaker. Felt the weight of it dangling off one shoulder, then grabbed it before it hit the pavement. He laid the jacket casually on the bench close by.

I watch all this, just go along, doing my thing. Talk, talk, talk. My God, how boring is that? How goddamn fucking boring. They sit around blabbing, taking the crap from every goddamn fucker that comes along. I'm the one that does things. Makes it happen. The ONE. I decide. She doesn't know it yet. Someday...

Amanda and Shelby suddenly emerged from the US Grant. The kid almost missed it. The two women dashed across the street toward Horton Plaza, directly toward the fountain. Watching them head straight at him, the kid slid to the end of the bench, then bent down as if tying a shoe.

At that moment, a young couple sat down near the kid on the bench. Fortunately, they blocked Amanda and Shelby's view. From his position, he felt Amanda and Shelby's shadows pass over the bench. Sneaking a peek, the kid smiled as the women strolled between the plaza arches and went up the stairs to the stores, oblivious. Lost in conversation, the two disappeared inside the mall. The tall, gray-haired man trailing them passed near the fountain and noted the variety of people sitting on the dozen or so benches scattered around. He even noticed the kid who was bending up from the ground, but he kept scanning and passed on, keeping the two women in his sights. He picked up his pace and disappeared up the escalator.

You see, invisible.

The kid turned and noticed the young couple making a racket at the end of the bench. They were playing kissy face. The greasy-haired boyfriend had rings in each ear. A scar slashed from his chin to his right ear. The girlfriend had purple hair with a beret on top; her tongue was pierced. Both had on tattered blue jeans topped by black leather jackets. The girl's cell was leopard skin. She was speaking loud Spanish into it as she sucked on a cigarette. In between puffs, the boyfriend was Frenching her like he was licking an ice cream cone. They suddenly realized someone was watching them. The pair turned to study the kid for a moment. The boyfriend opened his mouth to say something, and then hesitated.

The kid stared back, cold and calm. Slowly he reached into the left pocket of the windbreaker and fingered the Swiss army hunter resting there. The kid loved that camouflage knife. Loved the feel of the smooth handle, the camouflage stump, and the way the steel-gutting blade slid erect from it in one easy snap. Holding it lightly, the knife felt strong and sure in the kid's hand hidden in the folds of the pocket.

Pop had seen to that. Pop had taught the kid the art of the blades. Which one to choose for slitting an animal's throat versus the one for gutting its entrails before hauling the dead thing home. It was all in the blade and the twist of the wrist. The kid had been schooled. Proven. So the kid stared back at the greasy boyfriend, fingering the hunter, steeled in case the boyfriend chose wrong.

Behind them, a boy's yell broke the moment. The new teen had pirate tattoos up both arms; he screamed to his buddy as he scampered around the fountain toward the couple. Greasy boyfriend and his girl got up and loped across to their buddy, the kid forgotten.

Calmly, the kid squeezed the blade back into its home, and then dropped the knife into the bottom of the pocket. The pigeons were pecking for crumbs again. He watched the scroungy birds, deciding. Trail Amanda Carlisle through Horton Plaza or go home? The kid decided it had been a long day.

They still have no idea. Not even her. The kid chuckled, got up, and grabbed the windbreaker. *No one knows. Not Amanda. Not the others. Not even that cop. Clueless. Always the way. Anyway, I've got time. But this weekend is it. Yup, this is it.*

The kid moved across the square, toward the side street where the car was parked. A homeless man watched the kid as he passed. Gordy considered whether to beg a buck—or pass. Something about the kid made the homeless man pause, and he slunk back into the shadows. Waiting. Waiting until a friendlier mark happened by.

Gordy had been on the street a long time. Gordy knew how to read people. How to tell the ones who'd feel sorry for him from the ones who'd kick him in the groin if he got within three feet. Gordy knew. If anybody had asked him, he would've guessed the person passing by was a groin kicker. Or worse. Others might argue, but Gordy knew. He could smell it.

Chapter Thirty-Three

Names and Games

"Dig, Daddy!"

Tracy and Nick sat in the sand near the shoreline building sandcastles. The La Jolla sun was high in the Saturday sky. Nick could see boats tacking out a mile in the distance. A fishing boat headed out to deep water. Earlier, Tracy and Nick had paddled around in the shallows of the cove until Tracy got tired. Nick had been teaching her the breaststroke until Tracy called it quits.

"Daddy, stop. You're trying to turn me into a fish!"

The pair climbed out and made a wet trail over to the towels near the rocks. Father and daughter were soon drying in the warm air, sipping Capri Suns. Later, Tracy had decided she wanted to build sandcastles. Now, the child was busy shoring up the sides of her two-foot-high castle, while Nick worked on the moat.

"Dig deeper, Daddy. We have to keep Lord Farquaad and his knights out of Princess Fiona's castle."

"Well OK, but how deep does it have to be?"

"Oh about up to your knees!" She giggled.

"My knees! Tracy, that will take all day."

"Yup. Better get going or Princess Fiona will get you."

"How come I'm surrounded by princesses who can do martial arts and also catch bad guys?"

"Cuz you're just lucky, Daddy, I guess." She dissolved into giggles, and then swooped around to the front of the castle, which was about to get breached by the incoming tide.

Nick enjoyed his time with Tracy. She'd just turned seven. Tracy loved Shrek. She wanted to be Princess Fiona when she grew up. Tough, but pretty. His little girl had been three when Nick and his ex split up. Or more correctly, when Nick's ex had decided she'd had enough of cops and robbers. Nick's schedule—and his move up the ladder in the force—kept him relentlessly busy. Ultimately, the marriage ran out of steam. At least Lauren had waited two years before she married again. Now Nick got most weekends and one night a week with his little princess—unless a murder got in the way.

Nick wished it had turned out better. He missed coming home to a family, especially when Tracy had been really young. Lauren had grown restless. Nick couldn't blame her. She'd come from a wealthy family and at first loved Nick's groundedness, as she called it. Ultimately the pair became oil and mud. No amount of counseling could save it. So he did his best as a single dad and tried to make up for lost hours when he and Tracy were together.

He worked hard to make things normal. Cooking fun meals, doing everyday things, not just keeping things big like a Disneyland Dad. So sand castles were fine with him. And Tracy seemed happy, too young to really remember when Lauren and he had been in love.

Nick looked over to the rocks, covered in marine life. Gazing at the slick seals and bulbous sea lions while he dug, he heard them honking and snorting as they rolled off the rocks into the cold water. The big brown sea lions lumbered around on their huge front flippers. Then they collapsed for a snooze on the rocks like brown bags of blubber with whiskers.

The seals, on the other hand, were fast and sleek. They dove in and out of the water like mini torpedoes, cavorting around their big, lazy cousins. The animals were slowly taking over the entire cove while they "hauled out"—sea-speak for lazing about on land. Some of the locals thought the animals should be removed. The kids were getting crowded out, they argued. Others—mostly tourists hanging over the railing from the park above—thought the frisky seals and belching sea lions were a hilarious circus act.

"Daddy, are you watching Clyde?"

"Who's Clyde, Tracy baby?"

"Clyde. That big one over there. The one making all the noise and smacking his flippers."

"Yes, I guess I'm checking him out."

"He's flirting with Julie."

"Who's Julie?"

"That dark brown one on the other rock. Don't you see her flirting back?"

Nick studied the two creatures. Mostly he just saw one sea lion belching and the other one burping in return.

"Well maybe..."

"Daddy they're in love. And Harold is jealous."

"Who's Harold?"

"The cute little black one splashing water on Clyde."

"Oh, OK, I see. Well Harold is a seal, Tracy. Clyde is a sea lion. And Julie is a sea lion."

"Well Harold can still like her even if he isn't a sea lion, can't he?"

"Ummm, I guess so." Nick knew that breeding subtleties were mostly lost on a seven-year-old.

"So if Clyde is a sea lion, do you think Clyde can roar?"

"You mean like Simba? No Simba is a lion. Clyde is a sea lion."

She considered that for a moment. "So what do they call little sea lions?"

"Sea lion cubs."

Tracy laughed at that one, not knowing exactly why it was funny but definitely knowing it was. "Oh, Daddy, you're so silly."

"You too, baby. Is the moat big enough yet?"

"Nope, Daddy, keep digging." Nick kept on realizing Tracy's taskmaster inclinations didn't come from her mother.

Soon, Tracy sat transfixed, watching the seals and sea lions waddle over the rocks, playing hide-and-seek with the sea. Nick watched her out of the corner of his eye. "Daddy?"

"Yes, sweetie."

"Can I ask you a question?"

"Sure."

"If Julie likes Clyde and Clyde likes Julie, they'll get married, right?"

"Um, well, they'll become mates. I don't know if they'll have a marriage ceremony under the sea or what."

"OK, Daddy. I have one more question. When Clyde and Julie get married, they'll have babies, right?"

"Well, I guess so." Nick stopped digging, pretty certain where this was headed.

"So, Daddy..."

"Yes?"

"How do Julie and Clyde make babies? I can't figure it out."

"Hey you silly, babies are for later," Nick answered, and then scooped Tracy up in his arms and changed the subject. "Let's talk about why you give names to everything."

"Because it's fun, Daddy."

"What makes it fun?"

"I don't know. I just do it so they'll be my friends."

Something tweaked in Nick's brain and he frowned for a moment. But he let it pass. Tracy was being Tracy and it was her day, her time. There was plenty of time to think about work and crime and killers and killing. Nick went back to shoring up the castle since the tide was coming in fast now and Princess Fiona's home was about to be toast.

A few minutes later, Tracy looked up. "Daddy, I'm going to go throw our cups away, OK?"

"Yup, no problem. Got to keep the beach neat. You know where the trash cans are, up the stairs?"

"Yup. I know. Been there a dozen times, silly."

"OK, you come right back, you hear? I'll hold the fort down—or should I say up—while you're gone."

"OK, Daddy. Be right back."

Tracy grabbed the cups and trash, stuffed them into an extra paper sack and headed across the sand then up the cliff steps to the cans on the grass at the top of the bluff. Down below, Nick watched her go, and then he turned back to see a wave heading his way. He scrambled to toss more sand on Fiona's castle. When he looked back, Tracy had disappeared. Nick wasn't too alarmed. He knew the cans were just up a few feet farther, so he waited patiently for her to come back down. He kept on digging.

Up top, Tracy walked across the grass about to dump the garbage when someone smiled at her.

"Hi."

"Hi." She dumped the garbage in.

"Cool day for swimming, huh?"

"Oh yeah," Tracy answered, smiling back, intrigued by the cheap flower lei the person was wearing. "And for building castles."

"So you're building sand castles?"

"Yup. What are those flowers for? Are those from Hawaii? I was just there. That's a lei, right?"

"Yup. These are really cool. Would you like one? I can give you one, if you want."

"Hmmm," Tracy considered it. "Well they sure are pretty, but my dad says I can't take things from strangers."

"I'm happy to get you one. There's a bunch of them just over there."

Tracy considered it some more. "Naw. I better get back. Got to take care of Fiona's castle."

"Well OK, you snooze, you lose."

"Yeah, OK. Gotta go. Bye."

"OK, see ya next time."

The kid watched the little girl as she turned and ran back across the grass and down the stone steps. The kid stepped closer to the edge of the cliff and looked down at Nick in the sand and Tracy running toward him. By the time Tracy remembered to tell her dad about the stranger at the trash can with the lei, Nick looked up alarmed, and then raced up the stairs. But the stranger was gone. Scanning the grass and keeping an eye on Tracy down below at the same time, Nick could see no one out of the ordinary, certainly no one with a lei.

Walking slowly down the stairs, Nick had a sickening feeling in his gut, like a rope was being pulled through it. It could be nothing, he told himself. Then again, it could be something. Trudging across the sand, he looked up just as Tracy and her castle were hit by a low wave that rolled in fast, swamping the little girl. Then the swell swept out again taking half the castle with it. Racing to Tracy, the stranger forgotten, Nick spent the next half hour consoling her when the child burst into tears.

Doggedly, they began anew a few feet closer to the cliff. The detective and his daughter spent another hour finishing off an even better castle for Fiona. But Nick's heart wasn't in it. Something was bothering him. He just didn't know yet exactly what.

* * *

Later that night, around nine o'clock, Nick sat in his deck chair with his feet up, sipping an iced tea. He was in pain, nursing a hell of a sunburn on his shins. He'd stupidly spent most of the day in the sun with Tracy without a drop of sunscreen. Tracy was home now in bed at her mom's, satiated with Chuck E. Cheese pizza and two new books from the children's bookstore downtown. She also had absolutely no sunburn at all since Nick had slathered her with Solarcaine several times but figured an old surfer like himself could handle the sun without help. Wrong.

Now Nick sat muttering on his deck. He was deep in the evidence again. The stranger encounter at the beach was bugging him, but not nearly as much as the photos staring back at him from the deck table, giving no clues. He scanned them all one more time. Ed's planner lay next to him. He'd been poring over the pages, trying to make sense of Ed's scribbles, getting nowhere.

The name equations he could make out since Amanda had deciphered a couple of them. Dr. Michael liked to play verbal games. Making rhymes, little jokes, double entendres, about people and things. There were a couple of interesting ones that he thought he could figure out:

KL + TJ = OCD + Mom = Howard Hughes in the making.

Probably meant the man was obsessive compulsive and his wife or mother was making it worse a la Howard Hughes. Nick knew Hughes had lived famously obsessed and paranoid until the day he died.

But then there were other names and events linked together that made no sense to him.

Frankl football, Dreikurs coffee, Skinner POW wow. Enns eruption, Perls meltdown, Jung meet.

The notes were written like appointments but there were never any first names attached. There were other names like *Adler, Rogers, Beck.* He even found Freud in there a few times as in *Freud consult,* but to Nick it seemed like the guy was checking research or something. Then there were lots of other acronyms stuffed in there like APA, AAPAA, SCARF, and ABPN. Must be associations or drug names or something Nick guessed

Maybe I am making this too hard, he decided. The shrink used letters, words, verbal play to track his life and the things and the people around him. It made sense then that he left a message in blood. It must have been relevant, for God's sake, not some theory or idea. A real clue that was meant to lead somewhere.

After another half hour, he leaned back, exhausted. The last thing he looked at before shuffling off to bed were the photos. Ed's death face stared back, grimacing, ungiving. "You asshole," Nick said to

Ed's pasty face. "Give. If you were so damn smart do you want to leave your killer out there somewhere to do it to somebody else? Give me the answer, you dead SOB!"

Nothing.

Nick's eyes drifted over the photos and other paraphernalia one last time before getting up. His eyes landed on the card Thomas had given the shrink. Nick read the words again for the umpteenth time.

"Ed. I want to blow you. Many happy returns. Fondly, Jung."

Nick read it and read it.

Nothing.

"The hell with it," Nick bellowed. "I'm going to bed." He got up and dragged himself off to his master bedroom armed with sunburn spray. It was going to be a long night.

Chapter Thirty-Four

Finding Freud

Amanda woke up to wet sandpaper scraping her arm. "Emily, stop licking me." Emily sat back on her haunches, blinking. The feline clearly had no concept of sleeping in on a Sunday morning. She wanted to be fed.

Now.

Amanda slipped on her robe and sandals, and then padded out to the kitchen to refill the cat's bowl. Since she was up anyway, she abandoned the idea of a late-morning snooze and started the day. Amanda looked over at her brand new slider; it felt good to be home. With a new security system in place, Phil agreed to back off until later today when she planned to head out for groceries. For now, she felt safe in her own nest once more.

Opening the front door, she heard the security chime ding lightly as she saw two newspapers waiting outside on the stoop. The alarm's at-home setting allowed her to go in and out freely, but it gave Amanda immediate notice if a window or door were breached. She picked up the two papers, and then noticed a bulge inside one of them. Opening it, a plastic lei fell out. Amanda's heart froze. She looked around, but saw no one. She paused for a moment, and then hurriedly clasped the papers to her chest, scooped up the lei, and ducked inside.

Shutting and locking the door once more, she put the papers on her kitchen table but dropped the lei across the room near the slider like it was a rattlesnake. Maybe I'm overreacting, Amanda told herself. Maybe they're giving one to everyone. Some promotion. She watched it for a moment, but decided to put on a big pot of organic coffee. Periodically, she craned her head around the kitchen pillar to look at the lei, but it lay there, inert, exactly where she'd left it.

While the coffee brewed, she toasted a sesame seed bagel, buttered it with Lurpak, and scooped up the front page of the *Los Angeles Times* and dug in. An hour later, she took stock: two cups of coffee down, a bagel and a half gone, one paper to go. She was reaching for the *San Diego Union* when she heard a rattle behind her. She swiveled to see the lei snaking across the floor. Emily had it in her mouth and was dragging the thing toward the hallway.

"Emily!" Amanda hollered. The cat jumped and dropped the lei; then she ran into the office and disappeared under the desk. Amanda walked over carefully, and then started to laugh. "My God, this is ridiculous." Walking over to the slider, she hung it carefully on the handles and decided to forget about it.

Her cell went off. "Hello?" she shouted into it after she punched answer.

"Amanda?"

She instantly recognized his voice. "Oh sorry, hi, Nick. How are you?"

"Actually, I'm nursing a bit of a sunburn, but other than that, I'm doing pretty well."

"So your Daddy Day got the best of you?"

"Well, I would say my stupidity did, actually." He could hear her laughing. "I was wondering if you might be up for a consult later today, say around one o'clock or so? I've got some things I need to show you because...I'm stumped, frankly. If you haven't got anything else planned for this afternoon, of course."

"Oh, I'd be glad to help. One o'clock would be fine. Downtown?"

"Oh no. You don't have to come all the way down here. OK if I come up?"

"Sure. By the way, I'm back in my place. Everything's in place. Anything I should be thinking about in particular before you get here?"

"Just how we can put it all together and solve this thing."

"OK, will do."

"I'm bringing up copies of some of the evidence. I feel pretty sure there's something in there but I need assistance deciphering it."

"No problem."

Amanda ended the call, ditched the newspapers, and headed to the closet. "What do you wear to catch a killer?" she said to Emily who was now stretched out by the bedroom window soaking up sun. Emily glanced back at Amanda and slapped her tail, cat code for "whatever." The fur ball yawned and went to sleep.

Jeans, Amanda decided. Forty-five minutes later, she was fully dressed and out on the couch enjoying a glass of mango juice. Staring across the deck, at the pool area, her mind wandered. It had been days since they'd found Ed. Amanda knew Nick and Gail must be itching to close the case. But how could she help? She decided to call Phil. Dumping the dishes in the dishwasher she settled back out on the couch with a fresh cup of coffee and her phone. Amanda punched speed dial.

"Dad?" she said after the fifth ring when he finally picked up.

"Hello?"

"Hey. It's me."

"Is everything OK?

"Fine, fine. Dad, Nick Caswell's coming up in a little while. He's asking me to look over some things."

"I bet they're putting you to work profiling."

"Well I don't know I'd call it that exactly, but they want me to look at some things in depth. Any words of wisdom, Father dear?"

"Remember what I told you, Amanda. Murder is murder. Motive, action, payoff. Perps leave traces. In your shrink's case the mutilation is a giant road sign in my book. My bet is that's where he lost it. One thing to kill somebody. But to carve him up? That's personal."

"Makes sense."

"Who'd do that? Ask yourself. The killer's practically giving you his name. Look for it. It's there. Tell those detectives that. They probably got their noses so far up their arse they can't see the forest for the trees."

"Mixed metaphor, Dad, but I get your drift. They need to back up a bit."

"Yup. That's where you come in, I bet. Fresh eyes. Is it that Caswell kid again?"

"Yes, Dad. He's really pretty good, I think."

"Tell him to give me a call if he can't crack it." She heard him cover the phone so she wouldn't hear him cackling.

"OK, thanks for the help. Unless something changes, see you this afternoon."

"Yup. OK, punkin. Happy huntin'.'"

"'Practically giving you his name,'" she repeated Phil's words as she hung up, letting the sound reverberate across the room.

Amanda stared across at the bougainvillea and the palm trees and the pool, not registering any of it. She was doing her best to see the killer's face. See the killer's actions again. Feel the enormous force of someone driven to carve his or her ire on Ed's defenseless body. But someone who misstepped. In the throes of mayhem and murder, neglected to hide completely. Tipped their hand so to speak, the hand that held the knife...

A peal cut through her thoughts. Amanda jumped as she realized it was the doorbell. Cautiously, she padded to the door, checked the peephole, and then opened it slowly.

"Hi. You made good time."

"Yeah," Nick said sheepishly. "Guess I'm a little early. Brought lattes since I know you like them."

Amanda burst out laughing. "God this will be my fourth cup today! I'll have to go slow. Feel free to pull me off the ceiling later if you need to!"

"Roger that. Where can we work?"

Amanda gestured toward the dining room table. Nick moved over to it but some of the framed photos on the wall caught his eye. One was of an older woman in a red bandana sunning by a fountain. She was shelling peas.

"That's a nice picture."

"Thanks, it's my mother."

"Did you take it?"

"Yes. A few months before she died."

He stared at it awhile, and then looked around the room, noticing others. When he was here before, he'd been completely focused on the B&E and all the broken glass. "Are you a photographer?"

"Oh, amateur. I like doing it. Started in high school."

"Nice." His eyes moved around the room, gazing from one scene to the next. Tall, gray trees bending in a field of yellow grain, a sled standing empty in an icy lane, balloons rising up in the sky over the racetrack, her mother surrounded by sunflowers holding a basket loaded with persimmons. "There's something about them. Don't know how you'd say it. Personal maybe, but..."

"Intimate but distant. Like looking through a keyhole but not being part of it. Heard it before."

"They're still pretty good."

There was an awkward moment.

"Thanks."

"Well anyway, these are photos you might appreciate in a different way. Hold on to your stomach." Nick pulled photos and documents out of his briefcase and dumped them on the bare wood. With a flourish, he spread the photos across the table so they could both see them all at once. He placed the planner off to the side and sat down in one of the dining chairs.

"Ouch." His face contorted. "Sunburn. Ankles are the worst." He turned back to the photo spread. He waited, while Amanda gazed at them.

She was enthralled by the grotesque images so brutal it was hard to look away. The investigators had captured Ed's office, his computer screen, the crime detail—and his corpse—from nearly every angle. Here it was in living color, what she'd only recollected in the murky haze of a stricken bystander. Nick gave her a moment to adjust.

"Wow. It's...it's overwhelming." She sat down heavily.

"Sorry it's so bad," Nick said. "We see so much of this, we're jaded."

"I can see why you need to be."

"OK, at any rate, do you notice anything that stands out?"

"I guess as I look at it, it seems...like...overkill to me. Pardon the pun."

"Yup. Overkill would cover it."

Amanda studied the pictures of the bloody letters. It was the first time she'd seen them from several angles. "This looks to me like he was clearly trying to spell out *F-R-E-U-D*. I know Ed and this seems pretty likely."

"OK, so if it is *F-R-E-U-D*, surely it's the killer."

"Well that seems more apparent when I really look at it now. But for the life of me, I can't see how that makes any sense. Freud is dead."

"Maybe."

"Maybe?"

"What if he's not? What if Freud's alive and well, and murdered the dear departed doc in the cold, clear light of day?"

Amanda was stumped. "How?"

"It's in this mess, I think. The key to the perp's identity. Maybe not *your* Freud. But maybe *Ed's*."

Amanda's eyes drifted over the photos, searching. Over and over she scanned, sifting the images.

The desk.

Ed's face.

The grimace.

The computer screen filled with pornography.

The medicine cabinet.

The floor, the window cord, the conference table.

The splatters on the carpet.

The footprints on the floor leading back to the door.

The smudged fingerprints on Ed's neck.

The spilled liquid.

The smashed cup.

The implement slashed through Ed's hand.

The bloody blade stuck in Ed's crotch.

Then she saw it.

Something she didn't register at first. Something her mind saw but didn't perceive because it didn't make sense. She jumped up. "What's this?" Amanda pointed to the photo of the card.

"That? That's a photo of a card we found. Ed got it from one of the interns."

"What intern? It's a very suggestive card."

"You know it. *'Ed. I want to blow you. Many happy returns. Fondly, Jung.'* "

"Why do you think it's from one of the interns?"

"Because he admitted it."

"Who?"

"Thomas."

"Thomas?"

"Yeah, Thomas."

"That doesn't make sense!"

"Why?"

"Because that's not his name."

"What?!"

"It's Thomas Wong, not Thomas Jung."

This time Nick sat up. "So why would he sign the card that way?"

"I don't know...unless..."

"Unless?"

"Unless they were...playing a game."

"What game?"

"Some kind of psychological name game."

Names again. Nick's brain buzzed. "Ed Michael and his word play. Why would Thomas call himself Jung?"

"Well I can't say definitively, but maybe he was pretending to be Carl Jung."

"Carl Jung?"

"The famous psychiatrist."

"What? Another one?"

"Yup."

"Well maybe that explains what some of these other names are in Ed's planner. He's got 'em all over the place."

Amanda scooped up the planner and devoured the pages. "Oh my god. They're everywhere. I missed it before."

"What do you mean?"

"Famous clinicians. Jung. Adler. Enns. Masters and Johnson. Satir. Ellis. And look, he's got appointments with them." She pointed to several items.

Masters & Johnson – lunch.

Adler re: Johnson.

Enns + Skinner on Carl.

Satir – APA conference.

She paused. "Wait a second. Ed and I went to an APA conference last June. My name isn't anywhere on the specific dates though." She sat letting it sink in, then suddenly she sprang up. "Oh my God! Ed, you stinker. He gave us psychological nicknames...how he saw us. If I'm right, he named me Satir. Virginia Satir was an experiential family therapist. Masters and Johnson must have been Mark and Barbara—you know, the married sex therapists who pioneered sex research!"

"So how does that fit with Thomas and this Jung guy and the rest of the names?"

"Let's see." She reached for the pad and pen she always kept near the phone. "If we write it out: Jung = Thomas. Masters and Johnson =

Hustons. Satir is me. Nancy is...let me see. OK I see a consult with Enns on meds for the C.V. Raman family. I remember them. They're an Indian family with cultural integration problems that Margaret saw. Enns has got to be Nancy. Enns was a famous feminist therapist; Ed probably saw Nancy Davis that way too."

She flipped back through the pages and wrote feverishly. "OK, I think I can see Gary here as Adler. Ed shows a meeting with Adler to discuss Beckers and ADHD meds. That would make sense since Adler dealt with child esteem issues and birth order and Gary's specialty was children. The Becker family has two ADHD kids. OK, and here's one for Skinner lunch re: OCD + depressives. I'll bet that's Margaret. She saw lots of depressed people and used behavioral approaches. Oh, there's even a family client name attached: Fredrick. I know that was Margaret's client family so it fits."

"OK, so where does that bring us?"

"Well let's see." She moved the pad over to his side of the table and he read the following:

Hustons = Masters & Johnson
Nancy = Enns
Amanda = Satir
Thomas = Jung
Margaret = Skinner
Gary = Adler

"OK, so where's Freud? I know I saw it in there," Nick insisted. Amanda frantically pored over the pages scanning for the word. Then she saw it.

Freud re: A.N. – Sharp.

"Oh my God. Here it is."

"What?"

"*Freud re: A.N. – Sharp.* I remember the case. A dangerously thin seventeen-year-old who weighed eighty-six pounds. Belinda Sharp. Anorexia nervosa. A.N. *Freud re: A.N. – Sharp.* He nicknamed the therapist Freud—the only one who treated Belinda Sharp and the only one with a specialty in eating problems. Oh my God!"

They both looked down at the pad and realized the one name missing from the list.

Nick spoke first. "I need to go right now."

"Oh my God, I can't believe it. Wait! You may need me. Can I come?"

He hesitated. "Something tells me this could get very ugly. We actually *may* need you, counselor. But you'll have to keep your cool."

Amanda nodded.

"What's that?" Nick whispered in a dark voice, freezing in place.

"What?" Amanda gasped, and then she followed his line of sight. He was looking at the lei hanging off the slider handle.

"It was stuffed in one my newspapers this morning. I didn't know what it meant. Do you know, Nick? Do you know?"

Nick's face was hard and he was nearly choking as he spoke. "I was at the beach yesterday with Tracy. I only let her out of my sight for two minutes at the most. She went up to the trash cans to throw some stuff away. She says someone approached her. Someone with a Hawaiian lei. Asked if she wanted one." Nick was breathing hard now. Amanda instinctively moved into him and put her hand on his arm as he spat out the words.

"It was her. Ed's killer. Talking to my kid. Wanting Tracy to go with her. My God I'll rip her throat out if she's harmed one hair on her head..." With that, he raced out the door, flipping open his phone and speed dialing Tracy's mother as he tore down the walkway.

Amanda grabbed her bag and phone and tore after him. She heard Nick shouting, "Is she OK? Where is she? Keep her inside, Lauren. I'm sending someone over now. For God's sake, Lauren, be careful!"

As they climbed into his car and flipped on the siren, Nick got Gail on the line and commanded she meet him with backup at the address he was pulling up on his BlackBerry in Clairemont. Within seconds the pair was speeding down PCH to I-5. Nick looked grim, contemplating what had to happen next. Amanda sat next to him, silent as death.

Chapter Thirty-Five

Vene, Vidi, Vici

Twenty minutes later, Nick, Amanda, Gail, and a backup cop named Joey Riviera knocked on the door of a small white house on a cul-de-sac in Clairemont. The dingy structure was engulfed by dying rose brushes dumping white-brown petals all over the undergrowth. The grass looked like it hadn't been watered in a month; two old chairs thick with dust sagged on the porch. The door opened. Sandra Daniels stood in the entryway.

"Hello...what?...uh, hello detectives. Amanda! What are you all doing here?"

"We need to come inside, Ms. Daniels."

"Sure." The ponytailed girl in cut offs motioned them inside. She gazed at Amanda, alarmed. Amanda said nothing. The foursome entered the tiny hallway, and then they followed the girl into a modest living room. There was a sagging couch, two fading overstuffed chairs, and doily-topped end tables. The coffee table was scratched but had a bowl of seashells sitting on it.

"How can I help you?" She motioned the group to sit down. No one sat.

Gail snapped on gloves, moved into the hallway, and began searching. Joey stood by the door, hand on his weapon.

Nick spoke. "Ms. Daniels, we're here to arrest you for the murder of Dr. Ed Michael."

Seconds passed as the girl sucked in air and let it register. "But... but...I don't know what you're talking about! I didn't kill Ed! I didn't do anything...someone else must have...Amanda? You know I didn't hurt Ed...oh my God!" The girl gasped for air.

"We have evidence. Your prints are everywhere. Ed named you."

"Ed named me?" The girl hiccupped. "How could that be? I didn't do anything! I didn't! Couldn't..."

"Ms. Daniels, what was Ed's name for you?"

"Name for me...?" The girl looked stunned.

"You interns...you students. Ed gave you all nicknames...what was yours?"

"Oh...uh..." the girl searched her memory, confused.

"Come on. Thomas had one. Gary had one. Margaret had one. What was yours?"

"Oh...uh...er, it was, it was...Freud." She said it, plainly confused. "I like Freudian slips. Ed used to tease me. I don't understand. I don't understand why that's important. Ed kidded around. Amanda, you know how he was. I don't understand how that..."

"Because he identified you as the killer and we know you did it..."

Gail came around the corner with a workout bag. "It's here. Keys to the medicine cabinet. Weight lifter half gloves, with threads wearing off. Some hair fragments, maybe blood. Tennis shoes look to have traces of blood too. Found some hunting knives, quite a few rifles, and a couple of handguns."

"I forgot those keys were in my exercise bag," the girl wailed. "Those are my gloves I use to lift weights with...yeah, I noticed the tennis shoes had some red stuff on them...but I thought it was paint or something. I don't understand. I don't understand!" She backed up, her eyes wild.

When Nick signaled Joey to cuff her and read her her rights, the girl became hysterical. The screams were deafening, like some animal caught in a bear trap, bleeding to death. Amanda covered her ears. As Joey moved in, Sandra suddenly stopped screaming and stood upright.

Nick signaled Joey to hold.

With a sweep of her hand, Sandra pulled off the scrunchie and let her thin brown hair fall around her shoulders. She shook her head and sank down into one of the chairs, and then reached up to open the top buttons of her shirt. "Oh God, it's good to sit down. Well, hello," she said to Nick, her voice low and liquid. "I thought I might see you again, cutie."

Nick watched her, and then glanced over at Amanda. Amanda studied the girl closely, ignoring Nick.

"And I can see you've brought friends," the girl went on. "So nice to have company." She smiled broadly at the group and kept on talking. "I mean if I'd known you were all coming, I would have picked up a few things. You know, for a party...oh my, I must be a fright." She turned to Amanda, peering at her like Amanda was an alien.

"Hello. I don't think we've actually met. I'm Sandee. So nice to meet you." Amanda watched her, dumbfounded. "It *is* so nice to have visitors. It gets so lonely here what with my family being back in the Midwest and all. My brother used to live with me here, but he's gone off somewhere God only knows. Never could get him to do much around the house. Lazy little brat. Doesn't like some of my boyfriends. Got loads of 'em...but they don't come here too often." She turned back and winked at Nick. "I do remember you though, cutie pie, but for the life of me I can't remember where."

Nick signaled Joey and he headed around behind the girl as Nick answered her. "We did meet," Nick said, milking the moment. "Downtown. Remember? We had a nice chat." Out of the corner of his eye he watched Joey get ready to pull the girl up and cuff her.

"Oh yes, I remember now. Downtown. She seems familiar," Sandee said, pointing at Gail. "I think you were the one in a bun or something..." Before she could finish, Joey yanked her up and hand-cuffed the girl. This time the screams reverbed off the windows.

"Oh my God...oh my God...why are you doing this? Why are you doing this?" The girl suddenly lunged right, falling sideways to the floor. She thrashed around on the hardwood floor, convulsing.

"Sandra, Sandra, it's all right," Amanda shrieked, trying not to scream herself. "We'll help you. We will help you. You just need to go with these officers and we will get you help."

The girl was having none of it. She writhed on the floor; a lamp went over, then an end table. Nick and Joey lunged for her. She kicked out at both of them, nearly connecting with Joey's groin before he collared her around the neck and yanked her up to cuff her. She suddenly let out a bloodcurdling scream, this time in a new, very deep, boy voice.

"Just wait a fucking minute you son-of-a-bitch goddam mother-fucker asshole pig-faced fucker!"

Something told Gail to pull out her recorder.

Joey yanked the girl in place, but she strained against him and hunched over like an Indian on the hunt. "Get your stinking hands off me you goddam fucking beaner or I'll kick your nuts from here to Alaska!"

She turned so fast, Joey was caught off guard. The spit caught Joey square in the right eye. Nick signaled the officer to release a little and the girl stood up straight while Joey wiped his face with his hand.

"OK, you motherfuckers," the boy voice menaced. "Stop terrify-ing the girl. She's had enough. You godddam motherfuckin' pigs think nothin' of torturing people. Pricks." Suddenly the voice looked over at Amanda. "Hi. We meet at last."

Amanda looked at Nick, then back at Sandra and Joey. Nick signaled Joey to bring the girl, but Amanda stopped him.

"Um, Nick," Amanda started. "Hold on a minute, would you?" She answered the voice. "Hello. Amanda Carlisle. Nice to finally meet you."

"I always knew you were a lady, even if you were kinda hard on the pinhead," the boy voice said back. "Don't know what you're doing with these shitheads, but here you are."

"Why haven't we met before? Or have we? My memory is getting so bad. What...was your name again?"

"Danny."

"Danny?"

"Yup."

"Danny. Do you know why we're here today?"

"Suppose so. You sussed it."

"What did we suss?"

"About that motherfucker shrink. 'Bout how I sent that goddamn motherfucker to hell. He deserved it man. Deserved every bit of it. Asshole, cocksucking, shit head, pansy-faced, asshole PhD prick."

"What exactly did you do to send him to hell?"

"Everything."

"What? The poison? The stabbing? The strangulation?"

"Sure."

Nick looked at Amanda but she ignored him. Joey looked over at Nick who signaled him to hold a bit longer. Gail and Nick swapped a look; Nick was glad the recorder was running.

"Did Sandra help you?" Amanda asked.

"Naw. You must be joking. Couldn't fight her way out of a paper bag. All that clinical crap. No, that dickhead shrink had to go and I was the only one who could do it."

"So who else is there, if you don't mind me asking?"

"Sandra. Sandee. And me."

"And you're in charge?"

"Yup. Danny's in charge. Always in charge, man. Handle the tough stuff. Keep those two pinheads out of trouble. Not hard with Sandra. What a fucking wimp. Sandee's tougher. Such a friggin' slut. Bound and determined to fuck everything this side of Tijuana. Short, fat, skinny, old, young, creep, no creep. Every bad breath, dick-faced, shit head with balls. Gets her panties 'round her ankles faster than you can count to two. Hates it when I drag her home. Sometimes I have to handle the creeps. Usually no problem. When they meet me, they don't stay around too long."

Nick and Gail looked at each other, silent.

"But why Dr. Michael?" Amanda probed. "Why did he have to go?"

"Because of what he was doing. Because of what he was, the dick face."

"What was he doing?"

"That godddam doc liked porn, man. Screwed anything wet behind the ears. He was jacking off in that office, man. While he was working! Man that's wrong *and* bad. I wouldn't have come out, but then she showed up."

"Who?"

"Sandee, stupid bitch. She went back in that office after her workout. Sweat gets Sandee started. Saw the fucker's porn and took it as an invitation. Man was she mad when that shit-faced prick told her she was too old. He even laughed. Said something about how he'd missed it. Such a brilliant shrink, but that he missed finding *her*. She started to cry. Got really mad. That's when I showed up."

"When do you usually show up, Danny?"

"When I have to mop up."

"Mop up?"

"When I have to clean up the shit the other two leave. For God's sake, I thought you were so goddamned smart! Sandy thought you were smart. Real smart. That's why I told you to back off her, man; you were startin' to be a bitch to her. That's why I had to keep my eye on you. Now you're seeing who's smart, lady."

"So you had to clean up everything that was happening in Ed's office?" Amanda kept the voice talking.

"Oh man, you know it. Sandee sniveling all over the place, grabbing the knives in the kitchen, starting on her arms again. Holy shit, always having to watch her, stupid bitch. Man, when I see the knives come out, I spring it. Stupid cunt would have zotzed herself years ago if I hadn't been here. So I took the knives...and I went in to see that stupid shrink."

"And then what?" Nick asked.

"Hey, jerk face, I am only speaking to the lady." The boy voice turned back to Amanda and went on. "Man, it was easy. That asshole was only too ready to jerk off. 'It'll be fun to have a psycho watching,' the prick said, thinking it was her. Just didn't realize it was *me*. So I watched. And waited. Easy. And while the asshole was getting himself off, I swiped his meds and some Valium. Loved me bringing him a post-jerk-off cup of tea. So a half hour goes by and the guy's nearly a goner with all the stuff I dumped in there. Then I did my thing."

"You mutilated the man?"

"You make it sound ugly. It was a work of art, lady! Nailed that motherfucker to his own desk." The voice laughed. "Watched his face while I strung him up, then..."

"Then...?"

"Gave him the final pain off."

"What?"

"You know, come on. The guy loved S&M. Didn't you know? He knew I was doing it."

"Doing it?"

"He loved it—at first. Then he realized it was *me*. Not Her, Sandra. Not even her, Sandee. *Me, Danny, the man.* Laughed his head off at first—'til he *really* got it...when he realized I was..."

"What?"

"...killing 'em. That's when he finally got it. *As you sow, so shall ye reap*, I told him. That smug-faced prick finally stopped laughin' then."

The group barely breathed, watching the boy—no, the girl—who stood quietly before them, humming. "When did you leave?" Gail asked.

"Oh, man, I didn't get to see it to the end. Somebody came."

"Who?"

"You know, one of those other shrink heads. Can't remember their names. She knows. I needed to get out of there, you know, man?

Too many people around. Would have loved to see the payoff, so to speak, but I knew he knew I'd won." The girl stood there looking at the four of them.

"OK, Danny or Sandra or whatever the hell your name is, we need to go downtown. Now!" Nick said firmly.

"OK, man. Never rode in a cop car before. Should be fun. By the way, your little girl's really cute."

Nick's face contorted. He was about to lunge for the girl, but Gail stopped him.

"Relax, man," the boy voice said casually. "I'd never hurt a child. Only pricks. Just wanted to see."

"See what?" Nick demanded.

"What normal's like."

"You goddam psychopath..." The look of savagery on Nick's face was enough to wither a sequoia.

"Why the lei?" Amanda asked, stepping beside Nick and putting her hand on his arm to steady him.

"Man, I'm not in that stupid. That was Sandee. Stupid cunt always picks up crap like that."

"So you were on my doorstep too?" Amanda asked.

"Always," the boy voice answered. "I like to watch. You in particular."

Amanda shuddered, but kept her grip on Nick who signaled Joey. The cop finally handcuffed the girl behind her back, pulled her out of the room, and stuffed her in the backseat of the patrol car.

Nick looked at Amanda in the doorway and her heart twisted in her chest. He looked like an animal wanting to gnaw on something, but she kept looking into his eyes until slowly he softened and covered her hand with his.

"Sorry," he said. "I guess I lost it." He removed his hand and Amanda stepped back. She wished she could reach out and stroke his hair. Suddenly, Gail coughed. The two looked at her, and then broke apart.

Nick and Gail walked to the door and Amanda followed. The three of them watched as Joey's patrol car pulled away. Sandra stared out the window and waved to some neighbor boys skateboarding in the cul-de-sac.

Amanda stood watching, random thoughts filling her head. How horrible it had all been for them at the clinic, and now for Nick, too, it had become personal. Amanda was flabbergasted she'd missed it, all the turmoil going on in the psyche of Sandra Daniels. How she, Amanda Carlisle, seasoned, experienced clinician, had completely missed it. She wondered most of all what the ride downtown would be like for the pathetic creature about to show up at police headquarters, DID on arrival.

Chapter Thirty-Six

Me, Myself, and I

Amanda explained "DID" to Nick as the Crown Vic followed Gail down the freeway in her hybrid. They were about a half a mile behind Joey's squad car with the threesome in the backseat. Nick was calming down now that he was driving.

"Dissociative identity disorder."

"OK I've heard of it. It's that multiple personality thing, right?"

"Yes. It used to be called Multiple Personality Disorder. It's DID now."

"OK, counselor. So what exactly happened in there? Usually when I arrest someone, it's one perp in one body at a time. I take it we nailed the three-headed monster."

"It would seem so." Amanda sank into thought for a moment. "She's very, very ill, Nick. God I am absolutely shocked. I feel so sorry for her. I just don't know how I missed it."

"Which thing exactly? That you were getting three for the price of one every time she showed up for work or that you were coaching a vicious little killer treating people for low self-esteem and eating problems?"

"Oh, Nick. I can't be glib about it. I can only imagine what must have happened to her to have created this...incredible aberration."

"Sorry. Still jaded. What makes somebody...become...that...thing?"

"Her personality must have splintered, Nick."

"Unless she's faking it."

"Unless she's faking it. My gut tells me she's probably a true multiple though."

"How does that work?"

"Intense childhood trauma. It probably caused her to splinter, but not into just aspects of one personality system. It sounds like there are three separate personalities in there."

"You know this multiple personality defense doesn't hold up in court too well—especially when it comes to murder."

"Yes, but you saw the dynamic. Sandra Daniels—"

"...your intern, right?"

"Yes. She appears to have had no idea the other two personalities were in there."

"How do the other two fit?"

"Without doing further interviews I can only speculate, but I would guess that Danny, the boy killer alter, is probably the controller. The switchboard personality."

"The one in charge?"

"The one who monitors the others. It sounds like Danny knew about the other two—"

"Sandee the slut and Sandra the therapist?"

"Yes, but they didn't know about *him*. Or at least my Sandra didn't. He must have stayed hidden, letting the others take the lead. Unless he had to intervene. He must have been the one with full access to the memory bank."

"Memory bank?"

"The full complement of memories, normal and abnormal."

"And the other two?"

"Sandra, my intern, may have been behind some kind of amnesiac barrier."

"If she's telling the truth..."

"Yes, if she can be believed. Living her life, unaware there were at least two others in there. Maybe even more. I can't believe we all missed it. Freud, indeed."

"Weird. Give me a straightforward Breaking-and-Entering any time. One guy, one crime, one set of fingerprints."

"Oh God, I just realized something. Maybe Ed was trying to tell us multiple things when he wrote Freud across his desk."

"Such as?"

"Not only that *Freud* did it, but that Freud's theory took revenge on him as well. Sandra is a multiple. A multiple whose avenger persona transferred every last ounce of warped psychotic vitriol on a psychiatrist who was warped himself. And she did it in a Freudian way."

"How so?"

"I guess you could say she delivered the ultimate Freudian punishment: she castrated Ed's manhood *and* his life. Freudian revenge from Freud herself."

They both were silent for a few minutes.

"What turns a kid like Sandra into a multiple and then into a murderer?"

"God so many things could cause this, Nick, it boggles the mind. Early childhood abuse. Extreme sex abuse. Childhood torture. Parental cruelty. Drug use. Genetic predisposition. Sometimes all of them. Maybe her early childhood years were so horrific, her personality split so she could survive. The alters probably rose to protect her, to help her, Nick, to save the original personality—Sandra—from the debilitating memories. In Sandra's case, Danny maybe surfaced not just to protect her, but to avenge her. Maybe make up for all the terrible, horrific things that happened to her. I would guess she was molested, maybe viciously, repeatedly, in her early years. Maybe by her father or someone else close. Her psyche couldn't deal with it, so she split to cope. Perhaps seeing Ed's actions and his contempt triggered every latent, hideous memory in their collective psyche and Danny, the controller, went for it. Pure, demonic ID—with a superego charger. I guess when you combine pure impulse with an avenging urge to be judge, jury, and executioner, you get murder."

"Weird and weirder."

"I feel very sad for her. I always felt Sandra—or the Sandra part I knew—was a caring therapist. And actually, maybe she is. Under different circumstances, maybe..."

"No maybes now, counselor. The kid is a killer no matter how you slice her."

"Yes, I can see that. I'm sorry you and Tracy got involved." Amanda could see Nick's knuckles go white on the steering wheel. "If he/she/they can be believed, I don't think Tracy would have been harmed."

"Well, Amanda, I know you mean well. I just don't share your optimism. That kid brutally murdered your shrink and I don't have any faith it's the first time or even the last." He looked at her savagely for an instant, than looked back at the road and softened. "Sorry," he said. "I'm not taking this out on you."

"I know. I know you were frightened. Sandra will have to deal with what she, they, have done." Amanda grew silent, lost in contemplation of the sometimes-unfathomable universe of the human psyche. A universe, Amanda knew, that sometimes only gives up its secrets through the tortuous path of human experience—if at all. With Sandra and her Others, it was likely to be a long, very long journey.

Chapter Thirty-Seven

Reunification

Six weeks later, the clinic reopened to great fanfare. There were balloons, hors d'oeuvres and desserts from Harvest Ranch. Jazz played over the loudspeakers. Everyone got free stress management kits, gift bags with calming candles and herbal tea, and raffle tickets for a day of massage at L'Auberge. The press was there. Locals stopped by to check out just where the murder happened. A few neighborhood clinicians wandered in to assess the psychological climate and offer support.

When they walked inside the clinic proper, visitors learned that the infamous office was no more. To placate the powers that be, the murder suite had been cleared and sanitized. It was then blessed by a priest, exorcised by a rabbi, and saged by a Native American elder from one of the local Indian tribes who agreed to dispatch the dark energies to the great central sun. For good measure, Barbara had both doors removed and the whole office space walled in with new plaster and paint.

Most of Seaside's clients returned, first, from curiosity, then from familiarity. Some looked around the corner for ghosts they thought must be lurking there. But once they remembered how feeling depressed was driving them to Haagen Dazs or to drink, or how angry they were at their spouses or kids, the concern about a ghostly shrink paled, then faded.

The Hustons returned to the executive suite with a renewed commitment to make the clinic and their marriage go forward with positive energy, they said. That was code, Amanda Carlisle knew. She was the only one Barbara confided in about the six weeks of $200-an-hour couples therapy she and Mark had had. The pair had gone to an unnamed celebrity therapist in LA who helped them banish two specters: the ghost of a degenerate shrink threatening to undermine their clinic, and a haunting mistrust eating away at their marriage. By all accounts the marriage had made a full recovery.

The clinic also had a complete makeover, with new paint in eggshell and fresh furniture in the lobby. A smaller intern room was created out of the old kitchen nook. The former intern enclave now housed a no-nonsense psychiatrist named Dr. Helen Baumhaur. Dr. Helen, as she preferred to be called, loved working with kids, and even the schizophrenics didn't faze her. She was calm, cool, and collected. But she didn't get hired until senior staff had fully vetted her—twice.

Nancy returned with Margaret. Thomas chose to head north to complete his intern training with a serious mandate for continued supervision and ethics training. Nancy was happily interviewing for two new psych intern openings.

Gary returned to treat his loyal families who'd waiting patiently for the clinic to reopen. Jackie wouldn't set foot in the clinic until her preacher, Reverend Charles, did a walk-through, declaring it safe. Al laughed the whole thing off, but Amanda noticed he'd lost a little weight. He seemed less inclined to flirt now, more inclined to keep watch. Lila went to work in a law firm, steering clear of the "whackos" at Seaside. A young man named Jeff took her place while he worked his way through undergraduate classes at a local junior college. He had no tattoos at all—at least that could be seen.

Amanda Carlisle walked into the clinic the day of the party, taking the stairs this time. On that first day back, she saw five patients, had a two-hour debrief with Gary, attended a 3:00 p.m. staff meeting, and then headed out around 4:30. In the car, she fielded phone calls from Shelby, Papa Phil, and her aunt Lynn. When the phone rang once more, it was Nick.

"I guess you're back in the saddle again, counselor."

She laughed. "Yep, you know it."

"Sounds like you're driving. Where you headed?"

"You know."

"Are you going down there again?"

"Yup."

"You're nothing if not loyal."

"Nick, Sandra needs me right now."

"Think you're getting anywhere?"

"Her psychiatrist thinks it's a good idea to help her ground with things and people she knows."

"Beyond the call of duty, if you ask me."

"Maybe. But I believe there's always hope, Nick. Hope that she can integrate, bring the personalities together. Pull it together and do some good somewhere, somehow."

"In jail?"

"Yup."

"Or a mental institution?"

"Yup. That's what she wants. Part of her is a good clinician. She's getting to know the rest of her now."

"Hope springs eternal."

"Yes. It's what we do, I guess, Nick. *You* lock people up. We *unlock* them if we can."

"She's still a killer."

"Yes, you're right. I won't forget. I just still believe there's something in there to save. She's not a throwaway no matter what."

"Well I have to hand it you, counselor. You never give up."

"Nope."

"I enjoyed coffee the other day. I forget how relaxing Del Mar can be..."

"When you're not hunting a killer..."

"Yeah, when you're actually chillin'..."

"Your advice on the Crawford case was pretty cool, helping me with some referrals for the kids."

"No problem. Always glad to help."

"Hey, I've been meaning to ask you. Are you still taking pictures?"

"Absolutely."

"Uh...would you ever be interested in taking some pictures of Tracy for me? If you have the time, you know..."

"Sure, Nick, I'd love to. It'd be fun. Just let me know when."

"OK, cool. I'll check in with you in a few days. Thanks for your hard work, by the way."

"Sure, Nick. You too."

"Talk to you soon."

She hung up and drove on. She wondered if Tracy looked like Nick. If she had that same jaw, the determination. It would be fun to find out.

Suddenly she slammed on the brakes. A boy in an old car with a thin-haired, laughing girl sitting next to him nearly cut her off getting to the fast lane. It reminded her of Sandra. In a normal life, that might have been her. But for now, Sandra sat alone in a cell, closely guarded, just off suicide watch. At least the screaming and weeping had stopped. With medication, she was finally starting the long journey back and reaching out to people like Amanda.

"It's just what we do," she said aloud to no one as she headed downtown to join the girl's afternoon session. "The good, the bad, and the very, very ugly. It's just what we do."

About the Author

PJ Adams is a practicing psychotherapist and author living in Southern California. Her other works include *Intoxicating Paris* and *Daughter Wisdom*, as well as several business books. She stays (mostly) sane by learning French and writing about crime and other topics.

Acknowledgments

The author wishes to thank Cathy Lewis, Tom Leech, and Karla Olson for their support and wisdom; John Updike for his brilliant writing and gracious words during *Buchanon Dying* so many years ago; and John Birkhead for his tireless encouragement and unwavering belief.